WHERE WAS GOODBYE?

JANICE LYNN MATHER

SIMON & SCHUSTER BFYR

NEW YORK   LONDON   TORONTO   SYDNEY   NEW DELHI

SIMON & SCHUSTER BFYR

An imprint of Simon & Schuster Children's Publishing Division
1230 Avenue of the Americas, New York, New York 10020
This book is a work of fiction. Any references to historical events, real people,
or real places are used fictitiously. Other names, characters, places, and events are
products of the author's imagination, and any resemblance to actual events or
places or persons, living or dead, is entirely coincidental.
Text © 2024 by Janice Lynn Mather
Jacket illustration © 2024 by Adriana Bellet
All rights reserved, including the right of reproduction
in whole or in part in any form.
SIMON & SCHUSTER BOOKS FOR YOUNG READERS
and related marks are trademarks of Simon & Schuster, LLC.
Simon & Schuster: Celebrating 100 Years of Publishing in 2024
For information about special discounts for bulk purchases, please contact Simon & Schuster
Special Sales at 1-866-506-1949 or business@simonandschuster.com.
The Simon & Schuster Speakers Bureau can bring authors to your live event. For more
information or to book an event, contact the Simon & Schuster Speakers Bureau at
1-866-248-3049 or visit our website at www.simonspeakers.com.
Interior design by Hilary Zarycky
The text for this book was set in New Caledonia.
Manufactured in the United States of America
First Edition
2 4 6 8 10 9 7 5 3 1
Library of Congress Cataloging-in-Publication Data
Names: Mather, Janice Lynn, author.
Title: Where was goodbye? / Janice Lynn Mather.
Description: First edition. | New York : Simon & Schuster Books for Young Readers, 2024. |
Audience: Ages 14 and up. | Audience: Grades 10–12. | Summary: As she starts her senior year
six weeks after her brother Julian's suicide, Karmen struggles with strained family relationships,
a distant best friend, and the search for understanding, but new friendships and a budding
romance help her on her journey of healing and rediscovery.
Identifiers: LCCN 2023021416 (print) | LCCN 2023021417 (ebook) |
ISBN 9781665903950 (hardcover) | ISBN 9781665903974 (ebook)
Subjects: CYAC: Grief—Fiction. | Friendship—Fiction. | Family life—Fiction. |
High schools—Fiction. | Schools—Fiction. | African Americans—Fiction. | LCGFT: Novels.
Classification: LCC PZ7.1.M3766 Wh 2024 (print) | LCC PZ7.1.M3766 (ebook) |
DDC [Fic]—dc23
LC record available at https://lccn.loc.gov/2023021416
LC ebook record available at https://lccn.loc.gov/2023021417

For K., who showed me the shape of goodbye

TRIGGER WARNING

Dear Reader,

This is a story of navigating grief, loss, and the search for impossible answers. It is also a story of friendship, understanding, and unconditional love.

The topic of suicide is central to this story. If you or someone you know struggles with suicidal thoughts or feelings, get help immediately. There's a resource list at the end of the book.

Last, please read with kindness for yourself. You have the right to set down any book that pushes too far, that takes you somewhere you don't want to go, or can't go.

With kindness,
Janice Lynn Mather

CHAPTER ONE

My brother's room is a time capsule. The bed is made, smoothed down perfectly. The top of the nightstand is bare. The curtains are half-open, half-closed, making some type of daytime purgatory. Everything is exactly as he left it six weeks ago, before police-car lights strobed catastrophe through our life. I grip Julian's slim reporter's notebook in my left hand. White cover, hard cardboard backing, spiral-bound at the narrow top edge. The first third of the pages are covered in my brother's careful, upright cursive—notes for stories he wrote, the name of a song, a phone number. They stop abruptly. That's where I took over. Where I wrote those three questions the night Julian died. The questions I haven't been able to look at since then, and don't need to—they're burned into my mind harder than they're scrawled onto the page. Questions that follow me everywhere, demanding I find answers. Isn't that why I'm here, in his room? To find out why he isn't?

I pull open the nightstand's top drawer. His phone—police already looked through that, said there was nothing on there of interest, gave it back. The charging cord is curled around itself like a snake eating its own tail. Other stuff that doesn't mean much now: the passport he'll never use, his driver's license and student ID. I push it shut and ease open the bottom drawer.

Unfolded papers almost pop out. A bumper sticker shaped like a marijuana leaf, an empty windowed envelope, a cologne sample, the tip of one of his skateboarding magazines. I glance over my shoulder. What am I doing? Julian's not gonna come in and find me here. If he could, it'd be worth the epic fight we'd get into over me going through his stuff.

I hear my mother sigh from all the way downstairs, deep and sad for seven a.m. I don't have much time. I flip through the papers. One catches my eye: it has the Commonwealth University letterhead. I grab that. *Dear Julian Wallace, We regret to inform you that you have been placed on academic probation. . . .*

"Karmen?" My mother's tired voice drags its way up from the kitchen. I never knew, before, that a person could stay in bed almost all day and still seem so exhausted. Correction: I never knew *she* could.

"Hey—you ready?" Daddy calls from the bottom of the stairs. I dart out, snatch Julian's backpack from just inside my room, cram the letter into the notebook, and then shove it into the bag. Something soft catches on my finger—unfinished knitting. Why'd I even pack that? I haven't felt like knitting since . . . I cram down the pumpkin-orange yarn almost as hard as I push away the memory. My room glows, guilty with sunlight that pours through opened curtains and spills into the hallway. If I look back down the corridor, I'll see nothing but dark. Shadows. Just like when my brother was still alive. My heart races like I've run down the road and back, full speed. I wipe my damp hands on my skirt and close the backpack. As I let go of the zipper pull, my hand brushes against the embroidery on the front. The tiny silhouetted skateboarder is frozen mid-leap, knees bent, feet on the board like magic, arms outstretched. He's soaring.

"Karmen, time to go!" My father's annoyed now. I pick up the bag and run down the stairs. He's waiting. The day's waiting. And it all feels heavier than I want it to.

". . . think it's good for her?" Mummy's words float up to me. I take two steps lightly and listen.

"I don't see the sense in just laying around the house." Dad's voice is louder.

"You gonna make a dig at me?" Her voice raises now too. "You don't see I'm up?"

"I'm not talking about you. I'm saying she's been through a lot, and it might be good for her to get in some type of good routine."

I swallow and go down the stairs, letting my feet fall heavier so they hear me. So they stop.

"Morning, Karmen." Mummy switches to false cheer. "Ready to conquer grade twelve?"

"Morning." The air is still prickly from my parents' words. Mummy attempts a smile that comes out all wrong—gritted teeth and grimacing. She's in the blue bathrobe, of course, with the dingy sleeve edges and the broken belt loop.

I extract a granola bar from the box on the counter.

Uncomfortable silence. So much for us running late.

Daddy leans forward and drops a kiss on my cheek. "Last

year of high school. You ready to knock 'em . . ." He falters a moment. "Knock 'em out?"

I force a smile back to distract from what he almost said. *Dead.* "Not really."

"She's not a fighter—right, Karmen?" Mummy pulls me in for a hug. She tries, but her arms are still limp. I should hug her back, but I don't, and I hate myself for being grateful when she pulls back. "You're our maker of soft things. Right?"

I can't stop myself from flinching away as she tries to pat my cheek. "I guess." I follow Daddy to the foyer. Mummy trails behind.

"Sure you wanna do this?" she asks as she leans against the wall. I glance at the calendar just beside her. It's still stuck on July. If I flip it forward into this month, I'll see the party hat Julian sketched on the day of his birthday, right there in the middle of September. I look away.

"School's starting, so . . ." I have no justification for going to school beyond that, and the fact that Daddy stands by the open door expectantly.

"A sense of normalcy will be good for you." Daddy jingles his keys. "It'll be good for all of us."

"You can let her speak," Mummy says. Her voice is low, but I hear the taut rubber band in her tone. Daddy says nothing, just breathes out extra sharp. I look away from him, and my eyes go right where I didn't want to look— Julian's white-and-blue sneakers on the shoe rack by the door, the left one facing straight in on the shelf, the right one leaning a little to the side, its toe resting against its sibling.

"Can we just go?" My voice cracks. I clear my throat and shove my shoes on. "I'll be in the car."

I climb into the front seat, leave the door open so I can get some air. I lean back. This is normal. This is what people do. Dress for school, ride in the car. Tote a bag full of books around all day. If I just turn my head, I'll see Julian slouched in the back, legs stretched out so his blue-and-white sneakers stick up on the center console, in protest for losing the prime spot to his little sis. If I just look back, I can fix everything. *Karmen. Hey. Come on, Sis. Turn your head.*

I turn my face to the window, close my eyes.

After Daddy pulls off, I head for the entrance, but when I get there, I can't seem to go inside. Five girls from my grade bustle past, chatting, giggling. Do they know? Everyone knows, probably. Will I be answering questions all day? *How was your summer? Your family take any trips? Is it true your brother died?* The girls are gone, didn't even look my way. I don't know which is better—for everyone to pretend they don't know, or for them to wear their knowing like a sickly mask, those *sad for you* smiles, the sympathetic head tilts. For them to expect me to wear grief too.

"Hey, Karmen!"

I turn around to see Layla grinning at me, a new green messenger bag strapped over her chest. She stands close, and the hairs on her arm brush up against mine like tiny, gentle hooks. "Last year in bondage," she says to me. "Ready?"

"Yeah." I follow my best friend's lead, walk in time to her steps.

"You all right?"

I'm not, and she knows it. "I'm okay."

"I was supposed to get here earlier, but Isaiah was hogging the shower. Like an extra ten minutes preening and gelling is gonna make a difference."

"Mmm." Layla's familiar yammering pulls me along. Right now, it's just what I need.

"By the time he got out it was after seven, and I barely had time to shower and get dressed."

"Julian used to do that. Take forever tweezing his eyebrows or something."

"Yeah, I . . . yeah." Layla's words peter out like an abandoned path. We pass the music hall in silence and head along the walkway that loops around the high school classrooms. A couple boys walk past us, and we're stuck behind a gaggle of seventh graders, backpacks almost bigger than they are. They cluster like grapes packed too tight for the bunch, seeking safety in each other. Someone just behind us calls out a hail; in a classroom, laughter booms. Everything seems magnified.

Layla slips her arm into mine and leads the way down the stairs to the math block. As soon as we turn, it's quieter. Shadows cool me as we take the steps.

"Give me a second." I sit in the alcove halfway up. Mom was right. I'm not ready for this.

"Should I run back and see if your dad's still there?" Layla's face is so close, it feels like she's about to swallow me. I can see the fuzz that covers her face, feel her breath.

"No." My voice feels far, like my cotton-stuffed ears are

ten feet away. "No." Did I already say that? How can this place feel too . . . everything?

"Stay here." Unless she's got a portal to anywhere but here, whatever she's planning is too much.

"I'm fine!" My voice booms. I cover my face with my hands. My palms are hot and dry. I close my eyes, count to five. When I take my hands away, at least the sounds around me seem turned down a few notches. A little closer to normal. And my best friend isn't right in my face.

"You wanna go to Ms. Dorsett's office? Or the nurse's station?"

I shake my head. "Can you just . . . sit?"

She lowers herself onto the step beside me. Out of the corner of my eye, I see her brows furrowed, figuring hard. "You could skip today. Everyone would get it."

"Mummy and Daddy had it out over me coming. She thinks it's too soon, and he said let me go if I'm ready."

"Are you, though?"

Her gaze bores into me. Her eyebrows are still knotted up like a botched stocking stitch, and there's something in her eyes I can't bear. I force a smile and hope it looks sincere.

"Yup." I stand up and smooth out the back of my skirt. "Let's go."

Layla mirrors my smile. A shadow of worry lingers on her face, a slight rumple between her brows.

"So your dad's pushing you to be here?"

"No, it's just . . ." I sigh. The bell for homeroom trills and saves me from trying to explain the impossible.

Layla scrabbles around in her bag as we head for our class. "I snuck in my phone, just in case."

"I said I'm fine!" Layla flinches like I've hit her. "Sorry, I just—"

"It's okay." Layla's voice shakes a little. An ache begins in my belly, small and hard as a bud. It's not okay. We both know it.

"I just wanna—"

"I get it." Layla smiles bright as we step into the room. "Maybe we should sit somewhere new."

I follow her to the back of the class, but I wish she'd just gone to our old spot by the window. Wish she'd let me get my words out. I slide into the seat beside hers and drop my bag on the floor. We've known each other since grade seven, been inseparable since then. *You better get it together, 'fore you mess things up with your bestie.* My brother's voice sounds in my head, clear as if he's right behind me. I turn, but it's just Robbie coming in. I turn back with a smile, though.

"I just wanna feel normal." I say it softly. Layla reaches over and squeezes my wrist. It's so easy for her to let go, to move on. I reach down to my bag, and my smile fades away as I catch sight of the little boarding dude, his embroidered dreads caught mid-flail like a spider flying on an invisible thread. *Normal,* I think, as I unzip the bag. My fingers graze the notebook's silver spirals. I reach past it and slide out my water, take a sip as kids settle all around me. Layla's chatting to one of the boys ahead of us.

"Good morning!" Mr. Douglas' voice hushes the low chatter. "Welcome back for your last year, grade twelves."

There's a pause where he should ask how everyone's summer was. "So," he starts, instead, "before we get into our usual greetings, I think we'd all like to extend our condolences to . . ." He looks around.

I try to slide down an inch or two. *This can't be happening. Normal, normal*—I will it.

Mr. Douglas' eyes land on me. "Karmen."

I look away. My stupid eyes start the first watery swell, 'cause they know what's happening too.

"Karmen, we as a class want to extend our condolences to you and your family on the, uh, the tragic loss of your brother this summer."

The classroom is growing, like I'm Alice in Wonderland, proportions all off. His words seem echoey, and I can feel everyone's eyes on me. They know. They all know. Who told them? Do they know how he died?

I want to grab my bag and bolt. This was a mistake. This was the hugest mistake.

"Class, let's come together to support Karmen in this difficult time. I believe a few of you have some words of comfort and sympathy to share?"

I keep my eyes fixed on the top of my desk. I need to run out of here. The door feels so far away; maybe my legs won't work. Someone near the front of the class is saying something: *So sorry, I just can't imagine* . . . Her voice is breaking like it's her tragedy, like her brother is dead instead of mine. I just want this over—all of it.

"Anyone else? Yes, Tasha," Mr. Douglas is saying. It's going on—this torture is gonna last forever.

9

Before I can think of a way out of this mess, the classroom door bursts open.

"Ooooh!" someone whispers.

"Think she crazy?"

Layla sucks air in through her teeth, quick and sharp, all in an instant, and I look up. Head full of long, tiny braids; skirt rolled. Long legs flash mid-thigh. Blouse knotted into a crop top.

"She new?" someone whispers.

"Uh . . . and you a-are?" Mr. Douglas stutters.

"Pru Davis." The girl slumps into a chair.

"Right, right. Welcome. Class, please welcome our newest student, Pru." Mr. Douglas fights to regain composure. "Pru, please refer to your student handbook for details on the, uh, school dress code."

The classroom's air bristles.

"Probably rolled it and smoked it before she came in here," Layla mutters under her breath. I can just about feel porcupine quills rearing up on Layla's arm beside me. I lean away and sneak another look over at Pru. The most outrageous anyone's ever been before is wearing a slightly brownish-tinged shoe instead of regulation black, or a boy slinking in after lunch with his shirt still untucked from playing ball. She sighs, then languidly hauls her blouse down, then leans back in the seat.

"So, uh . . ." Mr. Douglas turns back to his desk. While he fumbles, I reach into my bag and slip out my math book, then wedge the tiny notebook in between its pages. I flip open the first page that Julian used. *Other settlements. Alternative histories. Other athletes.* I trace the words with my fingertips.

"Hey, you in my seat."

I glance up to see Robbie towering over the desk.

"Sit someplace else."

"I always sat here last year." He dumps his backpack onto the desk—on top of the notebook. I hear paper crumple and shove his bag away. It thuds onto the floor along with my textbook. The page—Julian's page—half tears away at the top. Robbie grabs his bag off the floor. "What wrong with you?" he barks at me. "You crazy?"

His words hit me like a slap, but before the sting's even sunk in, the new girl is on her feet and in Robbie's face.

"Watch your mouth." Pru's chin is lifted, her face just a few inches from him, like he insulted her, not me. Robbie takes a step back, brow crumpled in confusion.

"Where you come from? Ain nobody say nothing to you."

"You don't call people crazy. If you say it again—"

"Robert, Pru, enough! Both of y'all sit down, or you both start grade twelve in the office. Understand?" Mr. Douglas' voice is loud, but somehow it still feels far away. I try to smooth out the page. I close the book softly, but my heart pounds loud.

"Mr. Douglas, you ain see what Karmen do? She push my bag, and then this one in my face like she ain got no sense—"

Pru raises a hand. Her middle finger sticks up like a flag.

"Pru, enough. Go to the counselor's office. Robbie, keep going and you'll be at the principal."

Pru grabs her bag and swishes out of the classroom without a look back.

"That's an entrance," Layla says under her breath. Her

11

voice sounds like she's just seen someone squeeze out a turd on their desk. I can't look over at my best friend. I can feel the charge in the classroom's air—if I touch the desk, the chair's leg, anything, electricity might jolt right through me. Layla elbows me. "This year's gonna be interesting." I can feel her looking over. I don't answer.

The girl in front of me passes my textbook to me. I stare at the front cover, feel my fingers clench into a fist. I wish I had tape, something to fix what's been broken.

"Let Karmen get away with anything. Just because—"

I don't even let him finish the sentence. The textbook's in my hand, then Frisbeeing across the room before I can even think about what I'm doing. It lands with a thud.

"See? See?" I hear Robbie say. My heart is pounding in my ears. I snatch up Julian's backpack and dash for the door. Feet thudding, heart pounding, bag thumping, passing full classrooms, teachers calling names. I glimpse a head turning toward me.

Slow down, girl, 'fore you get everyone out here on ya case.

I listen to Julian's voice, drop down to a walk. I'm near the library—a little farther and I'll be at the counselor's office. Her email flashes into my mind. *I know we've got time scheduled together for two thirty, Karmen, but come see me any time you want to talk. Or not talk. Or just take a break.* I slow even more outside the lounge. Couldn't I even get through the first twenty minutes of the day?

I push the door open. Pru is there, clothes restored to uniform code—blouse tucked in, skirt hem below the knee. Her loafers and socks lounge below the low table, and one foot is cocked up on the edge, a bottle of nail polish beside her bare toes. The contents shimmer silver-white, like crushed stars. Pru shakes the polish twice, unscrews it, eases the tiny brush out. She strokes a layer onto her left big toe. She doesn't look up at me. "*Your* summer sucked."

"How would you know?" I snap as I slump into the farthest chair from her. Even someone brand-new, even someone whose only reason for being here seems to be to get noticed, knows what happened to Julian. *She ain fake, Karm,* Julian would say. *At least she's real.* I don't know if Julian's right, but, as I lean back, my head starts to clear just a bit. I'm mad at Robbie, not her. And it's true. *Sucked* doesn't come close.

"We aren't supposed to wear nail polish."

"Or extensions." Her braids are up in a messy bun, a few tendrils loose at the edges, snaking over her face and down her back. She dips the brush again and wipes it on the bottle's mouth. "Next year we can vote, though." Pru lifts the brush, holds it out toward me.

It's stone-silent outside the lounge. The whole school's in their classrooms now, except me, Pru, and whoever's on the other side of that soundproof door with Ms. Dorsett, having what must be another first-day-of-the-school-year breakdown.

"Why'd you do that? Get up in Robbie's face?"

"Robbie's an ass." Pru announces this like she's reporting the weather, like she wasn't ready to fight a boy she'd never met on her first day at a new school. Her hand is still extended, waiting, sure.

What you think ga happen? You get sent to the office?

I can't argue with Julian's voice. I can feel him, too, beside me. See his eyes meeting mine in a shared smirk at the way Pru's holding out nail polish like she's offering me a joint. I drop my bag and slide into the chair opposite her, then lift the brush from her fingers. She's wearing French tips. Not even subtle ones. There's a tiny stud embedded in the middle of each one. Like she figured she'd start September guns blazing, manicured middle fingers to the sky.

Pru lifts her other foot onto the table and grips the edge with her toes. She half smiles. I stroke a vertical line down the middle of my thumbnail, then even it out on each side.

"So, what, you just like trouble?" I ask, to break up the silence.

She shrugs. "I don't like that word."

"Robbie's an ass." I move to my pinkie nail. Painted, it looks like a tiny, precious shell, like some unexpected treasure. The office door opens and I scramble to hide the brush, and my hand. It's just another kid, who looks at Ms. Dorsett's closed door, then retreats.

"Shoulda done your toes." She holds her hand out and I pass the brush back. She screws it back onto the bottle.

"You still waiting to talk to Ms. D?" I ask.

"For, like, a minute. Supposed to journal a list of ten of my best internal attributes."

"Looks like you got far."

She laughs outright this time, short and loud. It comes out *Ha!* "How is it?" she asks.

"What?"

"Being back after what happened with your brother."

"You weren't even here last year. Who told you?"

Pru shrugs, holds my gaze until I drop it. "Nassau small. People knew Julian. I—"

A sound behind Ms. Dorsett's door cuts Pru's words short. She crams her bare feet into her shoes, slings her bag over her arm, then reaches on top of a bookshelf. My breath catches in my throat as I see what she brings down.

A skateboard.

She darts outside, and through the closing door I hear that sound I know almost as well as Julian's voice—the clack of wheels hitting the ground, whoosh-swish of a board gliding away. I stumble after Pru in time to see her skateboard down the empty hallway. She glances back a second before she swoops around a corner, out of sight. I stand there, motionless as a tree. What was she about to say? Something tells me she's more than just a stickler for respectful words. Nassau *is* small, and almost no one here skateboards. I keep staring down the empty hallway, questions circling me like birds looking to land. Wondering if she holds the key to the questions I carry. Wishing, more than anything else, it was my brother who'd just skated away.

The morning's classes pass in a blur. Ms. Dorsett's words ring in my ears: *Take it slowly. Step away when you need to.* At lunch I head to the cafeteria to meet Layla. The room teems with jostling, hungry bodies, and I strain to pick out her short brown 'fro and blue headband. Finally I spot her on the side by the water fountain with Joelle and Danika. I squeeze through kids toward them.

". . . he would do that," Joelle says as I come up behind them.

Danika sucks her teeth. "What's with the new girl, too? Who comes to school dressed like that?"

At least they're not talking about me, I think. I'm about to step forward when Layla says, "That's why they emailed everyone, obviously. So nobody would say something stupid."

"I think it's sad they gotta tell people how to act. I mean, her brother died." It's true, but Joelle says it so casually, it makes my breakfast threaten to rise.

"Not just died." Danika leans in close. "Like, died in the *worst way.*"

I hear the clatter of my lunch tray as it hits the floor, but it feels far away. Something cold runs down my shin. Layla spins around, and as our eyes meet, I see something in them I never thought I'd see. Guilt. Like she was gossiping about me. Joelle and Danika slink away.

"You okay?" Layla's voice sounds like hers. It sounds like she cares. But I can't look her in the eye right now. Her words are still sinking in. Someone—Mr. Douglas, I guess—sent our whole class an email about Julian? And she didn't even tell me? I stoop down and pick up my empty tray, but my hands are shaking. I don't want to shake. I don't want people whispering about me, hiding from me. I want last year's life. I want someone else's life.

I straighten up. "I'm gonna go sit."

"It wasn't like it sounded—we were talking about—"

"I heard what y'all were talking about. What happened this morning, and about how Julian died—"

"In here so crowded." Layla tries to take my arm, but I step away. "Let's go sit under the tree."

"Died by suicide."

"Someplace over there." She heads for a free table by the windows. I follow her, but my feet feel numb. I sit opposite Layla. There's clinking and chatter around us. Everyone else is going on with lunch, with life. I stare at my friend. She fiddles with the side of her tray, looks over her shoulder again. What's she looking for?

"What was in the email?" I ask. Layla's eyes are on her neatly sliced sandwich. My mind flashes back to Pru—disheveled misfit. I look down at my painted nail, smudged and sparkly. It doesn't fit in at this table either.

"Mr. Douglas emailed everyone to explain that—to say what happened with Julian. I mean, he didn't give details, he just said he had passed—"

"Passed? Passed what? His driving test? Passed the bar?"

Layla flinches at my words. I can't stop, though.

"Passed by the graveyard and dropped off a résumé? Passed on life? I can't stand that stupid term. He died. Say *died.*"

Layla's head is low. "Sorry."

Everything in me—blood, veins, bones—is shaking. "You couldn't tell me?"

"I just thought—it was supposed to be something nice. Mr. Douglas just emailed everyone—"

"Everyone except me."

"—and said that your brother had—he had died, and that we should acknowledge it at the start of the first day. Just to, like, show you we care."

I can hear Layla chewing on the inside of her cheek. This day's turning into a nightmare. Everyone—everyone—knew this was going to happen except me. Did Ms. Dorsett know too? It's like no one gets me. No one gets that I just want to slide into class, open my book. Be like everyone else around me. Be someone whose brother isn't gone.

Layla slides half her sandwich over to me. "I never meant to hurt you, Karmen. I don't know what to do. I think people just want you to know we care. That's all."

Her mouth is in a sad frown, and she's looking at me like a mistreated puppy. I'm even less hungry than I was before, but I pick up her peace offering and take a bite. Tuna with bits of pickle chopped up in it. I suppress my grimace and swallow it down.

"Thanks," I say.

She nods, her easy smile already starting to return. "You comin by me after school?"

"I dunno."

"Come on. We can go to youth group together."

Layla's brother flashes into my mind. I haven't talked to Isaiah since—no. I push the night away. Layla keeps chattering on, but I can't follow her words. Instead I force my mind in a different direction—a direction that matters. Back to the letter. Julian's letter from the university. Back to the answers I'm looking for. Back to the *why* of him walking out one night and never coming back.

"Just come." Layla's chirp breaks into my thoughts. She stands up. "I gotta get some water. You want anything?"

I shake my head. She slips off through the crowd, and I

sit there with my lunch. I push it aside and reach down into Julian's backpack. As I pull the letter out, my heart speeds up like I've broken into a jog. I unfold the paper and read fast.

Dear Julian Wallace,

This letter is to inform you that you have been placed on academic probation. Your GPA in the fall semester was at 1.90, and it fell to 1.75 this past semester. As you know, students with two consecutive semesters below 2.00 must be placed on academic probation.

In order to continue at Commonwealth University, we require you to retake those courses in which you obtained a D or F.

Commonwealth University is committed to your success. We encourage all students on academic probation to meet with both their academic advisor and Campus Wellness to plan a return to campus life at a pace that supports their individual needs and success.

Please directly contact your advisor, who will meet with you.

Sincerely,
Dr. Jackson Fox
Dean of Social Sciences

Even after I read it twice, the words don't make sense to me. Julian got straight As through high school. He had a scholarship. How could he have gotten kicked out of school? Is this why he ended his life? Do my parents know?

I push the letter away; Layla will be back soon. I can't make sense of the words I've just read right now. I feel the bench across from me shake before I see that Layla's sat down.

"What you think about clubs this year? I was thinking we could sign up for the paper and Arts Club, and Earth Club, and—"

"Sure, yeah." I sling Julian's bag over my shoulder. "I'll do whatever. I gotta go pee."

"See you after lunch," she calls after me. I can hear the forlorn in my best friend's voice but I have to keep going— through the cafeteria, out into the sun, just going going. Moving might be the only way to get through this day. To get to where I can understand what I just read. To understand how I got here—without Julian.

The end of the day can't come fast enough. When I see our car, I make a beeline for it like it's lined with million-dollar bills.

"Don't forget, youth group tonight!" Layla hollers after me.

Pulling the car door open almost feels like stepping into our front door—it's a little piece of home. I plunk down in the seat and lean back into the headrest. Daddy reaches over and puts his hand on mine.

"You made it through."

I look over at him. He seems the same as always—steady eyes, even, calm. It could be September of any year. How is that possible? He starts up the car and I close my eyes as we head home.

When I open our front door, Julian's sneakers still sit there, waiting patiently.

Bare bulb's glare, sideways lamp casts light over the closet door, bed thrown into strange dark. Tangle of prints, trampled map, flag pins strewn everywhere. My hands shake as I reach for the light, switch it off. I instantly regret it as police lights strobe our driveway blue-red, blue-red.

I squeeze my eyes shut as I let the backpack drop from my shoulder. When I open them, though, everything is still there, where I left it. Everything except him. I step out of my lace-ups without untying them. The house feels stagnant.

"Hey?" I call, not particularly loud.

"Karmen." My mother's voice floats out through her open office door. "I'm in here." Mummy sits on the pale blue sofa she favors during counseling sessions. She's still in the same bathrobe. There's a plate of half-eaten salad beside her on the couch.

"Mummy?" She never has food in there. There's a purple notebook beside her too. A bloom of black ink spreads over the center of the page. She's not written anything. How long has she been sitting here?

"How was school?"

I swallow down the words I want to say. "Fine." I notice the open patient file on her lap, near the notebook. She folds it closed and drops it onto the floor beside the sofa.

"You wanna talk about your day?"

Ink stains her thumb tip, too. I can't bring myself to ask her if she knew about Mr. Douglas emailing everyone else in the class. "Nothing much happened. It was okay."

She nods, looking through me.

The ink's smeared on her robe. How long has this been going on? How long did she stay, holding the pen that couldn't capture words she couldn't write anyway? "What happened to your paper?"

She looks down then, makes a small, startled noise. She fumbles for the pen cap, finds it in the groove between the sofa cushions, snaps it into place. "Come talk to me."

The awfulness in homeroom rushes back to me. I want to know if she knew, if she gave Mr. Douglas the okay. But she can't even remember where pens go. How to write. "I just wanna lie down."

She looks down at the school shoes dangling from my fingers, then back up at me. Lifts the plate of wilted greens. A tiny fly alights, then settles again. "You want something to eat?"

I shake my head. I should take the plate and throw that old food away, but I don't even have the energy. I glance back at the foyer. We've always left shoes on the rack by the door. It feels wrong to put mine down by Julian's now.

I trudge upstairs and collapse on my bed. I close my eyes, but snippets of the day whirl through my mind like dry leaves. *Academic probation. Died in the worst way. Your summer sucked. Nassau small. People knew Julian. Get away with anything. Just because.*

I take a breath, like Ms. Rhonda suggested at counseling

last week. Let it out. The thoughts are a little further away, but what comes rushing in is a memory of Julian. Julian, sitting on his bed, nose buried in a textbook. I'm holding my half-written history essay out to him. It comes easy for him.

"Hey. You want do this for me?"

"Stop playin. Go do your work."

I plunk down by the foot of the bed and heave a sigh. "At least read it for me."

He looks up. "It's due when?"

"Tomorrow."

He rolls his eyes and snatches the pages out of my hand and reads aloud.

"'There's been a mysterious disappearance of one of the artifacts from the Pompey Museum. Write a report from your professional point of view about what has taken place. Choose one of the following jobs: police investigator, museum curator, reporter covering the occurrence, thief, security guard, café owner across the street.'" Julian looks up. "And you chose . . ."

"Reporter."

"Think that was a wise choice?"

"What you mean?"

He shakes his head and carries on silently. I flop down onto the bed while I wait. "Okay," he says at last. "Couple things. First, you should write this over from a different point of view."

"Why?"

"You're not a journalist. You don't think the right way. You don't have enough detail. For one, you have to think of the five Ws: who, what, when, where, why. And how."

23

"How's not a W, and that's six."

"You want argue, or you want an A?"

I sigh. "Go ahead."

"You say, 'It was a grim day in downtown Nassau today when a valuable piece went missing without explanation.' A reporter would start off answering as many of those Ws as possible, straight off. 'Police and staff at the Pompey Museum are baffled after the priceless mill vanished inexplicably from the site on Bay Street sometime yesterday.'"

I roll over. "Agggghh. I already spent an hour on this stupid thing." I look over at Julian. "I'll pay you thirty to write it for me."

He throws the pages at me. "Lazy. Go do the work yourself."

"You think I should pick a different point of view?"

"Why'd you pick reporter?"

I gather up the pages. Why do you think? I want to ask. But it never pays for your big brother to think he has too much sway. "Not everyone's like you. Not everyone knows what they wanna be from the time they're ten." I wait for him to toss a jab my way, tell me that if I focused more, I'd know what I want to do. I get up to go.

He picks up his book again. "Just remember: who, what, when, where, why. That's how to cover the most important info. Every time."

I open my eyes and reach for the backpack, take Julian's notebook. With trembling fingers, I flip past the pages of Julian's handwriting, past the one Robbie tore. I stop at the questions. *Think of it as an assignment,* I tell myself. *Get answers like Julian would.*

Except I'm not Julian. He's always been older, smarter, *better* than me. I look at my bedroom wall, at the calendar hanging there. This one's turned to September. There it is, in the middle of the month—Julian's birthday. What if I could find answers by then? Understanding him. That would be a gift.

I grit my teeth and start to add to the list of questions.

Who would know how Julian really was those last months?

What did he do when he was on probation?

When did he start feeling like it was too much?

Where did he go?

Why did he end his life?

My fingers shake so much, I drop the pen. One last question swirls around in my mind, but I don't want to write it down. I grab my pillow and scream into it as hard as I can. It muffles the roar, the worst question of them all. Muffles it but can't silence it. I scream till I'm hoarse, but the question doesn't go away. I drop the pillow, pick up the pen again. I make myself write it down, but as I do, I feel so hollow. I'm his sister. I shouldn't have to ask these questions. I should know. I should have known, and he should be here, alive, getting a real gift.

How could I have missed this?

CHAPTER TWO

My body is done with this day, but my mind won't lie still. I have a notebook full of questions, and dozens more in my mind. What else were those other girls saying about me? What did they say that I didn't hear? What else did they say about Julian? How do I go back tomorrow and do it all again? Did my parents know Julian had to drop out of CU? Why didn't they tell me? Why didn't they do something? Why didn't I just know? Family knows—or at least asks. If only I'd done more, asked more, looked more, he'd be alive. He'd be here right now.

Suddenly I can't seem to get enough air. I sit up, put my feet on the floor. Still feel my chest tightening. I can't stay here suffocating in questions. I have to move. I have to ask. I have to go. I grab the notebook and wedge it into my skirt pocket. As I reach for the door, the house phone rings, two hollow chimes. I step into the hallway. I hear Mummy in her room. Her whimpers carry through the closed door. I can't listen to her—I might break.

I take the stairs in twos and round the corner to the front door.

"No, no appointments." Daddy's voice stops me short. "Mrs. Wallace isn't seeing any clients." He's on the phone. I sneak a look at his face. He seems normal, first glance: shirt tucked into jeans, his red-framed glasses perched high on the bridge of his nose. But his shoulders are slumped, and those new lines near his mouth look thick and well-worn. His jaw is clenched.

"No, not even for emergencies. Her clients are being referred to Brighter Days Healing Center. No, I don't know when she'll be available again. All the best." He hangs up. He looks down at the phone like it's a strange object he's not seen before. He seems unsure whether to snap it in two or launch it at the wall.

"Hey."

"Oh, Karmen." Daddy's face is bare and startled, the way he looked when I forgot to knock on the bedroom door and walked in on him in a T-shirt and briefs. I look away.

"Can I ask you a question?"

He puts the phone down on the chair. "What's up?"

"Did you . . ."

A muscle in his jaw twitches.

"Do you think . . ." *Think Julian was doing okay at CU?* The words are right there, but now doesn't feel like the right time.

"You want me to take you somewhere?"

I think fast. "Layla invited me over."

"You told your mother you goin out?"

I look back over my shoulder. "I didn't wanna bother her."

"You gotta tell her every time. You gotta say where you goin, say goodbye."

"I told you."

A low wail begins upstairs. Daddy's mouth lines deepen. "I'll drop you off. Go wait in the car. I'll tell her this time."

I grab the backpack and my shoes and take them outside to put them on, though I can't help but see the blue-and-white sneakers as I open the front door. I lean against the gate to the backyard. Then something catches my eye. It leans upright against the lime tree, wheels sun-bleached and worn, the logo of a bird with outstretched wings barely visible on the wood. Julian's skateboard. Cerasee twines around its wheels, the wiry vines trapping it. I wrench the gate open and push through—Julian would have never left it out here. I try not to remember the evening, the police inspector, voice matter-of-fact.

"*Sometimes we see this . . . unstable behavior in the counterculture youth.*" *The policeman sets Julian's skateboard down on the table like it's drug paraphernalia.*

"*Counterculture.*" *Daddy's voice is dangerously bland. "He was an honor-roll student through high school, not a criminal.*"

"*No offense intended, sir. I know you're upset, and I know it's disappointing that we can't find any leads, even a suicide note. I'm just saying, we see young people with unusual interests—*"

"*Skateboarding? Officer, you have something useful you found regarding my son's death, we want to know. Otherwise . . .*"

Later, Mummy shouting: "I wish that thing never even came in the house!"

"*Stop talking mess, Barb. You of all people know it ain that simple. Please.*"

"Me of all people?" The back door opens—then the crack of wood hitting the metal fence.

"Happy? It's out of the house now." Daddy's words make me flinch. "All better now."

I pull on the board until the vine snaps. The skateboard is freed. The wood is slightly swollen where the varnish wore thin at the back. I sit on the patio. Rock-warmth through my damp clothes and through my thighs, my hips, my behind. Sun beats down on the back of my neck as I bend over the board, unwinding weed tendrils. As the plant gives way, its leaves release their grubby musk. I toss them into the grass. As I hold the board, he is here again, alive, in our kitchen tearing open a wide white box.

"That's it?" Daddy peers over Julian's shoulder.

"Yup." He pulls the skateboard out and sets it down on the table, right on my English homework. "Look at those wheels."

"Nice. Red trim, too."

"Mummy, Julian have his toy on my papers!"

"On the floor, Julian! Remember, I got you a helmet, too."

Julian and Daddy spill outside, wheels hitting the patio, then skidding shoes, laughter, and shouts intersperse with thumps and yelps as Julian wipes out. I try to ignore the two of them, turn my back to the kitchen door, but their cheers still disturb me. I grab my books and head upstairs, still grumpy. But joy has feathers, and the sound of it floats up to me, through the open windows, and by the time my books are open, I have to smile.

My fingers touch the scuffed black deck, run over the once-white wheels. I lay the board on the driveway. It rolls slightly, almost alive on its own. It's instinctive to step up onto it with one foot. It rolls more, and I fight for balance, stumble off. I bend down, lift it to my chest. This thing, this feels like something. Feels like a way. To get into my brother's head. To understand.

I ring Layla's doorbell and wait. Daddy idles in the driveway behind me. I wonder if he's in no rush to get back home either. I keep the skateboard in front of me—Daddy didn't comment on it while we drove, but I know he saw it from the way he kept glancing over. Same as I kept looking over at him. I hear low laughter from inside the house. Isaiah. I run my hands over my hair, not that it'll help. I should have at least checked the mirror before I got out of the car. Layla's always tidy and neat, always has a compact in her pocket and lip gloss in her bag. In its own special compartment, no less. Sometimes I wonder why we're even friends, we're so different. I hear Julian's voice, again, singing now.

> *I take two steps forward*
> *I take two steps back*
> *We come together 'cause opposites attract,*
> *and you know . . .*

The memory comes over me then. He's crooning the song into the bathroom mirror as he pats his hair down low, turns his head this way, then that, checking every angle.

"Boy, when you cuttin that forest on your head?" I reach between him and the mirror to get my lotion.

"This a crown, girl."

I suck my teeth. "Who you tryin to impress?"

My brother tilts his chin up. "Just tryin to look fresh. Take pride."

"You goin skateboardin and have to look fresh all of a sudden? Who you tryin to impress?"

"Only you one out there scopin all the time." He gives an unconvincing snort. Tries to suppress a smile.

"It's a little lopsided over here."

"Where?" He twists his neck, eyes sharp as he scans for a dent in the carefully groomed Afro.

"Here!" I plunge my hand into his 'fro and yank up, making a big peak in the primped coils.

"Get out!" he howls, slamming the door shut after me as I run down the stairs, guffawing. Worth the smear of grease I'll have to wash off.

I raise my hand to my face now, half expecting to smell the rosemary zing of his pomade. There's only the faintest whiff of mustard from the sandwich I half ate at lunch. The door opens, and suddenly Isaiah stands in front of me, tall and wide-shouldered. I step back, like an idiot, and blink. It seems impossible that Isaiah's here in front of me, and I'm here, and that memory is here in my mind, and Julian is just—not.

"Hey." Isaiah's smile is the warmth I've wanted all day. With everything I've felt since morning, I didn't even know I was cold. I can't find words, just smile up at him—way up. His eyes, deep and dark, are on mine, and his beard gleams like it's freshly oiled and combed—and then he looks away, over my shoulder. "Hi, Mr. Wallace!"

Daddy. I even forgot he was there. I turn around too. Daddy peers back, gives a concerned wave. I don't need to think hard to guess what he's thinking. Then his face clears a little.

"You came!" Layla's squeal hits me seconds before she folds me into a hug. "Come in. Skateboard? You got plans?" She squeezes past Isaiah, waves at Daddy too, who eases out of the driveway, convinced I'm not here for an unannounced tryst. "I made cookies. You hungry? Mummy, Karmen here."

"Hi, Karmen. I'm on a call right now," Layla's mother hollers back. I push down a twinge as I follow Layla through the house, skateboard under my arm. Must be nice, having a mother who can take her own calls. In the kitchen, sure enough, there's a rack of cookies—chocolate chip. She's even got glasses and nice plates out. I remember why we're friends. Sometimes she loves so hard, it's impossible not to get caught up.

Layla snaps on the TV and pours out milk for us both. "What are you doing Friday after school? We might go bowling and get pizza for dinner."

I slide the board under the table, then sit. "I can't go." I rest one foot on the board, feel it shift. "I have to go to the counselor."

"Ms. Rhonda?"

"Yup." I bite into a cookie. It tastes like Functional Family.

"Well, maybe after?"

Chances of me wanting to do anything other than sleep, after talking with Ms. Rhonda for an hour, are low. Layla's trying, though, really trying. And her cookies are good, and I want this piece of time to be good too. I take a drink of milk. "Maybe."

"So, you ready for youth group?"

"I'm here, right?"

"Yeah, I just mean—I get it if you don't wanna do church," Layla says quickly.

"It's not that. Why you think I don't wanna do church?"

She gets an *oh shoot* look on her face. "I didn't mean that. I just meant—"

I feel washed over with heat, prickles of sweat under my arms, across my back. "We went before. What's the big deal?"

"I thought just 'cause . . . you didn't come all last month, and y'all ain been to church since . . ."

"Yeah, we ain been since Julian died."

The air between us feels like discolored water, contaminated, gone stagnant. I push my chair back.

"I gotta go pee." I reach down and grab the skateboard, then feel ridiculous with it as I walk past the bright, tidy living room. What am I going to do, skateboard from the toilet to the sink? In the bathroom, I set it on the counter, splash water on my face, grab a squeeze of the orange-scented lotion from the bottle that never seems to run out. I rub the thick cream into my hands, though my palms are already sweating again. Does Layla have to tiptoe around me? We've been friends for five years now. Why's she making things up for me instead of just asking? *Karmen, how come you ain been to church since Julian died?* Why concoct a whole story? What's the point? I'm right here. She doesn't have to guess. She can know.

When I come out, I'm still not ready to go back. I take a

few steps down to Layla's bedroom. Her white, metal-framed bed is overloaded with purple and green accent pillows. The hot-pink cushion I knitted for her last birthday is perched in the center. Light spills over the top of the push-down blinds. Her bag leans neatly against her desk. I use my tongue to poke at the compressed cookie bits stuck in my back teeth. It's not like Layla doesn't care—I still have her caring wedged between my molars. It just seems, some moments, like our two lives don't . . . fit. I step into her room. I don't know what I'm planning to do. Maybe verify that two very different things can exist together in the same space.

After that night, and the blur of days following—calls from one of the tabloids asking for a quote, for any recollections, Daddy shouting *Stop harassing my family!* and my parents disappearing to the hospital, to the morgue, to the funeral home—the house was oddly full. People streamed in and out. Auntie Laura flew in from Exuma, her two children perched on the sofa, staring obediently at cartoons, neither peeping nor wriggling like five- and eight-year-olds should. Layla's mom hugging me, Layla crying on my shoulder. Two of Daddy's friends came and sat out front with him, the dining chairs dragged out onto the driveway. Then there was the funeral, and then the repast, people crowding the kitchen and stairs, guys who graduated with Julian, a handful of teachers, others I didn't know but who seemed to know me. Layla there too, constant, at my side, maneuvering past people and finally up to my room.

Inside, we sat on the floor, music on low, the rumble of voices below, inescapable even as I edged up the volume. I felt outside my body, as if those legs, that chest, that head I leaned back against the closed door, were not where I was, as if I were somewhere up beyond them, a balloon tethered to a weight, bobbing. But when I try to think of us spending time since then, my mind draws a blank.

"Goin for a spin in here?"

Isaiah's voice sends me just about through the ceiling. I jump—and fumble the board. It slides across the floor and comes to rest right by his foot. "I didn't mean to scare you." He bends down as I do, too. Isaiah's faster—he picks up the skateboard. "You skateboard now?"

Heat washes over me. "It was Julian's. I found it in the yard."

He holds out a hand. "Can I see?"

I hesitate.

"You can say no," he adds, and that changes my mind all the way.

"I trust you." The words pop out before my mind realizes I feel that way. His grin is wide and warm as it radiates up to his eyes, out to his ears. Across the small space, and through me. I feel his joy in the middle of my chest. Feel it spread out and up. Make me smile. He takes the board, turns it over gently, then passes it back.

"Should shake youth group up nicely. How come you hangin out in here instead of with Layla? Everything all right with y'all two?"

"Yeah. I guess."

"Or you plan on unearthing the dark secrets in our house?"

"Ha-ha." The idea of anything being hidden in this house is too ridiculous to be genuinely funny.

"Oh, you don't know." He looks around like a bandit in an old cartoon, then tiptoes in, beckoning me. He lifts a corner of her bedspread. A tumble of shoes, clothes, a bit of a book. I burst out laughing.

"Can I help y'all?"

I spin around at the sound of Layla's voice. Isaiah drops the spread like a hot French fry. Layla's eyes go from him to me, then back. They land on me again. Mad? Annoyed? Full-on pissed? I can't get a read on them. She flops onto her bed. "Zaiah, you drivin us to youth group or what?"

He glances at his phone. "We should leave in ten."

I suddenly feel aware of how close we are—maybe it's the way he had to move, reaching, back. I sit on Layla's bed too. Isaiah leans in the doorway, one arm draped up over his head. It's awkward, and I bite my lip to hide my smile, and look away. That's for me? Pretty sure it's not a brother move.

"You goin tonight too?" I try to sound nonchalant.

"Yeah." Isaiah stretches. I can't help but notice his shirt slide up just a bit at the waist. It's tucked in well.

"How come you all dressed up?" I say.

"New job. At PK Accounting, right across from the university." He adjusts the collar on his dress shirt, then tugs at the tie. My eyes drift to his shoulders—wide and strong.

Layla snickers. "As an assistant. They didn't ask him to come in fancy clothes, though."

"You have to dress for the reality you want, not the reality you have." He winks at me, and my insides turn to mush. "Right, Karmen?"

"And the reality Isaiah wants is to be a tie model," Layla cuts in. "He bought *eight* separate ties for this part-time job, *and* he's going to class looking like that." She reaches over and opens her dresser drawer. "I gettin dressed to go."

Isaiah reaches over and snags the top Layla just took out—a pink T-shirt with GIRLS RULE printed across the chest. His arm brushes against the top of my head as he lifts the shirt up to him. Tingles shoot through my scalp. "This should fit."

"Get *out*!" Layla tosses a pair of socks at him as he makes his escape.

The room is extra still for a second, two, three. Layla looks at me.

"What?" I say, as if sweat isn't gathering under my arms.

"What was that?"

"Nothing! We were just talking—"

"Right." She closes the door and shimmies out of her school skirt, then pulls on a pair of jeans. "Okay, well, give me notice if you want me to design the wedding dress."

"Funny." More sweat now. I lean toward the doorway—he isn't in earshot, is he?

"Relax, he's in his room by now. You need help. You borrowing clothes or you plan on wearing uniform all night?"

I pick out a T-shirt dress and head to the bathroom again. Layla may not need to wash her pits after a school day in September, but I do.

• • •

Layla climbs in the back seat beside me. "I have something for you." She slips a hand into her bag and pulls out an emerald-green skein of yarn.

"Oooh! It came!" I snatch it up. I remember us poring over the catalog she ordered, cooing over the colors—gemstone-rich squares that almost sprang off the page.

"Pretty, hey?"

"What y'all talkin bout?" Isaiah turns around from the driver's seat.

"We ordered this back in June." Layla reaches over to slide the label off.

"You wanna split it?" I fish out the loose end at the center.

"I was saving it for you—but, okay. You gonna mix it or—"

"I only got orange in my bag. I'll see how it look on its own." I ease off a length—the yarn resists a little, then gives way, lets itself be pulled loose from its core. As I work the softness around and between my fingers, something settles in me. Layla leans in to check how I've looped.

"Ah, right, like that," she mutters, and something flutters up in me. Pride, maybe. We never really compete, but it feels a little good, seeing her need to look to me for how to get something right, even if it's just finger-knitting. By the time we pull into the churchyard, I've got a solid chunk of knitted rope. Layla's is snugger, tidier. My pride deflates a little, but I push that feeling away. "You need a stitch holder?" she asks, easing one out of her apparently bottomless bag.

"Nah, I'll wing it." I reach past the skateboard at my feet and root around in my backpack with my free hand until I finally feel a pen. I slip the four stitches off my left fingers and onto the pen, then lay it on the middle seat. "All good."

There are just a few cars parked outside the church. Isaiah eases in near the door and hops out. He stretches, and, from the back seat I stifle a smile as his shirt rides up just a bit.

"Are we early?" I check my phone. Most people start showing up twenty minutes before. "What y'all wanna do?"

"I'm gonna go practice. See y'all in there." Isaiah's already humming.

"You wanna hang out with Isaiah for a minute?" Layla hovers at the door, glances over her shoulder at no one.

"I'm not in the choir."

"Yeah, but . . ." Her excuse fizzles out.

"You tryin to get rid of me?" I step in first and head toward the activity room. The folding tables are still leaned against the wall, the chairs in stacks. "I wonder who's on setup duty."

"Why don't you go relax a bit."

"We at the spa? Relax where?"

She reaches for a stack of chairs and starts lifting them down. "The sanctuary . . ."

"I should go lay across a pew, put my feet up and nap?" I lean over and feel her forehead. "You got a fever?"

"Just suggesting." Layla trips over a chair.

"I don't know why you so jumpy." I step over to the schedule. "Who supposed to be setting up anyway? I mean, I don't mind helping, but if it's Jaya, she get kinda funny when people do her stuff—"

"Why don't you just—" Layla bounds over like some big secret's on the schedule. And there it is. *Setup, September. Layla and Devin.*

"Oh."

"I—sorry, I know we always do it but, I—I mean, I didn't want you to get stressed out or . . ." Layla's voice is getting tight and high. "I didn't even know if you wanted to come. And we had to sign our names up start of August."

"Right." I don't have to work to remember the start of August. Up and down to the funeral home, calls from the police, the newspaper, the cemetery. For a second I see Mummy on her side on Julian's bed, his powder-blue suit laid out. She's making this sound—like something deep in her has been hooked and twisted as it's being wrenched away. I guess I wouldn't have wanted to talk about whether I'd rather set out bottled water or pour chips into big bowls. On the other hand—here I am. Did she think I was that incapable? She could have texted Devin and asked him to switch with me. She could have even just said, *I'm setting up with Devin.*

"Hey, Layla, I thought you wasn't coming." Devin comes in with a pack of napkins and a stack of cups. "Oh, Karmen!" He side-hugs me. "We missed you. You arrite?"

"Mm-hmm." I feel squashed down with the weight of his question—he didn't ask Layla that. He knows *she's* good. The thought is like a loose thread on my skin: persistent, irritating. I brush it away—at least *he's* honest. "You good?"

"Yeah, yeah, I'm great. You helpin set up? Three of us could finish faster." He looks from me to Layla, who's frozen over by the chairs, like she got caught throwing a party without inviting me. The room is stifling; it feels too small. I pick up the skateboard and step out without answering. To the left, snatches of conversation waft out from the foyer. I turn right. The hallway leads past the kitchen—the youth leaders, Ms. Elaine and Mr. Chris, are here now and chatting. I slide past them, then by the offices and the choir entrance to the stage. Practice hasn't begun, but the musicians are warming up, haphazard notes that meld, then clash, then meld again. Isaiah's off to one side, singing low. I take a step back—I really just want a second for me. I don't want him to think I'm following him.

I reach into Julian's bag with my free hand. My fingers find the notebook's cold spiral. I slip a finger between its curls, feel the metal give and bend. I slide on to the emergency exit. Lean my back against the metal door and pause a moment.

"All right, who here for Youth Night, come on in, almost time to start." Behind me, Ms. Elaine's voice is sweet as always. I can picture her round-cheeked face getting rounder as she beams, waving folks in. I hear Layla's voice. "I don't know. She was here a minute ago. Let me go see . . ."

My own best friend, who doesn't know how to be around me—how to even talk to me. I lean back into the door, hard this time, and step outside.

The air is humid and heavy, too weary to shrug off the day's heat. The sun stretches shadows out long. There are a handful of guys on the basketball court. I recognize Elrin: he and Julian used to be friends long ago, long before they were even in double digits. I grip the notebook like a lifeline. My questions loom. Who knew? Elrin? Any of these guys?

"Hey," I call, and all eyes are on me. My chest pounds like I'm the one who's been running up and down. "Any of y'all used to hang out with Julian?"

"Nah." Elrin answers for the whole group.

"He never used to skateboard out here?"

"Court always full, and the driveway too rough. He used to go off that way when y'all was here for group and stuff." Elrin points vaguely through the back parking lot and into the neighborhood beyond. I nod.

"You know where?"

Elrin shakes his head. I start walking the way he pointed. I'm not sure where I'm going, but the thumping in my chest feels different, now—scared. What if no one knows anything? No—it's too early to think that.

"Where you goin, girl?"

I know Isaiah's voice even before I turn around. "I thought you had practice."

"I thought you was in with Layla and them."

"I had to get out." I don't look at him. I don't have to. There's a feeling I get from him, all around: a listening, an understanding.

"What's on your mind?"

Between the notebook and the board, my hands feel awkwardly full. I set the board on the ground. It rolls a little, like it's moved by its own life. It seems wrong, the skateboard moving without Julian's feet on it. Without Julian here to make it go. Tears prick my eyes. I look down, hope Isaiah hasn't noticed. "Long day."

"You must miss him."

The tears give up teetering and start to fall, hard. I wrap my arms around myself, hold the notebook to my chest. Isaiah's arms are around me—a large tree, branches gentle, strong, steady. I close my eyes, lean in. He doesn't say anything, just lets me stand there, soaking up his strength, till the crying eases away. Holds me a minute longer.

"That's a reporter's notebook."

I ease away. His warmth is still imprinted all around me. "It was Julian's."

"I figured."

I flip to the page I wrote on. I hand it to him, my heart beating fast again. I want him to know. The way he held me—I figure he can help me hold these questions up. "I'm trying to figure stuff out. I just thought someone must know . . . what happened? Know why it happened."

Isaiah nods. "You wanna sit? Or you wanna walk?"

I need to move. "Walk."

Isaiah and I walk along in silence for a couple minutes. *Say something,* I think, but my mind goes completely blank. It's Isaiah, I've known him forever, but my feet suddenly don't feel like mine, like I have to think extra carefully to keep walking.

"What's it been like?" Isaiah asks, after a while.

"I dunno. Weird. Like a really bad dream."

"You sleeping at night?"

I think of my mother's fitful rest, how she cries out sometimes. "Mostly." I feel like I should say something else, let him know it's okay for him to ask—that I like him asking. "Home just . . . doesn't feel like home, I guess."

We turn left. It's all just houses through here. I can't imagine there's anyplace Julian would have come, except to glide through quiet streets. Maybe to think.

"How's your mum?"

"She got up before I left for school today. That was kinda momentous."

"Sounds like all of y'all are having a hard time." Isaiah reaches down to touch the notebook a second. His fingers send tremors through. I feel them in my hand. "You and your mum close?"

"I mean . . . she's my mother. I'm closest with Julian, mostly." *Was closest,* I think. As we walk in silence, I think of my brother and me. Of the things we tell ourselves. How I always *knew* we were close. Were kind of best friends for each other.

"Those questions you got written down. You know it wasn't your fault. You know that, right?"

I keep my eyes on the road ahead. I don't know that at all. I know I'm here, and Julian isn't. Everything else is uncertain, now.

"Karmen? You know that, right?" Isaiah's voice is more urgent this time. I nod just to end this conversation thread.

"Good. Hey—look there." Isaiah points ahead of us.

"The primary school." I let out a breath. "I didn't even think of that." I squeeze the notebook. "See why he was supposed to be the journalist? He'd have thought of it right away. Empty parking lot in the evening, walkways and stuff. A few steps. He was good at solving problems."

Isaiah's fingers squeeze my shoulder lightly. "And what you were supposed to be? Orange-wool wrangler?" The smile's back in his voice again. He's thinking about the night—*that* night. Soft string twined around my fingers and tumbling to the ball of yarn on the floor, the warmth of him standing close, and me. I push the memory, all its unearned softness, away.

"Still figuring that out."

"You got time."

We've gone in a loop now. The basketball court is in front of us, the sky dimmer, the guys jumping and dribbling little more than silhouettes. We both slow as we reach the edge of the parking lot.

Out of nowhere, the hard swish of wheels against asphalt. I turn my head to see a figure glide toward us, then across our path. Frayed shorts, sleeveless shirt, long fine braids piled on top of her head. Second time in a row. It can't be an accident.

"Pru!" I call.

She waves, glittery nails defying the dusk.

"All the skateboards out today," Isaiah says beside me.

"New girl at school," I tell him as Pru turns and rolls toward us. "You live near here?" I call as she slows down.

"Not really." She steps off her board and looks from me to Isaiah. "Hey, boyfriend."

Her words make heat rise through my cheeks. Does she mean mine or hers? Is she trying to flirt with him? "This is Layla's brother," I say.

Isaiah extends a hand. "Isaiah."

Pru smirks as she shakes it. "Nice to meet you, boyfriend."

He doesn't return her smile. *Take that,* I think, beaming inside.

"Don't you have youth group?" Pru asks.

"Are you stalking me?"

"Is it a secret?"

"Karmen, you wanna talk to her or you wanna go back inside?" Isaiah touches my arm, light but sure.

Pru looks up at Isaiah again, as though he's stumbled into the girls' bathroom and is obstructing the tampon dispenser. *Who knows? What did he do?* "I have to talk to her," I tell Isaiah. He nods and heads over toward the court. I feel suddenly cool in the evening's warmth. The skateboarding, her standing up for me against Robbie, then almost literally running into her again—it can't be coincidental. "You knew Julian."

"Yeah. I mean, we met."

"How? From skateboarding?"

Pru folds her arms across her chest. "You could say that." Like she's hiding something. I don't have time to try to pry answers out of her.

"What's with you? You wanna tell me something about him or not? 'Cause I'm looking for answers, and you seem like you know something."

"I hadn't talked to him for a while. I didn't see him at boarding meetups like I used to."

Julian had mentioned meetups before—a bunch of boarders gathering in a freshly paved parking lot, a subdivision with ramps and low sets of stairs, things they could jump over or stunt off. I try to remember the last time he mentioned one. "Since when?"

"Stopped coming early this year."

"What was it like? Did y'all ever talk?"

"Not a lot of talking, really. He seemed like a cool guy. Sorta quiet. Okay boarder."

I don't believe this is it—this is all she has to say. "It was Julian's board." I hold the skateboard up.

"I recognize it."

"I guess everyone he used to board with heard what happened."

Pru reaches into her back pocket and pulls out a phone. Rhinestones form a swirly letter *R* on the back. She taps at the screen like I'm not even there.

"Did he ever say anything to you?" My words come out desperate and I don't care. I want to snatch the phone away and toss it on the ground. *Hey, bring it down.* Julian's voice, in my mind, calms me. *Since when you so hype?* I force myself to take a breath. To imagine Julian. If it were him, notebook in hand, questions jotted down, how would he get someone to trust him? To talk to him? To peel their eyes off the screen? "Did he?"

Pru's phone-holding hand shifts slightly. The cheap glass stones glint like the real thing. Her eyes flash up to meet mine. "I heard what happened." She leaves off the *sorry* most people add. The sentence hangs, bare. It feels raw. But it *is* raw.

"How'd you hear?"

She purses her lips. "I read. I listen to the news. What's your number?"

I tell her, and she taps again. My phone buzzes.

"Sent you my friend Cardo's number. He's taking history at CU. He might know more." Pru drops her board and puts one foot on.

"Why are you helping me? Just showing up now—"

"It's a public road, no?"

"But in class today too. Why?"

She looks back at me, all traces of smirks and boredom gone. It's like a mask's been wiped away. Just a girl like me. Not avoiding my gaze, not whispering, not tearing up over my sad life. Just looking back at me. She lifts her chin toward the board under my arm. "Stick together. That's how we do."

Does she mean her and me? Or her and Julian, the real skateboarder in our family? Before I can ask, she's pushed off and flying away into the night.

"It ain made for holding like a purse," she hollers back before she turns away. "Use it sometime."

I watch her go. Maybe Pru's right—whether that was an invite to help, or an order for me to figure skateboarding out. Maybe the board can tell me something. That was Julian, wasn't it? Flying down the street that same way?

Part of me wants to step on and fly like Pru did too. Instead I walk toward Isaiah. When he sees me heading his way, he comes forward to meet me.

"Everything okay?"

I nod.

"That girl's . . . different," he says.

Julian's words echo in my mind. "She's real. She knew Julian. I think she can help me." The choir's singing drifts out to us. "Guess you missed practice for nothing."

Isaiah looks at me, surprised. "You think that was nothing?"

"Not exactly. I . . ." My words fizzle out. We're at the church door now. Isaiah swings it open, pauses, waiting for my move, for my words. There's a chorus of laughter—I can pick up Layla's trademark squawk. I step back. "I'll wait out here. Gonna text my dad to pick me up."

"I can drop you."

I want more time with Isaiah—want to sit beside him in the car, want to talk more. But I'm not ready to face Layla. "It's okay."

"Wait out here with you?"

It feels good to smile. "Sure."

He leans against the wall. I lean too—then wonder if I could have gone a little closer.

"Sure you up for this? Digging around, going where your brother used to hang out? Talking to all kind of different . . . characters?"

I look into Isaiah's eyes. They're concerned. Ocean-deep. Sun-warm, even in the dark. Can a person ever be sure?

On the court, there's a swish of ball gliding into the net. The guys cheer, laughing; hands clap at the shot. They're so loud, so sweaty they glisten, even from this far away. So alive. The tears that fell earlier are back, hovering this time. Promising to fall, but still teetering on the edge.

"I have to," I say.

Isaiah's hand is on my arm. He pulls me close again. With my ear against his chest, his words rumble into me. "I'll help." Breath so low I can imagine its damp heat, and the fine hairs on the back of my neck bristle against my will. "I'll help you every way I can."

CHAPTER THREE

The whole drive to school, I feel Daddy staring at the skateboard as I slip it in beside my backpack, but I can't be bothered to care. At school, I get out and tuck it under my arm. I don't know what exactly I'm doing, but I feel a tiny bit closer to Julian, and that feels right.

"Hey." Layla's voice behind me. I don't slow or turn around, but she catches up anyway. "I didn't get to say bye last night before—" Her eyes get wide as she takes in Julian's skateboard. "Is that allowed?"

"I need it, so I brought it."

She nods. "Makes sense. Oh yeah, I think I heard about that."

"Heard about what?"

Layla hesitates, then pulls a book out of her bag. There's a picture of a guy, back hunched over, face in shadows. When I see the title, I have to catch my breath. *Everything to Know about Grief.*

"What are you reading that for?"

If she hears me, she pretends not to. "It says it's normal to get attached to stuff that belonged to someone who's gone."

"Well, at least I'm normal."

"I just meant—a lot of people go through it. Are you mad?"

"No." My voice doesn't sound convincing even to me. The closer we get to our classroom, the more heads start to turn. It's as if I'm carrying a miniature rhinoceros under my arm.

"You ran off at youth group last night—"

"You even noticed?"

"Of course I noticed. You okay?"

"Perfect." I push past her into our classroom. "Never better."

Layla follows behind me. " I know you're not *okay*, obviously. But did I do something? I'm just trying to find out why you acting so—"

"How exactly do you think a person is supposed to act when their brother dies?"

Layla swallows. "I don't know. I don't wanna say something stupid—I'm just trying to understand."

I stop. Kids carry on around us, jostling, laughing. I'm not mad at Layla—not really. What am I really mad at her for? *That stupid book. Acting like I'm too fragile to help set out chairs at church.* I push the thoughts out of my mind. "I had stuff on my mind."

"I didn't want you to be upset about the setup, I just . . . I heard sometimes people need space away from extra commitments when they're grieving."

Her words sound oddly stilted. "Heard or read?"

"Sorry." Layla slumps into her seat, shoulders curled like a wilty flower.

I sit down too. "It's okay about the setup." The words don't feel true, but I need to move on. That's what I'm supposed to do, right?

"Hey dude, surf's up?" one of the boys says as he passes my desk.

"That's her brother own," someone whispers to him, and the smile melts off his face. I slide the board under my seat. If fitting in is the goal, this was a mistake.

"I get why you have the skateboard, but you're gonna get in trouble." Layla hooks her bag on the back of her chair.

The skateboard. Would it kill her to say *his*? Say *Julian's*? "I don't see why it should bother anybody." What I really want to ask is why *she* thinks I have it. What does her grief manual say? That skateboards make perfect security blankets for the bereaved? "I'm not using it in class."

"Yeah . . ." Her voice peters out as Mr. Douglas comes in. His gaze goes to my chair, and his eyebrows go up.

"All right, grade twelves. Take your seats, let's see who's here. Karmen, no athletic gear in the classroom, please." He flips open the attendance book. I don't budge from my seat. Where am I supposed to put the skateboard? I'm not leaving it outside class for someone to steal. Mr. Douglas is onto the Cs now. Pru slinks through the door. Her eyes find mine, then drop down to the board. Her face opens into a smile I've never seen on her before as she eases into the seat beside mine.

"Nice wheels," she says.

"You're gonna get in trouble," Layla hisses.

"Take a breath, Prissy." Pru opens her backpack with a loud *zzzzzzziiiip*. Mr. Douglas fixes his gaze on us.

"Girls, is there a problem? Karmen, I've spoken to you about the skateboard already. Bring it up front."

"No."

A small gasp goes through the classroom.

"Miss Wallace. Do we need to step outside the class-room—"

"It's her brother's skateboard." Pru's voice cuts through our teacher's. Everyone ahead of us turns to look back too. Then they look up at Mr. Douglas. My legs are jittery under the table. Why'd I even bring the board here? What if I lose it? At the same time, I didn't feel like I could leave it at home. It felt like I had to have it with me today. Like it's the link I need to the most important thing for me to learn.

Mr. Douglas opens his mouth and closes it again. He shakes his head. "Karmen, I'll see you before you go to first period." He looks back down at his attendance book. "Where were we?"

The door opens again. Robbie slumps into the closest chair, basketball under his arm.

"Robbie," Mr. Douglas snaps. "Lose the ball."

He sheds his bag and slips the basketball onto the desk.

"Get rid of it!" Mr. Douglas is loud now. "Y'all wanna have in here like the equipment room."

Robbie stands up and grabs the ball. Then his gaze lands on my skateboard. "How come you lettin her have a whole skateboard in here?"

I keep my eyes on my desk. I don't need another day like yesterday.

"Take it outside, please, Robbie." Mr. Douglas' voice is lower again. "You can rest it down by the door and come back in."

Robbie knocks into his desk on his way out. He doesn't come all the way back in, just lurks by the doorway like he'd rather be anyplace but here. Mr. Douglas finishes up attendance, then goes on to remind us about the college fair next month. Layla leans over.

"You could call your mom from the office and ask her to come get it."

An image of Mummy pops into mind: right now she's probably in her room, curtains closed, under the sheets. The TV might be on for company. "She's busy."

Layla looks like she wants to say more, then changes her mind and closes her mouth. At the front, Mr. Douglas is talking about volunteer options for our graduation requirement. Around me, the class is quiet, kids facing forward, listening. Planning for the end of school. Planning for beyond. What's the point of all this, sitting in this room listening to how I can pick up trash off the beach so I can graduate? Julian did all that. Look where it got him.

Out the window, puffs of cloud drift across the blue, pushed by a wind I can't feel. The trees edge the field, nodding yes to a question I can't hear. A splash of yellow shows, then disappears, then shows again, shifting as the leaves move. Everything's having a conversation I can only lip-read and half guess at from in here, but I know it means more than listening to how many hours I should wash stray dogs at the shelter. I need to be out there. Living. Finding out why Julian couldn't.

The bell rings for first period. I grab my bag and Julian's board, then hustle out the door. I hear Layla call, "Karmen, wait up," hear Mr. Douglas call out too, but I can't seem to make myself turn around or even slow down. It's all I can do to move through the halls. To stop at the math classroom and go in.

At morning break, I wait till the classroom's empty to step into the corridor. Most kids have drifted off to benches or the café. Perfect. I drop Julian's skateboard and step on. It rolls slightly, but it might as well be careening down a hillside as I try to get my balance. I step one foot onto the ground. I try to imagine what Julian would do, if he were here. For how much he boarded, he never snuck and brought it to school— it's not an easy secret to keep. Or did he? Just because I didn't see it doesn't mean it never happened. But I know—knew— him. Right?

"Watch it, sorry." Someone jostles me and I teeter back for a moment before I right myself. I pick up the board as my heart hammers in my chest. As I pass the chemistry lab, I feel my shoulders start to relax. I lean against the bench by the art classrooms. I've needed this quiet. Though it's just past ten, its seat is sun-warmed already, so it feels alive, like blood pulses through veins buried deep in its concrete core. Slowly, my breathing settles. I slump onto the seat. I feel like a twisted-up plastic bag, all wrung out.

"You got art or you just tryin to duck people?"

I look up. Pru smirks at me from the studio doorway. I look away, but she walks over and plops down beside me, undeterred.

I squint over at her. "What happened to you?" The sun

behind her obscures her face, but I can see the rest of her—the hoop earrings each at least half an inch larger than school rules allow, blouse untucked, middle button undone.

"What? Food in my teeth?"

"You look rumpled up."

She rolls her eyes. "I can't stay nipped and pressed in here." Pru sits on the bench beside me. "You pretty bold, bringing a whole board out in class. I thought Dougie was gonna confiscate that. I stash mine in Dorsett's office."

My stomach flips at the idea. "Thanks for what you said. For telling him."

She waves a hand, brushes my words away like a few gnats. "Let me see?"

I hesitate. Julian only ever let me touch his board when he was alive. How'd he feel if I let someone I hardly know step on?

"I can show you couple things," Pru says. "It ain hard. You just gotta keep at it." She holds her hand out, so sure I'll give in. It feels like less work to pass it to her than to say no. And right now, I need easy. I put the board down on the ground—that feels less traitorous. Pru steps on. "Okay, first, you gotta position your feet right. Then you use one foot to push yourself, and step back up to glide. Just try a short glide first." She steps off the board, then looks at me.

I step on. I try to remember how Julian used to stand, but my mind comes up blank.

"Here." Pru taps the board with a disco-ball fingernail. I put my feet like hers were. "Bring your right foot down and push off, then glide."

I ease along a few feet, then bring my foot down. I skid to a clumsy stop and step off.

"Try it again."

This time I make it halfway to the chemistry lab. The wheels clatter over cracks in the concrete, tiny shudders my whole body feels. The third time, I make it even farther; I even pick up a little breeze. I glimpse my reflection in the window: my mirrored smile is wide. "Look, look!" I call as I glance back at Pru.

"Yeah, good!"

"Hey, watch out!" a voice calls as a ball hurtles across my path. I stumble off and the board tangles around me. I tip forward, then hit the ground. My whole body jolts—hands stop my face from hitting concrete, but there's a pain in my hip, in my knee. Blood pours down my leg. Pru runs over to me.

"You all right?"

I push myself up. My ankles feel okay, but my knee's pretty scraped up.

"Probably just need a Band-Aid." I touch my hip.

"You fell on it." Pru looks over her shoulder. "Way to go, idiot," she shouts back. I turn my head that way. Robbie. His basketball on the ground, halfway between us and him.

Robbie.

"I wasn't tryin to hit her." His voice seems far away.

I pick up the skateboard. It's in one piece, far as I can tell.

"Y'all ain even suppose to be doin that in school. I don't know why Dougie let you—"

"You throwin blame and you 'most kill the girl?"

"You hear her say she all right?" Robbie shouts back. How

can *he* be mad? He isn't supposed to be playing ball here either. Was it even an accident? Did he mean to hit me? I want to drown out the questions flooding my mind, and I can't.

"Look at her leg!" Pru's voice is raised too.

"I already tell her sorry. Get over it. Ain nobody dead!"

Heat spreads over my face, chest, armpits, deep in my belly. *Ain nobody dead?*

Something in me snaps. I'm running, the ball is in my hands, my arms rise over my head, then forward—and I let go. Orange blur. Then a crash. Then broken glass.

The ocean roar in my ears is gone. I feel like something vital, something that keeps my body churning forward, is suddenly gone. A teacher asking, "What happened?" Pru says words I can't quite follow; Robbie protests loud. There's a high, powdery ringing in my ears now, and the air around me is going fuzzy and black. My knees buckle as I go down.

The nurse's office is quiet and smells like lemon cleaner and rubbing alcohol. I hold an antiseptic wipe over my knee. Red blooms thin through the square's translucent white.

"Let's get a bandage on you," the nurse says. She holds out a small garbage can and I lift the wipe away. She spreads a wide beige Band-Aid over my knee. "How's your head?"

"It's okay."

"Lucky you didn't hit it. That can happen when you pass out. You'll be home for the rest of the day, I'm afraid. I know how heartbreaking it can be to miss class." Her smile tells me she doesn't know what I did. If she did, she wouldn't joke with me. I look around the office again, strain to hear anything from the other room, but I'm still the only one in here. At least I didn't hurt anyone else.

"How are we doing in here?" Ms. Dorsett peers around the doorway.

"All fixed up," the nurse says cheerily.

"Good. Come on, Karmen. Your parents are here."

My parents. My stomach backflips. I can't imagine what Daddy will say. Mummy's face flashes into my mind, contorted with tears, this time because of me.

"I'll help you out, Karmen." Ms. Dorsett holds out an arm.

"What broke?" I ask.

"The chemistry lab's window."

I stand up and wince. "Is everyone okay?"

"No one was in there, luckily."

Her words don't ease the knot in my stomach. "Can I get my bag and—"

"We'll get it from the office on the way out." Ms. Dorsett's voice is firm. I know there's trouble waiting for me in that office.

I follow the counselor outside. We have to pass by the lab. The glass is swept up, but the whole middle pane of glass slats is jagged and broken. Yellow caution tape lines the area.

"Did anyone get hurt?"

"Luckily, no one was near that window, and none of the chemicals broke or spilled."

I bite the inside of my cheek. "I didn't mean to—I never. I'm so sorry. I don't even know what came over me. Robbie, he just . . ."

"Let's talk in the office." Ms. Dorsett sets a brisk pace, and we walk the rest of the way in silence. We bypass the counselor's office, and my heart sinks. It's straight to Principal Gardiner, then.

We step inside. Ms. Lightbourne at the front nods for us to go right in.

We walk into Mr. Gardiner's office. Julian's skateboard leans up beside the tall mahogany bookshelf. His backpack slumps, dejected, beside it. My parents sit opposite the principal, heads down. Daddy glances up at me and makes a low sound in his chest. He turns away, arms folded. Mummy looks in my direction and starts to cry quietly.

"Karmen," Mr. Gardiner says. "Have a seat."

I sit.

"I've discussed with your parents what we've heard from the other student involved, and a bystander. Would you like to tell us your side of what happened?"

I shake my head. I want this over, and I already know—nothing I can say will erase the rage Daddy's stifling. Nothing I do could ever stop my mother's tears.

"You better speak up." Daddy's words are clipped.

"I just—I was on my skateboard and I tripped over Robbie's ball. Then he said something to me and I . . . lost it. I didn't mean to break the window." The words come out as a low mutter.

Daddy leans back in his chair. "Who told you bring that thing to school? Shouldn't even have it here." His hands grip the table's edge. "What was said?"

His fingers are so clenched, I almost expect him to snap

off a chunk of wood. If I tell him what Robbie said, it'll make everything worse.

"Karmen, we'd like you to share what the other student said." Mr. Gardiner leans forward.

"No," I say. I feel Daddy bristle. "No, sir." On the other side of the table, Mummy moans, sad, low. I can't bring myself to look her way.

"Are you sure?" Ms. Dorsett says softly. "If someone said something bad to you, Karmen—"

"I don't know what words could justify breaking a window," Daddy cuts in. I slouch down in my chair. *Ain nobody dead.* Julian was nobody, then. Not according to him. And I was wrong, apparently, for flipping over that.

Mr. Gardiner clears his throat. "Very well. Karmen, you've attended here since grade seven, so you're familiar with our code of conduct. Intentional property damage and violent outbursts toward fellow students—each of these separately warrant serious consequences. You know that."

I look down at my shoes. I just want this over. I just want to go home. Not for the day, but for the month. Forever.

"Answer the man," Daddy snaps.

"Yes." My voice comes out quiet.

"Stan." Mummy's warning is soft. I wonder if anyone else even heard, but Daddy doesn't say anything else. Maybe her word reached him, too.

"Someone could have been seriously, seriously hurt. Broken glass—chemicals knocked over in the lab. All told, we're fortunate the only damage is a window to be replaced."

"I'm sorry." My voice comes out as a whisper.

"I accept your apology." Mr. Gardiner looks over at Ms. Dorsett. "We also appreciate your family's unique circumstances. I don't understand firsthand what it is to lose a brother, but I know grief is a powerful thing. Normally, your actions would warrant suspension, or even expulsion. I'm considering your clean record up to now, and the challenges you're facing after Julian's death."

The room is silent.

"Karmen, we care about your well-being," Ms. Dorsett says. "Mr. Gardiner and I have agreed that the best way to support you, while acknowledging the seriousness of you breaking that window, is an absence from school. We are requiring a mandatory personal leave of three weeks. Rather than view this strictly as a punishment, I would invite you to view this as a time for you to heal, and to get help and support that you very understandably need."

"No . . . ," Mummy moans, louder, this time. I don't have to look at her—I can hear the way her voice comes out squeezed through her tight throat, feel the tears already spilling down her cheeks. "I said it was too soon for her to come back, I said that, I—"

Daddy exhales sharply, and her words stop.

Mr. Gardiner looks at a space somewhere between my parents. "I understand it's a shock, Mrs. Wallace. As Ms. Dorsett said, this is not a punishment for Karmen. Her grades don't need to suffer either—we'll have her teachers assign work so she can keep up in class during her absence."

"If she's well enough to do work, she's well enough to be in school," Daddy says.

"We have three stipulations for your return," Mr. Gardiner continues. "You need to commit to regular counseling with a professional of your choice."

"She's already seeing someone." The calm in Mummy's voice shocks me.

"Lot of good that did," Daddy says, not quite under his breath. My stomach clenches.

"Second," Mr. Gardiner carries on, "we require your counselor to sign off that he or she believes you are ready to return to school. If they are not able to provide this confirmation, we will review your situation after further weeks, until you are ready to come back."

"*Review?*" Daddy's voice flares like fire.

"If she's not deemed ready after six weeks, what then?" Mummy's voice is so soft it nearly disappears. "Or nine? Or twelve?"

"She *needs* routine!" Daddy's on his feet. "Have you *dealt* with a kid who's lost a sibling before, Mr. Gardiner?"

Mummy reaches over to touch him, and he thumps back into his seat, recoiling from her touch.

"We all want to see Karmen thrive, and, ideally, graduate on time." Ms. Dorsett sounds unsure that's an option anymore. "I promise you, we *have* helped students navigate grief and loss during their studies here. Let's start with this three weeks, and see where we are after that. I think Karmen's—" She shifts her gaze to meet mine. "Karmen, your well-being is what matters most here. This time away is meant to help support you in that way. And I'm happy to connect with your personal counselor as often as needed to give you the best chance when you're ready to return."

I look away. *Ready to return.* That's a feeling I can't imagine, any more than I can imagine repeating Robbie's awful words. They play over in my head again anyway. *Nobody dead. Nobody dead.* Across the table, Mr. Gardiner continues. That's what people do, I guess, when it isn't their world that's been broken open.

"Karmen, when you do return, you need to return ready to comply with our school rules and standards. That includes respecting other persons and property. That also includes leaving prohibited sports equipment at home or having it confiscated without discussion. We all deeply sympathize with the loss you're adjusting to. That said, bringing a skateboard to school is not appropriate—"

"That's my son's skateboard," Daddy cuts in.

"I understand, Mr. Wallace—"

"My *dead* son's skateboard."

Mr. Gardiner flinches at *dead.* I clench my teeth. "I'll do it. Can we go?"

Ms. Dorsett opens the door. "If any of you want to talk in my office, or if you want to speak privately with Mr. Gardiner—"

"Let's go." Daddy stands up so fast, his chair tips back on its rear legs, hovers a second, then crashes down on all fours. He pushes through the open door. Mummy gets up slower. The calm she had on for a minute has slipped. She moves now like she's in a dream.

"Mrs. Wallace, let me walk you out," Ms. Dorsett says. "Karmen, can I carry Julian's skateboard for you?"

I shake my head and pick it up first, then the backpack. My knee feels like it's on fire as I step outside. Daddy's far ahead of us, already halfway to the parking lot.

"Thank you," Mummy says to Ms. Dorsett. "I'm fine now." She looks back at me. Her eyes shine with tears.

I walk beside her. My shoulders feel like my backpack is full of boulders and cement blocks. The board is coffin-stiff under my arm. The walk to the car feels like an eternity, but I almost want it to go on and on. I know once I get in the car, it'll be worse.

It's silence most of the way home. The only time the quiet breaks is when someone runs a red light ahead of Daddy. He pounds on the horn.

"Get off the road, you sack of wet pigeon crap!" he shouts at the closed window. His rage bounces back in on us.

There's a second—half of that, a quarter, an eighth— when I look over for Julian. My brother's dark eyes dancing behind wide rectangular glasses, lips miming, *sack of wet pigeon crap?* His signature smirk-chuckle, his shoulders shaking with suppressed delight.

I catch myself fast—almost fast enough not to see the empty seat, the unbuckled seat belt. The way Daddy's seat is pushed back far, so far Julian's legs would never fold into that space.

I look back at my own feet, the board, the bag in between. He's not here. He never will be. And between Daddy's rage and Mummy's ever-present tears, figuring out how we got here all falls on me.

65

At home, Daddy shuts off the car. *Are they gonna talk to me?* I wonder, half wanting an answer, half wishing we could keep pretending I'm invisible back here.

"It's not gonna be three weeks' vacation." Daddy turns around to look at me as if he's read my mind.

"I know."

"You get every piece of work your teachers assign turned in and done on time. Don't make sense you sit idle at home. School would have been the best place for you. You need routine—"

"Stan." Mummy's voice is soft. "She could have hurt someone. She could have—"

"I don't need to review. Karmen, you get up every morning, you come to CU with me. Sit in the library and stay there. You need to occupy your mind with sense."

"But I have to do counseling," I venture.

"Yeah." He ugly-laughs the word. "That's helped."

"I'll see if Ms. Rhonda can see you tomorrow morning as well as Friday afternoon, since you'll be in the area." Mummy's even voice is unsettling. I don't want to hear her cry, but she's too calm. "An extra session a week would be good."

Therapisted. Julian's voice rings in my ear the same time as my mind finds our word. "Jinx," I whisper.

"What's that?" Daddy's ears miss nothing.

"Extra session," I say.

"As far as punishment," Daddy continues, "the school might not be penalizing you, but you can bet your backside we are. No phone—"

"You can't take my phone! I can't just be home by myself and not talk to anyone."

"No phone, no computer, no TV, no friends. And that starts now."

"That ain even fair! Mummy—" I protest. I can't be trapped here without a lifeline. "Tell him!"

"Stan, you don't think that's too harsh? She has to have some type of social contact."

"How am I supposed to do homework?"

"Write it by hand." Daddy flings his door open and all but hurls his body out. He slams his door so hard, the whole car shakes. The same rage I felt earlier flares as I slam my palm into the back of his seat. Then I catch sight of my mother, rigid in the front of the car. I want to tell her sorry, but I can't even choke out a single letter.

My mother reaches a hand back. I lean forward and take it. Her fingers are cool. They feel dry. I press them into my palm, try to give her some of my heat.

"You'll get back on track. You just need some time away." Her voice is far-off. Therapisting Mummy is fading. Sad Mummy takes form. "What did that boy say?" she asks.

For the first time ever, I want Therapisting Mummy back. She might be able to handle hearing what Robbie said. "He . . ."

"Yes?" Mummy turns around to look at me. Dark half-moons curve under her eyes. Her skin looks dry, and too loose for her face, made for a fuller version of herself. *Ain nobody dead.*

I want those words out of my memory; I want someone else to help hold them up, not just me. I look at my mother, the flaky skin across her forehead, slivers of raw red flesh at the corners of her cracked lips.

"Was it about Julian?" Mummy's bloodshot eyes are glassy again. The therapisting mask is gone, but she, the real Mummy, isn't there. The person looking back at me is somewhere in between, slipping toward the bathrobed mess stumbling out of the dark bedroom at four in the afternoon, dried tears trailing forever down her cheeks. I can't tell her. I know she can't take it.

"Just something stupid about my shoes," I lie.

She looks unconvinced. "That's not like you, Karmen. Losing it like that. You sure he didn't say something more?"

The lie leaves my throat burning. But the truth won't make things better. It'll just pour my sadness into her, and she already looks soaked through. "Stuff just makes me madder now, I guess." It feels like a line from Layla's stupid book.

Something like relief passes across her face and she nods.

"Before you go back, you're gonna have to tell him you're sorry."

I nod.

"Saying sorry is part of resolution." Her voice sounds like she's speaking to someone outside the car, not to me.

"Of course, Mummy." Right now I'll agree to anything. "Can I go inside?"

"You go ahead. I'll be in."

Outside, I look up at the sky. The clouds I watched that half lifetime ago in homeroom are gone. I try to let it sink in. Three weeks. Three weeks away from school. No phone, no computer. How am I going to get anywhere with what I need to know?

I feel through the backpack until my fingers close around

the notebook's spiraled top. Three weeks to find out my *who, what, when, where, why*. My answers to why he ended his life, to what I missed. To understand why Julian didn't think he could talk to me. Somehow, I'll find a way to figure it out.

Inside, the kitchen is a microcosm of our lives. Breakfast dishes are still piled up in the sink, sunlight forcing razor-thin slivers of yellow over the counter. *Tuesday,* my brain registers. A pot crusted with grits, gone cold on the stove. My parents' not-hushed-enough voices spill from outside Mummy's now-defunct office space.

"Why you had to challenge me like that?" Daddy, a whisper-shout. "I'm trying to hold it together."

"It's too much. You can't isolate the girl like that."

"It works for *you*." His insult makes *me* flinch. I grab my phone out of the bag—I can text one person, at least, before they take a break from bickering long enough to remember to take it away. I send a message to Isaiah. 'Bout to lose phone. Can you still help?

A message flashes in. Layla. The bolded preview reads Remember, you didn't lose . . .

I open it. Remember, you didn't lose a brother, heaven gained an angel. Picture of an almost cloudless blue sky, a pair of hands outstretched. I feel the bottom drop out of my stomach. Is she dumb or just clueless? My head swirls with comebacks. *Good for heaven. I didn't lose a brother? Guess it was rocks and sticks in that coffin we buried, then. If I didn't lose him, why isn't he here?* I feel my hands shaking and I can't stop them.

"Pass it here." Daddy's voice is suddenly right behind me.

I fumble the phone onto the counter. "I just—"

He holds out his hand.

"Daddy, I just wanted to—"

"Wash up these dishes. You should have done it this morning."

I pass the phone over. Why'd I even open Layla's dumb image? I could have sent something more to Isaiah. *Miss you. Need you.* Or maybe that's too much to say.

He powers my phone down and pushes it into his work bag. "You can say goodbye to *that.*"

The *ssshhhk* of the closing zipper is like my world, shrunken in, shutting down around me. That panicked feeling rushes over me—I need out, even a window of time when I'm not just stuck here, suffocating. If I have to miss more than three weeks of school . . . then what?

"Can we still have people over for Julian's birthday?" I blurt out.

Daddy drops his work bag on his chair. "What?"

"The fifteenth. It's his birthday. Can we have something for him?"

"You just got yourself kicked out of school—I can't even think about that. Do the dishes, that's all."

I blink back tears, but they're more angry than sad. I plug the sink and turn on the hot water; a memory tries to creep into my mind. I push it away and reach for the dish soap. My elbow bumps into the purple glass, not enough to knock it onto the floor, but enough to jar something loose. To take me back to when Julian and I were younger. When the glasses were a set of four.

"Mummy, can I be excused?" My brother's voice is smooth, his smile for our mother sweet, as always. Mummy looks up from scraping the rest of the rice onto Daddy's plate. Her face is already transforming into that special joy she saves up just for him.

"Got a reason?"

"Yeah, it's Tuesday. He know he supposed to do dishes Tuesday, Thursday, and Saturday," I pipe up.

"I wanna put the finishing touches on my Cultural Studies presentation. I just want it to be the best it can be."

"Please. You don't want to scrub burnt barbecue sauce off the pan."

"What you mean, burnt?" Mummy fixes me with a quizzical stare.

Julian swoops down on the chance to suck up, like a hawk aiming for a dawdling mouse. "Dinner was excellent, Mummy," he says, so syrupy I almost gag.

"It was a touch crispy at the edges." Daddy forks rice into his mouth. "But I like it that way."

"Karmen, you all can switch dish duty this once, can't you?" Mummy still has me pinned by her gaze. "You had your math test today."

"Yeah, and I had to wash dishes and take out the garbage last night."

"Julian, you'll do Karmen's dishes the rest of this week."

"That's only tomorrow and Friday!" I protest.

Julian ignores me. "Of course! I just wanna do my best on this paper."

"You just say it was a presentation?"

"It's a really big part of my final grade."

Mummy nods at him. "Go ahead."

I shove my chair back and push past Julian's so I elbow him in the back as I pass. I clatter my plate into the sink. "You always pick his side," I fling back at Mummy.

"Mummy, you saw that?" His tattling whine follows me as I stomp upstairs to the bathroom, lock myself in, and perch on the edge of the tub with the last book to be left in there. Of course it would have to be one of his dorky history books. I swat it onto the floor. When I'm calm enough, I emerge. Down the hall, Julian's practicing his speech. I march to his doorway. He stands in the middle of the room, papers in his hand like he's some great orator.

"You better do dishes for the next month."

Julian shoots me a scathing look. "Matter of fact, I think I have big assignments every day for the rest of the school year."

"Watch when your alarm magically don't go off tomorrow."

"Watch when—"

"Yeah? What?"

He snorts. "You so proud 'cause I can't get you back like that. But guess what? It's you who can't get back at me, Miss C-minus Average. Get used to scrubbing dishes. One day someone'll be hiring."

He picks up a glass from his nightstand. Through the purple glass, I see milk crusted on the inside. "Don't forget this one."

I reach a hand out. As he lets go, I pull my arm back

too. The glass falls against the bed's footboard and cracks, its translucent purple splitting in two.

"Mummy!" I shout, sprinting for the stairs. "Julian had a drink in his room and broke the cup!"

The tap's water starts to run extra hot, bringing me back to the present. I hate myself for remembering Julian that way now, when he can't defend himself. Then again, I'm the one who's stuck here. Missing him. On dish duty every day, forever. *Get used to scrubbing dishes.*

No. I can't be mad at him now. I run the water hotter, its near-scalding sting scolding me. I force myself to remember something good. Beach picnics on Labor Day. Playing Fish for my tenth birthday when I had laryngitis and my party got canceled. Making Mother's Day waffles at six a.m. The sound of his laugh.

But those memories feel as flat as Julian's picture on the front of his funeral program, and the words I don't want to relive keep coming back up like a plastic container inverted and submerged in the dishwater.

Julian, how could you do this to me?

You happy now?

You finally won?

A shudder brings me back to the kitchen. Daddy is on the other side of the sink. His hand rests on a drawer handle. A yellow dish towel dangles from his hand like terry-cloth sunshine. He lifts a plate out of the drainer and wipes it off. *Found something else to confiscate?* I think.

Daddy looks over at me for a half moment before he sets the plate down. "I wasn't thinking. It's Tuesday."

73

I nod. I bring the glass up to the running water, wash off the bubble slick and all the other things that covered it, unseen. I wonder what Daddy thinks as he takes it from my hand. I don't ask. For now it's enough to have someone here, washing dishes with me on a day that isn't my turn.

CHAPTER FOUR

I wake to glaring light burning through my eyelids.

"No . . ." I groan.

"I have an early meeting." Daddy's voice reverberates from the hallway into my room. "Be ready to leave in forty-five minutes, please."

He's still mad. I reach over to the nightstand for my phone. My fingers close around paper, and yesterday comes flooding back—ball, broken glass, Principal Gardiner's office, Daddy's hand out for my phone. I grab the notebook and hurl it across the room. It lands with a small thud.

"I don't even know what time it is," I complain.

"Look at a clock," Daddy calls back. Helpful. I grab clothes and shower, then dress. My scraped-up knee stings when I take the stairs. As I near the kitchen, a familiar oceany smell greets me. Boiled fish. Mummy made boiled fish. My stomach lurches.

At the table, I dip my spoon into my bowl. Ghostly bits of onion swirl through the broth like translucent jellyfish.

"Hot sauce?" Daddy's eyes meet mine and he slides the bottle my way. I grab it, grateful, and shake a dollop in.

"I didn't season it enough?" Mummy leans forward. She

has the fish head, the prized piece according to 50 percent of my family, between her left thumb and forefinger. She hasn't taken a bite yet.

"It's fine, Barb." Daddy reaches for the black pepper. "It's good."

He doesn't look at me again, but I can feel him willing me to pretend to like this brothy breakfast. I answer Daddy in my mind: *I get it. I know. First family breakfast since* . . . I don't even want to finish the thought. Or don't need to finish what we already know, what we're all living every second of the day.

Mummy smiles brightly, but the sparkle doesn't go farther than her lips. "I needed to use some snapper up. Anyway, it's something healthy to fill your belly in the morning."

I look across the table at the fourth chair. We've arranged ourselves around Julian's space—hot sauce, lime wedges, black pepper, salt, all skirt around where his place should be set.

"He loved boiled fish," Mummy says, so soft she could be talking to her food. I lift the spoon to my mouth and try to swallow the liquid without tasting it. *I can do this,* I tell myself. *This isn't the hardest part of today.* "Loved boiled fish." This time barely a whisper. Why won't she just say his name? Say *Julian*? If she won't say it, maybe I should.

"It's September," I start out. No response. "So . . . are we gonna do anything for Julian's birthday?"

Daddy exhales through his nose, short, loud, and reaches for three pieces of lime. He squeezes them into his bowl, then stirs it. His expression is that trying-too-hard neutral.

I try again. Maybe she'll forget how much Daddy and

I hate her boiled fish. "Mummy? What you think?"

"What would we do?" Mummy directs her words toward the empty chair.

"Have some people over? I could make a cake, we could play songs Julian liked . . ."

Mummy watches Daddy take a tentative spoonful. He cringes—could be the lime, but it probably isn't.

"Guess I didn't season it at all." Mummy looks from Daddy to me. The fish head dangles from her fingers as if it might fall at any second. I drop my gaze back to my bowl and shovel another spoonful into my mouth. So much for changing the subject. "Stan?"

"It's fine. It's good. You know I'm more of a chicken souse man."

"You know where the stove is. Next time, *you* get up at five to cook." Mummy drops the head in her bowl. Fish water splatters across the table; a drop lands on my shirt. "Shoot. Karmen—sorry."

Daddy draws a breath in, then lets it out in a sigh. Why can't he just . . . be quiet right now? Why can't he *not* make this worse?

Mummy pushes her chair back and picks up her bowl, then mine, then Daddy's. She swoops over to the kitchen sink. Her bathrobe swirls like wide peach wings. She flings the bowls into the sink. Then the crack of crockery on metal, the din of clattering spoons. She turns around to look at me. The tears are gone, evaporated under hot rage. "That boiled fish was *good*. Julian would have eaten it." Then she stomps out. A moment later, her office door slams shut.

Daddy gets up without a word. He picks the broken pieces of the bowls out, wraps them in a plastic bag, sets them outside the kitchen door. "Remember, you have counseling."

I get up. I want out of here, out of this place. It's only six, but I can't stay in this house a second longer. "Are you gonna punish me like this every morning?"

"It's not punishment." Daddy fills a water bottle, then a second one. "I have an early meeting. Library opens at seven—you can do schoolwork in there." He points to a stack of printed papers in front of the toaster. "Assignments. Your teachers emailed them."

I pick up the pile of papers. It feels like a stack of boulders. "I have to tote all this?"

Daddy shoots me a look like I should be grateful for the chance to build my upper-body strength. "Yup. And you have an appointment with Rhonda you need to walk to. I have a class, so—"

"But my knee—"

"Let me see it." Daddy looks at the uncovered scrape. "Clean it with Dettol and put a bandage on it. You gotta be there ten o'clock."

"How am I even supposed to know what time it is? You took my phone."

Daddy looks momentarily stumped, and for a second I'm hopeful. "There's clocks on campus. One on each floor in the library, one in each classroom. You'll find a way. Let's go."

My knee still stings a bit when I arrive at the campus library. I follow signs up to the fourth floor, then walk through the stacks until I find the history section. It starts near the middle, then goes all the way to the building's windowed edge. Skylights show pure blue above me and cast squares of early shine onto the mottled green carpet. I gaze up at the titles, row after row. I recognize sections from classes Julian talked about his first semester—apartheid, the history of wars, ancient Egypt, the early Caribbean. *When did you stop talking about your classes? Why didn't I notice?* More questions, and I still can't find good answers. I can't think of a great moment of change—him jabbering about the great war of whatever one day, then falling silent the next. It all merges: Was he studying the Aztec empire a term before that probation letter was written, or a month? I just don't know.

I close my eyes. It's already too quiet, and that makes it worse—a silence I can see. I want to open my eyes, but to something different. I want to open them and see Julian here, crouched down to examine the bottom shelf, blue sneakers, red laces, orange jeans. I blink my eyes open. I'm alone. Too alone. The stacks are closing in on me, threatening to crush me. I backtrack toward the stairs and down two levels, then collapse into an empty chair. *He's not here,* I tell myself. *He's not here.* I don't know if I'm expecting this truth to console me or just give my brain something to do besides look for my brother, but it calms me somehow, its factual rhythm, the knowing what comes after each word, and before. *He's not here.*

I reach down for the backpack and take the notebook out. I have questions to answer. I have a number for Pru's friend Cardo—but that's stuck in my phone, so I'll have to find another way. I have Julian's probation letter. If I remember my questions, if I find the right people, I know I'll get somewhere.

I turn to a new page to write down my plan. Who, what, when, where, why, and how. That's what Julian said. It's what he'd say now. I take out a pen, then start jotting down my ideas. I can start with grades. I remember Daddy talking about students getting transcript copies from the registrar's office. That's my first step. Those will tell me when his grades shifted. It'll give me a timeline for when things changed. After that, I can look for Dr. Fox—he's the one who put him on probation. I grab my stuff and head for the office. For the first time in a long time, my mind is clear. I know what I'm going to do.

The administrative offices share a wide room with one wall painted an orange that feels loud for this early in the morning. One section declares FINANCIAL AID, another PAYMENTS. On the far side, there's a counter with four spots, but just one person behind the desk. The sign says REGISTRAR. I walk toward it. My footsteps feel too loud. This place seems more hallowed than the empty library. All the secrets held here. Grades earned and lost. I step up to the desk.

Successes. Failures. Answers.

"Good morning." My voice comes out as a croak. I clear my throat. "I came to get some transcript records." Transcript records. It even sounds bulky. I should have said one or the other. If I sounded stupid, the lady doesn't register it on her face.

"You have your student ID?"

"I have the number." I pull out the probation letter. "It's nine-four-eight—"

"Let me see that." She extends a beckoning hand, fingers impatient for the paper in mine. Her nails are the same shouty color as the wall behind me. I pass the letter over. She scans the letter and immediately I feel like I've betrayed Julian. I've let something private be seen by this orange-fingernailed stranger. Her eyes flicker over the number, then Julian's name. "This isn't you."

"It's my brother."

She raises her eyes to my face. "Why are you requesting your brother's transcript?"

"He's, uh—" The word sticks in my throat. I've said it before, feels like I've said it so many times, I *know* how to say it. But for some reason, here, now, I can't say it. I can't say *dead*. Can't even say *passed* or *gone*. "He's sick." My tongue is thick. "So he can't come in himself." The lie feels like a cop-out.

The woman slides the letter back across the counter to me. "The information is confidential. You'll have to wait until your brother's better and he can come in himself."

"What if he can't come in?"

"He'll have to wait till he can."

"So . . ."

She presses her lips together so tight, she might never be able to speak again. Or maybe she doesn't want to. I've lied myself into a corner—nothing I can do now. I grab the letter and head for the door. I'm so mad, I feel my hands shaking.

How stupid am I? How dumb is she? All that information, how Julian was doing—really—the months before this letter, and after, all trapped behind a few keystrokes of those Halloween fingernails. Why'd I say he was sick? If I'd said what really happened, she might have felt sorry for me, instead of looking at me like a would-be bank robber too dumb to demand the cash. Then guilt stops me in my tracks. How could I even think about using what happened to my brother for sympathy?

The walkway is suddenly dense with students. I press my back against the wall so they can move past me. For a moment it feels like high school—the rush of bodies all knowing where they need to be, laughing and jostling, some weaving in and out of the crowd, focused on their destination or intent on avoiding chitchat and eye contact. I scan the passing faces for someone familiar. Layla, Pru . . . right now, even Robbie would be welcome—

I know you can't be serious. Julian's face—left eyebrow rumpled, right eyebrow raised, lip curled like he smells bad fish—is so clear in my mind, it almost overshadows his voice. *Not that bey you gone ballistic over?*

Julian's reality kick is just what I need. I didn't even want to be back at school the two days I was there. I square my shoulders and slip across an opening in the crowd of students, then step onto the grass that grows under old fig and almond trees that have been here longer than the buildings themselves. I take a minute to get my bearings. The library's over to my right, and the big parking lot behind that. The science block is straight ahead, and the business block is to the left.

If I cut between them, social sciences will be just a bit away.

I head toward the history department. This is going to be better. This is where he really spent his time. I'll figure out something here. There are people here who knew him, who saw him—or who didn't. They can tell me something I don't know.

I pull the door open and step into the narrow corridor. There are eight or so doors on each side. I start to walk, not even sure I'll know when or where to stop. An empty office with a plant trailing along a bookshelf; a closed door, a low voice: "—unacceptable. Why would you cheat?" I pick up my pace and come to a half-open door with a sign at the top. DEAN. I don't need to look at the letter to remember the name at the bottom. Dr. Jackson Fox. I raise a hand to knock.

"Someone looking for me?"

I turn around to see a short, paunchy man with a big forehead and huge glasses.

"Didn't mean to startle you. Are you looking for Dr. Fox?"

I nod. This is him. The man who banned Julian from school. Of course, he didn't make Julian mess up assignments or flunk tests, but I still feel like he's responsible somehow. Couldn't he have seen he was struggling? Wasn't there some way to help? I thought he'd be bigger, more ogrelike. Not holding a muffin and a mug that says #GIRLDAD with a blurry picture of a beaming toddler on the side.

"Come on in, I have time before my next class." He elbows the door all the way open. The room doesn't look very deanly. It's small, and seems darker than the empty one I passed. Bookshelves stretch up to the ceiling on two sides, and a huge file cabinet looms behind where I'm supposed to sit. Dr. Fox eases behind his desk and settles in his chair. "What can I do for you?"

Before I open my mouth, I promise myself what I say will be the truth. "I came to get any information you can give me about my brother, Julian."

The smile on his face sort of hovers, then fades.

"Julian Wallace."

"Yes, of course." He pushes the mug away. "I remember Julian well. We all do. You are—"

"Karmen. His sister."

He extends a hand and we shake.

"Have a seat, Karmen."

Which chair did Julian take? The one on the left, closest to the bookshelf? The one on the right, by the door? I pick the one by the books and set the bag on the other chair. Something changes in Dr. Fox's face and I follow his gaze to the bag. It's just a moment; he's looking at me now.

"We are so heartbroken about your brother. Just devastating. How are you holding up?"

How *am* I holding up? I want to laugh, except for the feeling of cotton stuffed in my throat. I try to swallow past it. "I'm okay. I just—" How much does he know? He must know how Julian died, too; it was in the paper. Would someone have told the school? It's a small department—people would have talked.

There's a clock in here too. Clocks everywhere—why? This eternal ticking, this counting down, measuring, like heartbeats being doled out. All these hearts, ticking and ticking. And somewhere, wherever Julian's clock is kept hidden, it's stopped. Did someone grab it off a wall and smash it? Did the battery run out?

What told him to walk out of our house, that day? Did he walk? Did he run? How fast could he go, on bare feet?

"Karmen?" Dr. Fox's voice is worried.

"Sorry, I—I came prepared." I open the bag and take my notebook out. "I came because I have questions. I can't seem to get the right answers—I thought maybe someone here might know."

"What would you like to know?" The dean's voice is kind. I sense something in it, though—a hint of what I felt with Orange Nails. Something he stands behind that I can't reach through. Something he knows but won't tell.

"I found this letter. It was from you, actually." I rest the letter between us on the desk. "I didn't even know Julian was having problems in school, and I just was trying to figure out if that's why . . . if he was having a really hard time." Not the full truth, not the *if that's why he ended his life* truth. Still, close. Close enough.

I watch Dr. Fox's face as he scans the page. His eyes give nothing away. His Adam's apple shifts as he swallows slow. He reaches for a sip from the mug before he meets my gaze.

"You want to know about Julian's time here."

"Yes."

Dr. Fox taps his fingers against each other, thumb to thumb, baby finger to baby finger. I already know what he's weighing—what he's going to tell me. What I'm allowed to know. He opens a drawer in his desk, closes it. Then a drawer in the cabinet beside him. "Here we go." He pulls out a small magazine, lays it on the desk. *Annals*, it says, across the top. I recognize it. Julian used to read it in grade twelve. Layla and I called it *Anals*.

Dr. Fox flips through the booklet. "He had a piece published in here. Have you ever read it?"

I shake my head.

"It was a fascinating piece on the villages formed by Africans freed from slave ships in the mid-1800s. They were bound for the US, after emancipation had come into effect here." He slides it over to me.

Free Towns: Echoes in the Present. By Julian Wallace. There's a page and a half, and four photographs. A battered stone building—pitted walls, square gaps that would have been windows, the roof long since blown away. A portrait of a family from at least a hundred years ago: mother, father, two serious children. Something taken recently—an older woman and a girl a little older than me, in front of a brightly colored building, smiling. Then a beach, and Julian on it. He's awkward and overdressed—his same blue-and-white sneakers on the sand, jeans, his long-sleeved red shirt, a cap shading his face. His eyes are hidden. He isn't smiling.

"It was a beautiful article. Here—you take it."

I close the magazine, but I can't seem to let go. Or to look up at Dr. Fox. "Did he write any others?"

"I think things got busy. First year's a big adjustment."

Is that why? School was too hard? But school was never hard before. "How come he was on academic probation?" I blurt out. If Dr. Fox is startled, he doesn't show it.

"The university's policy is that students are placed on probation when their academics are not as high as we need them to be."

"But Julian always got As in high school."

"It's hard to take in. College is different. Every student has their own circumstances."

"What about Julian's?"

Dr. Fox looks away, then back at me.

"I know you want information about your brother, Karmen. I'm so sorry that I can't get into specifics of why Julian wasn't doing well here. Sometimes we don't even know why a student doesn't thrive. Some struggle with the workload; some have other circumstances in life. Some simply stop coming to class."

"That was him. Right? He wasn't coming to class? Because he was always smart. School was easy for him. I went to get his transcript and they wouldn't give it to me—they said it was confidential. . . . He's not even here." It feels like someone else saying those words. "How can it be confidential when he's gone?"

There's a quiet in the room. Just *he's gone*, swelling up, billowing out, translucent and large. I feel defeated. I'm no closer to understanding my brother. And I never will be.

"Karmen." Dr. Fox speaks low. "There are policies the university has in place for student privacy. It's not the same as high school. Even a student's parents aren't entitled to information, even when the parents are the ones paying tuition. I wish I could tell you everything there is to know. I don't understand everything you're going through, but I'll tell you this. Everyone here agrees with you that Julian was smart. We were lucky to have him in this department."

"Even though he flunked out."

Dr. Fox keeps going, as if I haven't said that. "Your brother must have talked about historical investigation with you. Are you a historian yourself?"

"Not at all."

He nods at the notebook. "It's a lot like journalism, actually. It's about looking for answers. Digging, extrapolating. Unearthing, asking questions. Looking for unbiased truths. I remember Julian talking in a seminar. He spoke so eloquently about how, even though there are splinters and fragments, missing information, and—at times, it seems—a dearth of artifacts, the knowledge may be there waiting to be found. And how sometimes, in his studies, he was frustrated when a trail fizzled out and the information simply wasn't there."

"But—I just want to understand."

"What do you think you'll find?"

"I just . . . Was school why? Why he—" I swallow. It feels important to say it. "Why he ended his life?"

The words are out of my mouth. The words are in the room. I've said them, and if Dr. Fox didn't know, now he does. If he's uncomfortable, now he can't look away. Neither can I. No one can pretend.

"I don't know."

We sit in the silence again, for a minute. That clock ticks on, the only one with anything to say.

"I've been working on the pre-Columbian history of the Lucayans. I wanted to understand the first people who lived on this land," Dr. Fox says at last, his voice low. "I started out with the plan to gain a deeper understanding of their spiritual practices—what they believed in, who they prayed to, if they prayed—that kind of thing. I didn't get far. But as I was trying to find this really obscure information, and not getting there, I realized I was learning a whole lot else. What they ate, where their food came from . . . how they spent time in these underwater pools, in these caves. How they became these skilled divers. I found I had so much information— enough for an entire large project."

"What does that have to do with Julian?"

"If you can't find out about Julian's grades, what can you find out? If this institution has rules about giving you his records and grades—and it does—then try talking to people. Sometimes human stories are even more interesting than facts."

"Aren't you supposed to be all about facts, in history?"

Dr. Fox laughs then, and the room brightens a little. "You would think so, wouldn't you?" He cranes his neck to look up at the clock. "I have a meeting shortly, but I'm so glad you stopped in. My door's—well, it isn't always open, but any time it is, you can come in. We can chat."

I unzip the bag and slip in the copy of *Annals*. "Thanks for this." I stand up.

"Good luck in your search. You know, every copy of *Annals* lists the professors who helped edit the issue. Those professors do work closely with the students who contribute. Some of our students enjoy History Club, too. A student, of course, isn't bound by privacy policies. You understand?"

I nod. I do.

"Look for the stories, Karmen," Dr. Fox says as I step out of the door. "That's where the heart is."

Outside, the air is warm again. The ground holds me up strong. My head is clear now. I feel a smile stretch over my face. I think of those stories about my brother, wrapped up in people still walking around here. Carrying around their own small versions of him, each keeping a tiny Julian alive.

I settle under a tree across from a building with a series of musical notes graffitied on the wall. I like it, even though I have no clue what the notes mean. They are playful colors— teal, fuchsia, tangerine. Shadow-gray figures with trombones and flutes and guitars are producing them, but it's the music itself that is hot with color, prancing up the wall, skipping around the building's corner. I lean my back against the tree's rough bark. I'm hungry already—consequence of having been up since before dawn, thanks to Daddy. I take out my cheese sandwich and wolf down a few bites, then reach for *Annals*. I flip through the pages. There are eight articles, some pictures. I turn to the back cover.

There, again, are the student contributors. A serious-faced boy with dreadlocks pulled back from his face. A smiling girl who looks about twelve, though she can't be, really. A guy with bad acne and braces. An older woman, her straightened hair combed and curled under.

Julian.

It's not the same photo included with his article. They took this picture for the magazine especially. It matches the other students' pictures, each with the history building in the background. He's wearing his Obama T-shirt, the one Uncle Ellis brought back for him years ago. He used to sleep in that shirt—men's medium, meant to go in a drawer until he hit a few more growth spurts. Instead he ditched his basketball pajama shirt on the spot while Uncle Ellis laughed from the sofa. Julian didn't care, his bony nine-year-old body wriggling as he pulled the new shirt on. It came down to his knees almost. Then the election, him sitting cross-legged, back curled like a comma, head lifted to the screen, face bathed in the white glow.

"It's history—again—y'all watching?"

"I see, darlin." Mummy, at the table, hunched over something. Daddy sits by Julian. The two of them gaze, their profiles identical—focused frowns, chins lifted, heads tilted just a little to the left. I look over at Mummy. She reaches into the purple glass with her fingers.

"What's that? I could have some?"

"It's just paper clips. I have to file some paperwork."

"Mummy, I wanna watch something too."

"This is on now, Karmen."

How come I'm not darlin? "But this been on all night."

Mummy glances up at the clock. "You should be in bed, now."

I tiptoe to see what's on the table. Mummy has her papers spread out in front of her. The glass is a jangle of wires, all tinged plum, but each hinting of other colors they still retain.

I reach up. "I want a paper clip."

"They're sharp, Karmen. They're not for playing."

But I can already feel the smooths and sharps, the way the thin, twisted shapes would bend between my fingers. My fingers brush the glass—smooth, cool. Bump it out of reach. I try again.

"Karmen—no!"

Contact—and then teetering. I look at it spin. I can't raise my arm out fast enough to grab it, and all I can do is watch. Then the crack, and bits of purple scatter across the floor. The paper clips—red, blue, yellow, green—lie among the bits of broken glass.

"Come, Karmen, come." Uncle Ellis hoists me up by the armpits, then onto his hip. "Let's go. You still like the story about the little girl and the magic mango tree?"

"It's apples." My voice is small. I bury my face in his shoulder as he walks upstairs. Cocoa butter and the nose-sting of pine and lime and flowers that always clings to his neck.

"How much times I have to talk to that girl?" Mummy's voice is vexed. "We had those glasses from we got married!" Daddy's voice rumbles low in reply; the broom cupboard opens.

"Accidents happen. Don't worry about that, little miss." Uncle Ellis lifts me down and sets me on the floor. I grab the book from the shelf and settle at the picture window. Together we sit, read the book twice. Downstairs, my real family carries on without me. I lean my head on Uncle Ellis' arm and wonder if it would be better if I weren't here at all.

My sandwich slips from my fingers and lands on my lap, my hand forgetting I was even holding it. I remember that feeling so well—my parents settling back into their places after my catastrophe, Julian letting out a bark-laugh at something on the TV. Everyone happy as ever, or at least comfortable, somehow right, even though I wasn't there.

Can Julian see us now, somehow? Is that how he feels?

Was that how he felt?

I pick up my sandwich and take a bite. My hunger's gone now anyway. I look back at the picture. I don't remember seeing that shirt as I went through his things. It must be there somewhere, in the drawer, or in the closet for some reason. What do we do with all these memories that we gather up over time, all the stories twined into our shirts' cotton, twisted through socks, laced through a pair of shoes? What happened to Julian's memories? What would he have said about that night? Probably that his little sister was making a commotion while history was unfolding, spoiling the experience. Would he even remember me being carried upstairs? If I'm the only one who remembers that stinging shame, is it even real? If Julian is gone, what does it mean that he was ever here? In seventy years, when I'm gone, and Mummy and Daddy too, will it be as if my brother never existed? Is that what he wanted? How he felt? Like it would be better to just . . . not?

I swallow the last of the sandwich and shove the foil back in my bag. I need to focus on my task—find people who knew Julian. I thumb through the notebook, scan Julian's tidy handwriting. Two names stand out: Professor Gibson and Professor Demeritte. Did they teach him? If I had my phone, I'd track them down easily. I hold on to the book and get up. No point worrying about what I would have done. I'm here now. I head back to the history block. There are four classrooms on the bottom level; the door to each is wide open. The first has a short, round woman at the front, talking. She catches my eye with a quizzical gaze and I keep moving. The second and third rooms are empty, chairs jostled out of place, then abandoned. I hear voices as I approach the last. I walk up to the door and listen. Light chatter trickles out. It sounds casual—no class in session there yet. I take a big breath, then step in. There are eight or so students. I flip *Annals* over to see if I can pick out any of these faces. No one stands out.

"Uh—morning." My voice comes out with a squeak. "I was looking for some people in the history department—"

"You in the right place," a guy sitting on a desk, facing away from me, shoots back quick. Apparently wisecracks don't dissolve into thin air after high school.

"I wondered if any of y'all knew Cardo?"

Wisecrack guy hops down off the desk and turns around. "Who's looking for me?"

I step forward. "I'm Karmen. Pru gave me your number."

"Yeah, yeah, she told me about you." He heads toward the door, away from the chatter that's already started up again. "You were looking for people on campus who knew Julian." He tucks his hands in his pocket. "I wouldn't say *knew*. I remember Julian."

The room seems to split in two. There's everyone else, chatter suddenly far away. Then there's me and my brother's name spoken out loud—by someone who admits he remembers him, someone who maybe isn't all that different from him.

"You remember him how?"

Cardo pushes his hands deeper in his pockets. "We had

some classes together. He boarded with me and some other guys a few times, but he didn't come out often like that."

There's the thumping in my chest again, like my heart isn't sure whether it should live in my body or out. Cardo's words give me a seed of hope, and a twist of fear. He remembers Julian. "You heard what happened to him?"

Cardo folds his arms across his chest, shoulders hunched forward, and that's my answer. He knows Julian died, and he knows it was suicide.

"Does everyone know?"

Cardo glances back at his friends. Someone's just cracked a joke; laughter lifts through the room. "Not in here. Most of them are first-years—they only heard there was a student who . . . passed away. The ones who were in our classes last year, they know, but . . . I guess he wasn't in touch much. He stopped coming to class. I didn't even really know; I ended up doing sorta bad in class too. That's why I gotta redo last year's classes."

Why couldn't Julian have done that too? He was always good in school, but failing isn't the end of the world—is it? Couldn't he have just tried again? He could be here, as alive as Cardo is now.

I force myself to keep going. "When did you stop seeing him skateboarding?"

He looks down at the ground. "Spring, maybe. Probably the same time he stopped coming to school."

"You think any of the other boarders ever saw him after that?"

"I don't think so. I can ask, if you like."

I nod. "Please."

"You could talk to his teachers. Mr. Demeritte just got a class ending now. Right upstairs."

"Thanks." My feet carry me out, then up and along the hall. Before I reach the first classroom, I hear footsteps. When I turn, Cardo stands behind me.

"You board?"

"No. Maybe."

"You probably see how they look at Pru at school. People think if you doin something a little unusual, you weird. Something automatically wrong with you."

"I don't think that. I'm not into it like Julian was, but I knew him." Or thought I did.

"Yeah, but I don't want you think that any of us—me, Pru, any of the other guys we hang with—that we had something to do with it. We didn't cause Julian to kill himself."

His words feel like a slap. What's better—saying it hard and straight, *kill himself,* that way, or the cotton-fluff crap Layla spouts about angels' arms? "I wasn't blaming you. I really just wanted to know if you could tell me anything."

"If I find out anything, I'll let you know." He disappears back down the stairs. And I keep going up.

The first classroom is empty, but the second has a class in session. The teacher's at the far end instead of near the door. I take a few steps forward and peer in.

"So, as you would have seen from the reading, this era was marked by—" The teacher sees me as I see him. The same face as on the back of the magazine, faint lines hinting at the smile creases by his eyes. Heads turn, looking back at me. Professor

Demeritte extends a hand toward the row of empty chairs at the back of the room. I step in and take the first seat from the door. The teacher continues and I sit still, listening. Imagining, for a moment, that I'm somehow closer to my brother as I sit in this room. That even though I'm not exactly following what the teacher is saying, I feel like I can understand Julian, just by sitting in this seat. That I'm in my brother's shoes.

There's no bell to end the class—Professor Demeritte just says, "We'll pick up again on Friday. Don't forget, essays due a week from today. Come see me during office hours if you need support. Don't wait till the night before and come emailing me about extensions, folks."

I weave between desks and students on their way out. I know they're not much older than me, but they seem so much more settled. Out of uniform, picking their own classes. I can't fathom being here in a year's time. Not that it matters. I have no plans to be.

"It's not every day I get a guest dropping into my lecture on race, gender, and class in post-emancipation Bahamian society."

Professor Demeritte's greeting stuns the words right out of my mouth. I don't even know how he rattled that phrase off unless he practiced it beforehand.

"What can I do for you, auditing student?"

"I—uh." I hold the magazine out to him. "I saw you did this last year, with my brother. I wanted to know if you could tell me . . . anything."

"You're Julian's sister."

"Yes."

A look crosses his face—sadness? Pity?—and then is gone. "You must have a lot of questions." He draws in a long breath. "I have to head over to my office right now. If you come around eleven, we can talk then. I just have a ten o'clock meeting first—"

Ten o'clock? Ms. Rhonda! "I have to go!"

"I'm there tomorrow, too," he calls as I run down the stairs and toward the gate, but it seems like every class on campus has let out all at once, and I have to settle for brisk-walking in between milling bodies. At the road, I zip along, then down onto Ms. Rhonda's street. The one place I had to be today, and I'm about to be late.

I ring the doorbell and let a smile take over my face. This appointment is something I'm supposed to do. But finally getting somewhere with information on Julian? That's something I *need*.

CHAPTER FIVE

Ms. Rhonda holds the door open for me, her trademark bright pink lipstick perfectly painted on. The pink lips stretch into a wide smile.

"Karmen! Good to see you, come in." She always greets me like I'm a long-lost friend who's come by to eat cookies on the couch. I follow her to her home office—frosted window that still lets in sunlight, a plant hung from the ceiling, trailing down onto the bookcase below, tendrils reaching for the ground like touching earth will give it power to get up and walk away. I sit on the pink sofa. Ms. Rhonda closes the door, then maneuvers around the oval coffee table and to her swivel chair. She lowers herself, then leans her green cane against the armrest. The carved parrot head at the top seems to be staring at me.

"Let's turn Rupert the other way. He can be a distraction." She tucks the cane under her chair, then straightens up, smile still in place. "How you doin?"

I wonder what she knows. Did Mummy tell her what happened at school? "I'm okay."

Ms. Rhonda's carefully drawn-in eyebrows go up. Her thick lashes open up wide, too. "Mmm?"

"Right." I sigh. Ms. Rhonda doesn't like it when I use *okay* to answer her questions. She says it's a placeholder for what

I'm really feeling. What are the right words? "I'm . . . tired."

"Grief tired or sleep tired? Or back-to-school tired?"

Maybe she doesn't know about my suspension. "Yeah, all of those."

She smiles. "What's it been like being back at school?"

My mind goes back to the first few minutes of that first day, then to what happened with Robbie in homeroom. "Sorta rocky."

"How?"

"Just people being weird."

"I notice you're not in uniform, and you're here at"—she glances up at her clock—"ten fifteen."

Fifteen minutes late. Oops.

"Let's talk about what happened."

"I guess my mother told you I got kicked out of school."

Ms. Rhonda's eyes widen. "What happened?"

Part of me knew, I think, that we'd have to talk about this, but my mind's been so full with figuring out how to answer Julian's questions, with trying not to replay Robbie's words in my mind. Now, after the registrar's office, and Dr. Fox, and Cardo, and Mr. Demeritte, even yesterday feels far away. The school corridors, Robbie and the basketball, Pru guiding me through balancing on the skateboard—even the skateboard—all feel like something a different Karmen did, in some other universe. Here in this cosmos, though, Ms. Rhonda clears her throat and waits for me.

"I got in an argument with a kid at school and it kind of got out of hand. The principal told me to take time off until I'm ready to come back."

"Out of hand how?"

Broken glass—Mummy's tears. Daddy barks across the table, *My dead son.* I don't want to go back. But counseling's part of the deal. I know I have to do this. "I broke a chemistry-lab window by mistake. This boy, Robbie, he's been . . . just messing with me since the first day back. Saying rude stuff, just being mean. I was practicing skateboarding at break time, and his ball made me fall. He said something stupid and I got mad and just threw it."

Ms. Rhonda nods. "Keep going."

I sigh and look up at the clock again. The long hand's barely crept past the three. "So now the principal and the school counselor think I'm unstable, and I'm on punishment at home till I sort out my messed-up self." My words sound angry, even to me. I slouch back into the sofa. This is why I don't like counseling. Everything I put away is right back at the surface now, being dragged back up.

"That's a hard, hard start back."

I look up to meet Ms. Rhonda's eyes. Her face has softened. It's one of the things I like about her: she's not a poker-faced counselor.

"What'd Robbie say?" she asks.

Ain nobody dead! His words surge up even before Ms. Rhonda's question is out. I shift on the cushion—is it always this stiff?

"He said something about Julian. Not about him directly, but it was toward him. I just felt like a switch flipped in me. Like I was outside myself."

Ms. Rhonda jots something down in her book. Does she

have to take notes, like she's prepping an article? Her eyes meet mine. "That must have been painful to hear." There's something behind the sympathy in her gaze. A waiting. "That doesn't quite answer my question. What did Robbie say?"

"I don't wanna repeat it."

"I have to ask, Karmen. Did he say something that suggests he knows something about Julian's death? Not aware that it happened, but that he knows something *else*?"

My impatience flares. "He said something *toward* Julian!" My chair's cushion feels like it's full of bristles. I shift in the seat. How much longer do I have to be here?

"I know it's painful, Karmen. It can also be useful sometimes to say hurtful words out loud."

"How would that help?"

"For some people, it's a chance to respond. A measured response, after the fact, where you have more power—the benefit of knowledge and time."

"Well. I threw the ball, so. I'm good."

"That's a glib reply."

"I'm not glib about it." I crane my neck to see the clock. Just past 10:20. Is time moving backward in here?

"I can tell your mind's elsewhere," Ms. Rhonda says gently. "Where?"

I don't want to be here. I don't want her making notes about me. I don't want to relive what happened yesterday. I want to be outside, asking questions, talking to real people. I don't need to understand the finer points of why Robbie is a dick and why his dickiness upset me. "It's just—a lot happened. I found out that Julian was on probation from his classes. I guess I just need to understand Julian's choice." No, that's not even right. "I need to understand why he felt like he didn't *have* a choice. And why he didn't say something to me."

"It's a tremendous weight, Karmen—being the one left behind. And when someone dies by suicide, it's sudden, it's traumatic, and it's complicated. I can tell you those questions are so valid, and so common among families. I'm curious— did you look at any of those resources I gave you?"

Our first session was right after Julian's funeral. I can't even remember what we talked about. I shake my head.

Ms. Rhonda sets her notebook down on the table. "Let me try that again. There are some wonderful resources I'm going to ask you to look at, *in addition* to our time together. I think it can be really useful to be among people who are walking, or who have walked, this hurtful road you find yourself on. This road you didn't ask for." Ms. Rhonda grasps Rupert and presses his base into the floor hard as she pushes herself to her feet. She takes a few steps toward her desk and slides the drawer open, then rummages around. She pulls out a piece of paper, then returns to her seat and lowers herself back down. She holds the page out to me. I glance at it as I take it; the words swim before my eyes.

"There's a support group for grieving teens, and another for families who've lost someone by suicide. There are other supports too—would you like to talk about those now, or look at them at home and we can talk next time?"

I stuff the papers into my backpack. "We can talk next time."

There's a long moment of quiet. "We still have time today,

Karmen. We can take this in so many directions. What's foremost in your mind? What this Robbie said, being asked to step away from school? Your questions about Julian's path before he died?"

I let my eyes wander around the room. Her walking stick is under her chair, Rupert's parrot head turned away from me.

"I just have Julian on my mind. I tried going to the office to find out how bad his grades were. Did you know they won't give you transcript records for another student, even if you're family?"

"That's standard procedure, unfortunately. Would you like to talk about what you hoped to gain, or feel, by getting that information?"

"Julian was the smart one. Always. I just don't get why a smart guy would end up on probation."

"I sense there's an 'and.'"

"And why someone who had it all together would . . . just not wanna live anymore."

"Those are valid questions. Let's talk about that last one—how someone who, as you say, 'had it all together' could die by suicide. How are you coping with this uncertainty, and Julian's death?"

"I'm fine. I'm the one who's alive. I'm gonna celebrate my next birthday come December. Julian's not even here for his birthday this month. I sorta feel like . . ."

"Go on." Softly.

"Like I owe it to him to understand."

"That's a huge responsibility, Karmen. How do you think you'll cope if that's not possible? If you can't understand?"

I don't answer. I can't. I guess I haven't thought that far, and I can't bring myself to start now. I only know I *have* to understand. "I wanted to ask my parents if they knew Julian was on probation."

"What's stopping you?"

Daddy, holding the house phone. His tucked shirt orderly, his jaw tense. In the principal's office shouting, *My dead son.* The way his chair teetered, on the brink of landing flat on its back, then righted itself. Mummy isn't even an option—how can I ask her anything when she can barely get out of her bathrobe, and when she does, half the time she's in tears? "They have a lot on their minds."

Ms. Rhonda nods. "This is such a painful time for each of you. But I would encourage you to speak up. Talk to your parents about these questions you have. You're looking for answers, and that's part of your journey. Leaning on your parents for comfort and for information can be part of that journey too. Have you all talked about how you might honor Julian's birthday this year?"

"I asked. My dad just shut it down."

"And your mum?"

"She's not . . . I don't wanna bother her."

"It sounds like she's struggling."

I don't reply. Talking about my problems is one thing. Telling Ms. Rhonda that my mother can barely get out of bed? That her attempt at breakfast ended in shouting and broken bowls? That feels too far.

"It can be a great comfort for grieving families to remember a loved one's birthday. Some families meet at the graveside; some go out for dinner and share memories. Some find an activity that the person loved doing. Some even have a party." Ms. Rhonda sees me chuckle and mirrors the smile. "Something brought you a glimmer of joy?"

"Picturing my parents on skateboards."

At the end of our session, Ms. Rhonda walks me to the front door.

"Remember, two pieces of homework for you. One, talk to your parents."

I nod.

"Two, look at those resources. I think connecting with others on this road would be helpful for you."

I take my time walking back to campus. The sun is strong and the road feels shadeless. Even my own body barely casts a shadow in the near-midday heat. Just inside the gates, I sit under a bench by a tree that miraculously provides some cool. A few students stroll past me. Then I'm alone.

"Karmen?"

I know the voice even before I turn around. Isaiah.

He sits down beside me. His pants are neatly pressed, a crease ironed down the middle of the front. His shirt is a button-up and sky blue. I look back down at my shoes. I shoved on ratty sneakers from last year. I never thought about them—till now. When I look into Isaiah's face, though, he doesn't seem to notice my tired shoes. There's a smile in his eyes. "How'd you know where to find me?" I ask.

"I got your text yesterday. No one answered at home, so I went to your dad's office and asked him. He said you had an appointment at ten. Figured if I hung around by the gates, I might catch you."

I lean toward him before I know what I'm doing. His arm goes around my shoulders, and he feels like the first sure, strong thing I've found in forever. I didn't know my arms felt so weary—they take him as permission to ache. It feels like a moment I should let out tears, but none fall. I sense Isaiah has questions, but he lets them lie silent, for now.

"I got kicked out of school."

"Layla told me."

"I guess the whole grade knows."

"She said you got in an argument with Robbie, and broke a window."

"People talk too much."

"It's school. What else people gonna do?"

This is not how I want Isaiah to see me. "I don't normally break windows, but Robbie—anyway, he had it coming."

"What'd he do?"

I sigh, resigned. "Robbie threw this ball at me and I fell off Julian's skateboard. Pru told him he should apologize properly, and he said, 'Why? Ain nobody dead.'"

"Wow."

"I lost it. I lost it all the way, like . . . everything in my head that thinks straight blurred right out. I grabbed the ball and threw it, and I broke the chem-lab window."

Isaiah's eyes widen. "Did you get hurt? Is everyone okay?"

"Yeah—my knee's a bit scraped, no big deal. But Mr. Gardiner and Ms. Dorsett said I need to take time off."

"Like suspension?"

"They said to get my head together."

He nods. "That's not a bad thing."

I snort. "It's working like a charm."

"Day one, Karmen." His voice holds so much softness, I feel almost worthy. "How come you're here, though? Shouldn't you be taking it easy at home?"

"Oh, you mean like Mummy? In my bathrobe with the curtains closed till midafternoon?"

Isaiah doesn't respond, and then I wish I'd kept my mouth closed, but how am I supposed to know? There's no guidebook on how much to say about your messed-up family. Especially when we were just a normal family until six weeks ago.

"I don't know what my mother would do if something happened to one of us." When he speaks, Isaiah's voice is low. "I can only imagine."

I like that he says it that way. *I can only imagine.* Like he doesn't know, but he's willing to guess. "I never thought she'd be this way. I mean, she's a counselor."

"You're a counselor's daughter."

"Not by choice!"

"True. I just mean . . . when you live it, it's totally different from other people living it. At least I think so. I think a lot of parents would fall apart if their child died." He looks over at me. "A lot of siblings, too."

"I'm not falling apart. Actually, I found out something interesting. About Julian." I reach into my backpack and take out the history magazine. "Julian has something printed in here."

Isaiah takes it. It falls open to the start of Julian's article, as if I've had it, been looking through it, for weeks. "That's amazing, Karmen. How'd you get this?"

"I went to see the dean in the history department. I met one of his teachers, too. I feel like I might actually get some answers. Even without my phone or computer."

"Confiscated?"

"That was Daddy's idea."

"What does he think about you coming here to ask around about Julian?"

"He doesn't exactly know. He just thinks I need to be out of the house and go sit in the library all day and do homework to keep out of trouble. Plus my therapist is close to here." I wait for that awkward pause, the one Layla always gives, like therapy is a below-the-waist doctor's exam and it's better not to say or ask about.

"Oh, that's the appointment you had. Does it help?"

I stand up and pull the backpack on. Isaiah gets up too. He must think I'm offended because he hastily adds, "I hope I didn't—overstep or anything. Just now."

"No." The word comes out too loud. "You just took me by surprise. Some people get weird if I even say *therapy*."

"Awkward, with your mum's profession."

"It's different when it's about you."

There it is again, that look on his face. Something past just caring. Something that draws me in.

"Which way are you walking?" I ask, and he jerks his head to the left. We move that way. "Therapy was okay. Ms. Rhonda gave me yet more homework, in case I didn't already have enough."

"What do you have to do?"

"For one, read over these resources she gave me. And pick one, I guess. The paper's in my bag, if you wanna see."

We stop walking. Isaiah unzips my backpack carefully. I can feel every shift of papers, every shudder of books moving around as he slides his hand in.

"It's a white paper, folded in half," I say.

"Got it." His voice seems extra close to my ear a moment, breath warm on my skin. I feel a grin blooming deep in me. I try to suppress the smile so he doesn't see, so I don't look too eager. I hear the rustling of a page being unfolded.

"Did you find it?"

"Yep." He zips the bag closed and opens the paper out. It feels easier, reading the words knowing that he's reading along beside me. *Resources for Families Impacted by Suicide. Suicide Survivors Network. Support Group for Families of Suicide. Life after Suicide: Online Support. Teens Against Grief.* It goes on.

"Look at this one." Isaiah draws a line under something near the bottom. "Art therapy at CU. Thursdays, six to seven, pottery studio."

"Layla would like that," I say. "Not that she needs therapy, I guess."

"Weren't y'all two holed up in her room half the summer, doing something arty? I remember there was yarn."

Isaiah starts walking again. I do too, but the memory that flashes in my mind makes the path, the trees, the little blossom of joy, all fade away. Suddenly I'm back there, back in *that* night: standing too close to Isaiah, the soft scratch of yarn on our skin, my phone's buzz, and ignoring it—and it's too much—too strong, too sharp, too soon. That night is too bitter and mixed up. I push it away. I'm here. Beside Isaiah. This is now. I close my eyes a second, pray he doesn't notice.

"Pottery's great, though," Isaiah carries on. "If it doesn't do anything else, it might relax you."

"How would you know, Mr. Button-Down Shirt?"

"I joined the pottery club last year."

"You? Mr. Business?"

He bursts out laughing. "Mr. Business!" He says it with an eyebrow wiggle. "I'm multifaceted, all right? And one of my facets happens to be that I occasionally dabble in the clay."

"How did Layla not mention this to me?"

"Take that up with her. It wasn't a secret, though."

"So, you like . . . do the whole spinning thing at the wheel?"

"I tried it. I really like hand building, though. Where you cut and roll and shape the pieces at a table. It's a totally different mindset than my classes, or work. It kinda balances me out. Everyone has something like that, though. Maybe like you and knitting."

I consider this. Julian had his skateboarding. Layla's always been artsy, but there's soccer, too, and she loves organizing at youth group. I like to knit, though it hasn't held my interest as much since Julian died. Being his sister—that's something else that brought me balance. And it's something I can't ever get back. I start to feel aware of the silence between Isaiah and me.

"I guess so," I say.

"Do you wanna try some pottery with me? See what you think?"

"Yes!" The word leaps out of my mouth before I can rein it in, before I can sound less cheerleader-eager. Maybe it's okay, though. As if he agrees, Isaiah reaches down for my hand. He rubs the back of it with his thumb, then lets go. We stop walking—we're outside a building surrounded by tall trees. "I should get to class, even though I really wanna skip it now." He holds the paper out to me.

"I'm glad we ran into each other."

"I'm always happy to be into you—run into you." He looks embarrassed for a second. "Anyway . . . I'll be on campus tomorrow at one, if you wanna check out the pottery studio with me."

My skin still feels the warmth of his, and when my smile starts, I let it take over my face. "Tomorrow at one. Should I meet you here?"

His grin mirrors mine. "Let's do that."

CHAPTER SIX

Daddy waits in front of the library for me. It can't be time to go home yet—it's barely noon. As I near him, his eyes flicker over me and he does his contemplative face, frowny eyebrows. "Where were you?"

"I went to Ms. Rhonda; then I was just walking around."

"I'm sure Isaiah found you."

I nod, and brace for a lecture. I try to tamp down my joy as we head for the parking lot. Above us, poincianas arch tall and cast a corridor of shade. Flecks of late red blooms interrupt the green. "I was in the library for a bit." I consider telling Daddy about my visit to the registrar's office and the history department. How would that go? Do he and Mummy know more about Julian being on probation? What do they know that they didn't tell me?

"You need lunch?" Daddy asks.

"I already ate." We're at the car now. I open my door. "Did you get a lot done?" I ask as Daddy gets in. "I thought you were gonna be here longer."

"I met with my advisor. Talked about possibly teaching a class next term. Right now, my focus is on getting back into my dissertation."

I glance over at Daddy. "You ready?"

He starts the car up and clicks on his seat belt. I reach for mine too. How does he always seem so together, so organized? Nothing out of place, nothing forgotten. "Gotta keep my mind occupied." His eyes are focused on the dash-cam screen as he eases back in one smooth motion. Then he shifts into drive and slides through the parking lot, steady, not speeding, not crawling. "It's good for you, too. I know you think I got you up early as punishment, but it's important to keep in a routine when things are . . . when you're . . . struggling."

Daddy never seems to be struggling, though. Well, aside from losing his cool in the principal's office, and that was more about him being mad at me. Even his rage is mostly tucked away, out of sight. Ms. Rhonda's words flash into my mind—what she said about leaning on my parents, that being part of the journey. If Daddy can handle driving, can handle getting on with his work, maybe he can handle my questions, too. "I didn't just go to counseling," I begin.

"Really." I know by his unsurprised tone that he thinks I mean spending time with Isaiah.

"I went to the registrar's office."

Daddy glances over, the only visible hint of surprise a slight wrinkle in his eyebrows. "What for?"

"I found this letter. It was about Julian. About him being on academic probation."

"Ah." His gaze is back on the road ahead. It's hard to read Daddy's expression in profile when he's driving. His eyes narrow, but that could be for the truck that swings in front of us. He slows down, adjusts his grip on the steering wheel.

"Did you and Mummy know?"

"We knew." His voice is steady: we could be talking about whether he noticed that the laundry soap's getting low. Something flickers in me—disappointment. Anger.

"How come no one told me?"

Daddy doesn't answer right away. When he does speak, his voice is lower. "You keep secrets for your children sometimes, Karmen. It wasn't easy for your brother. He didn't want you to know."

Daddy's words feel like a slap. "It's not like I would have teased him."

"He was having a hard time. I'm sure you know that."

"Well, it's obvious now." I don't mean for my words to come out sarcastic. "I thought we were close, is all," I add, but it stings. Julian didn't trust me with his secret. And everyone in the house knew but me.

"You know school records are confidential, though. I couldn't have gotten them myself, when Julian was alive. And I wouldn't now."

"Why not? Wouldn't you want to know how bad it was?"

"He's gone, Karmen. It was too much for him—everything—and he's gone. We know how bad it was."

I don't know how that's enough, how that's an answer. Julian's death doesn't answer everything for me—it unfolds everything. It undermines everything. Was he ever happy? Were we ever close? Did he ever trust me? What was the point in me being in his life, if he couldn't talk to me in the end? Before there was an end? Daddy doesn't see it that way, though. He doesn't have questions. I wish I felt the way he does. Wish I could feel that matter-of-fact. That resigned.

We drive on a few more minutes before I get up the courage to keep going. "Ms. Rhonda thinks it's a good idea to do something for Julian's birthday. She gave me a whole bunch of ideas, but I think we should just have some people over."

"Mmm."

"Maybe Aunt Glenda and Uncle Ellis could come over, and Isaiah and Layla."

Daddy drives on in silence.

"So . . . can we?"

He sighs. "Your mummy got pretty upset this morning. You gotta think about that."

"I know. But we always do something for birthdays. Remember last year we went to Blue Lagoon Island for the day? And the year before, for my birthday, we did the aquarium and got sushi after?"

"I don't mind celebrating, Karmen. But we can't just think about you and me. You know? And Julian's gone. He won't know if we have a shindig or if we just try to . . . move on."

His words feel like a too-tight jacket, squeezing me. *Move on, move on.* What does that even mean? Forget about him? Pretend September fifteenth is just another day? "Ms. Rhonda said it might help us move on." I don't think Ms. Rhonda would mind me stretching reality in her name.

"Why's it so important to you?" Daddy looks over at me.

"It just feels wrong to pretend the day doesn't matter. It's bad enough he's not here—we have to still remember."

Daddy's eyes are back on the road. "I remember. Every hour of every day. It's been a lot these past few days. And I don't know that your mother's up for that yet. Let's shelve it for now."

I look away from him. He just doesn't understand. *It doesn't matter*, I tell myself. *I'll keep thinking about it.* I'll put together a plan on my own if I have to.

I glance down at his phone in the drink holder between us. The old me would text Layla. I could ask Daddy to borrow his phone, ask her to help me pull something together, something to help Julian's birthday feel right—or less wrong. I turn away and lean back in my seat. Right now, the silence between me and her feels like a respite from not fitting in with the kind of friend she wants me to be.

At home, Mummy's car is in the driveway, but she's nowhere to be seen. Upstairs, I pass her bedroom door. It's closed tight. I put my bag in my room and lie back on the bed. I can hear Daddy moving around downstairs. I can imagine what he'll think when he sees the door closed. *It's important to keep a routine. . . .* Is it, though? Right now it feels more important to lie down with a pillow over my head to block out the world. Then the doorbell rings. Whatever. I stay where I am. Daddy can answer it.

It rings a second time. I sigh and head down. When I open the door, Layla stands on the doorstep with a heavy-looking bag in one hand.

"Oh, so you *are* alive," she says; then a guilty look crosses her face. "I mean—"

"My phone and computer got taken away." I cut her off before she can make a bigger fool of herself.

"I heard you got suspended. What happened? Everybody was talking about how you broke a window and you went after Robbie. . . ."

I step outside and close the door. "It didn't happen like that. You saw how he was messing with me since the first day back. Pru didn't tell you what gone down?"

Layla makes a face like she's tasted rotten fruit. "Her? She don't talk to me."

I sit on the step. Layla does the same. "It's a whole thing. Robbie started it, and he said something stupid—"

"What'd he say?"

"He . . ." I bite my bottom lip. Why am I hesitating? It's Layla—my best friend.

"Tell me," she urges. When I don't answer, or even move, she reaches into her bag, pulls something out, and sets it between us. The ball of yarn from the other night on the way to youth group. Its brilliant green nearly glows against the step's dull gray. She takes her end and slips the stitches off her holder. She works a few, then looks over at me like she's offering up a piece of the normal I used to have. I lift my end and slide the stitches off the pen and onto my four left fingers. We work in silence for a few moments. It's familiar, it's right, just hanging out, making something.

"So?" She keeps her eyes on the wool.

"He said—well, he tripped me up with his ball and I fell off the skateboard. Pru was yelling at him and he just brushed it off—"

"What a jerk. Said what, though?"

"You keep cutting me off."

"Sorry."

"He said, *Ain nobody dead.*" I wait for her to react—a flinch, a gasp, something.

"Then what?"

"That was it. I just lost it, and . . ."

"And what?"

I don't know what to say. I've missed my best friend, but now that she's here, she just doesn't get it. Do I have to spell it out? *It would appear you do,* Julian's voice whispers. "He said it like Julian was nobody."

"Ohhhhhh." She sounds legitimately surprised. "You think he really meant that, though?"

"Yeah, I think he really meant that," I snap. "Why else would he say it?"

"Maybe he meant it like *you* weren't hurt that bad."

The wool slides over my fingers. It's the thing keeping me going. If I stop, I don't know what I might say.

"I get it. What you did, though."

"What *I* did?"

"It's totally normal."

"What is?"

"Acting out as a symptom of grief."

I shake my head. Am I hearing this right? "Meaning what?"

"So . . . you know, I really think you should look at this." She slides out a thin paperback.

Ah. That book again. I barely suppress a laugh. "*Everything to Know about Grief*? Everything?"

Layla keeps going as if I haven't spoken. "It says it right

here." She flips open to a dog-eared page. "'Erratic behaviors—fighting, skipping school, avoiding extracurricular activities—are normal and understandable responses for teens.'"

"Where did you get that?"

"I ordered it." Her face is dead serious. "I thought it would help me."

"You need help?"

"Help me with understanding your grief," Layla rests a hand on my arm. "I want you to know I'm here for you."

I pull my arm away. "Your book tell you to say that?"

A look crosses her face like she's been caught digging in my bag. "Why you say that?"

I fight the urge to roll my eyes. "When's your mummy coming back?"

"She went to the store for one thing. Maybe fifteen minutes, half an hour." She pushes her stitches back on the holder again and stretches out her fingers. "Can we go inside?"

"I'm not supposed to have friends over."

"No phone, no computer, *and* no friends?"

"Have you never actually been grounded before?"

"Never mind." She reaches for the bag. "The breeze outside is nice. I brought over some stuff from school."

Of course she hasn't been grounded. Perfect girl, perfect life, perfect record. I try to push the thoughts away. "There's more? Daddy already printed off like a hundred pages of assignments."

"Did you do them?"

"Not a one."

"What'd you do all day?"

"Poked around CU. I was trying to talk to people who knew Julian."

Layla studies her shoes.

"What?"

"Is that a good idea?"

"I dunno. Check your book."

She swallows. "Anyway, Mr. Francis suggested I get some books for you from the library. He suggested a few, and I picked out the rest."

I slide my fingers out of the yarn. The moment's gone anyway. I pick up the first book, a thick self-help paperback on overcoming anger. "Whose idea was this one?"

"He picked that one out."

The next is on the stages of grief. "Oh goodie. Something fresh." I toss it on the step beside me and it tumbles onto the ground. "Whoops." I reach for the next one. "*Loving through Loss: Opening Your Heart After a Beloved Dies.* Who actually thinks of these titles?" I reach for another. It's agonizing, and I want to keep going just to see the ridiculousness. "Oh wait. *On Our Own Together: An Anthology of Loss.* They serious?"

"Okay—you don't have to be like that. You want me take them back?"

I watch her stuff the books into the bag, torn between anger and relief. I do want her to take these atrocities back. Even more, I want her to know not to bring them in the first place. Why can't she be like Isaiah? I wish he were here. Then instantly I wish I didn't want that, wish it could feel right to hang out with my best friend. Like it used to.

Layla zips the bag closed.

"Sorry."

She shrugs. We sit in silence for a few moments. Both our eyes land on the first book, still on the ground. Layla scoops it up and stuffs it in with the others. I wish I could make myself tell Layla I was wrong, tell her I want to keep even one of these awful books. I wish we'd talked about something else—wish I'd told her about bumping into Isaiah instead, the zing between us. Even told her about the pottery class we might take. But I don't want to hear if crushes are normal for a Grieving Teen. I don't want to be told that learning a new hobby is a useful healing technique.

The swish of skateboard wheels makes my head snap up. I crane my neck; everything in me feels like it both speeds up and freezes, waiting. Waiting for the skateboarder to come in line with the house. Waiting to see Julian fly up the driveway.

Pru sails into view. She's a sight for sore eyes and disgruntled headmasters: blouse untucked, shoes dusty, top button undone. I feel Layla bristle beside me. Pru rolls toward us, then skips off her board. She does a flick thing with her feet, so fast I can't follow it—one moment she's on the board, and the next it's in her hand. She takes the last few steps to us, chin high like she's on the runway. She grins wide.

"Hey, jailbreaker. How's the outside?"

"Hello, Pru," Layla says pointedly.

"Hey." Pru glances over at Layla, then back to me. "What's up? Your people locked you out?"

"She's not supposed to have friends over." Layla leans hard on the word *friends*.

"Tell them I'm your court-appointed bad influence." She pushes the mutually abandoned yarn aside and squeezes into the narrow space between us. "You missed it. Our whole grade got a lecture on anger management. It went right through the first half of English."

"You did?" I look to Layla for confirmation. She grimaces. So. She must have heard something after all. Why did she act like she hadn't?

"I hadn't done my homework, so for me they could name a holiday after you." Pru rubs a bit of the soft green between her fingers. "Robbie is a jackass, though. I don't know why they didn't give a lecture on not being a dick."

Layla gets up. "Can I use your bathroom?"

"Sure." I start to get up too, but she's already inside. I don't know if I should follow, but Layla's been in and out of my house for six years now. She knows the way.

"Thought you couldn't have friends inside."

"You want me ban her from using the bathroom?"

"Don't leave that choice to me." Pru peers into the bag Layla brought. "What's all this?"

"Don't look in there."

"Now I have to look." She practically shoves her head in. "Oh. Required reading?" She holds up the same book I tossed.

"She's trying to help."

She looks around. "Where's the skateboard? Confiscated?"

"It's inside. Not in the mood. Robbie say anything to you today?"

Pru shakes her head. "It's BS they didn't suspend him, too."

"Technically I'm not suspended. I'm supposed to be taking time to heal."

"So they gave you forever off?"

Her words refresh and terrify me at the same time. I don't want to think about how I'll feel about Julian being gone in a year, or five, ten. Will it really take forever to feel like me? Will I ever feel like myself again? "Try three weeks. But really, it's when I'm ready."

Pru stands up. "If everyone followed that, school would be half-empty." She stands up. "You better get back on that board."

"My knee's still sore from yesterday."

"So that's why you sitting around knitting like arthritic Grammy?"

"It's relaxing."

Pru yawns.

"I found Cardo." I hope the words will keep her here a little longer. It feels like ages since I talked to a real person. "They took some classes together."

"Did it help?"

Polite answers lie just out of reach. "Not really," I say instead. It feels like finding a rock in my backpack and tossing it onto the ground, admitting that. I still feel heavy, but I've shed a little something.

"What'd you talk about?"

"He mentioned he's retaking couple classes right now. I just couldn't stop thinking, Julian could be doing that. And he's . . ."

"Not." Pru pokes at her skateboard with her foot. "Life's vicious that way. Always showing you how it ain fair. Showing you reminders of who you lost." She stands up. "Wish I coulda been Julian instead."

Her words sting like a slap. "What you mean by that?"

"Nothing. Just a joke, I guess." There's no laughter in her voice.

"It wasn't funny."

"Guess not." She retreats down the driveway.

I watch her disappear. How could she wish to be Julian? Was she really joking about Julian being gone? I shake my head to clear away the thought. After that, Layla bringing over that ridiculous book seems almost saintly. At least Layla gets that it's not a joke. I get up and head inside. I follow the sound of voices—Layla's and Mummy's. I make my way to the kitchen, praying my mother is at least dressed.

". . . think I should check out?" Layla says. I pause just before the doorway to listen.

"Not really." Mummy's voice sounds normal. She always sounds normal, though, when she's talking to other people. "It means a lot that you want to support Karmen so much."

"I've been listening to this podcast too—it's called *Walk Beside You*. The guy on there, he's a really famous psychologist, and he said sometimes when someone has a death in their family, they pull away from other relationships. How do I help her if she doesn't wanna be around me?"

"Hey!" I say, maybe a little too loudly. I set the bag down on the table. Mummy looks relieved to see me. She fiddles with the tie on her bathrobe.

"We were just talking," Layla says. She sounds almost guilty.

"I'll give you girls some space." Mummy scurries out of the room like her hair is on fire. I kind of wish I could do the same.

"What were you talking about?"

Layla takes a long drink from the purple glass. "I was just asking her advice."

"Advice?"

"As a therapist."

"You can't do that!" My voice bursts out of my throat in a shout. I don't want Mummy to hear me yelling, to know we're talking about her, but it's too late and I can't stop myself.

"I was just—"

I force myself to talk more quietly. "You don't see she's still in her robe and the day's almost over?"

"I thought she might have just showered." Layla sounds defensive.

"Yeah, you *would* think that."

"What does that mean?"

"You don't get it!" My voice flares again. "My life isn't *like* yours. We're not like you, Layla. She doesn't even work anymore. She's not doing therapy, and if you wanna figure something out, you can go find a therapist and pay them like other people do."

Layla looks about to cry. "You ain gotta yell at me. I'm just trying to help you."

"By stressing out my mummy? You realize she had a death in *her* family too, right? Were you born yesterday, or you legitimately that stupid?"

Tears stream down Layla's face. "Why are you being so mean?"

Her tears should make me apologize, should make me take my words back. *Stop!* a distant voice whispers. Trouble is, I'm not sorry, and I want to keep going. "Why are you being so stupid? You can't bring Julian back with a bunch of books on grief."

"I know he can't come back, but I'm trying to help you!"

"I don't want help!" My throat is raw with the scream. I feel myself shaking, feel like something in my blood is about to burst out through my veins. My body can't hold my rage in, and my throat can't let it all out. "I want my brother back!"

Layla and I look at each other for a second. When she looks away, it feels like we're strangers.

"I was just—" she starts, and a horn toots outside. We both look. Her mother's car eases into the driveway.

I want her to know she can't ever come here and ask stupid questions, come and make stupid comments, come and scare Mummy into living in her bathrobe for another six weeks. I almost cry with relief when her mother honks from the driveway again.

"I'll just go." Layla ducks back into the front room. I know I should follow her. I should say I'm sorry. Say goodbye. Instead I stand by the window, watch her open the passenger door, see the car pull away. I don't know what it means that I just want her gone—if I'll feel this way tomorrow or just right now. I only know that, now, the feeling I've been trying to ignore is creeping back over me. The feeling that not only have I lost my brother—there's still more I stand to lose. My friends. What's left of my family. I lean over the counter and rest my head on my arms, try to will the last of that boiling rage away, so I can feel like me. My heart slows a bit; I'm not shaking anymore—that's something. I straighten up, and my eyes land on Layla's bag of awful books. Heat starts to rise in me all over again. This feeling isn't going away, not for good. What if I can't hold it together?

What if I lose myself?

I'm back in my room, surrounded by souvenirs of the day—the history magazine, my notebook, the bag of books, the flyer from Ms. Rhonda, and all the memories that go with them swirling around me—when my bedroom door opens. Daddy appears with a frown on his face.

"Young man wants to talk to you." He holds out Mummy's office phone. "Two minutes."

I put the phone up to my ear. What would make Isaiah call me here? Is he trying to get me in trouble? On the other hand—he's calling me! After we saw each other just a few hours ago. "Hello?"

"Hi, Karmen."

The voice isn't Isaiah's. "Yes?" Is it Cardo? I try not to notice Daddy's scowl.

"Someone told me you were looking for people to talk to about Julian. My sympathies, by the way."

It isn't Cardo, then. "I was. Who's this, though?"

"Alan Jackson. Someone passed your number on to me. I'm out by the softball field right now, by Ocean Drive, if you're willing to talk. It can be confidential, of course. Can you come out here?"

Confidential. Why would this Alan want it to be confidential? Does he know something? Five minutes' walk from here. So close—but I'm grounded. I look toward the doorway, but Daddy's gone, no doubt somewhere watching my two minutes tick down.

"I'll try." Will Daddy let me go? I know I have to at least ask. "Can you hold on a second for me?"

I mute myself as I rush downstairs. My parents' voices float out from the living room.

"It's too far," Daddy says. "Not one, but two friends over here. Now she have people calling on your line?"

"We shouldn't be isolating her." Mummy's voice is low but strong. "So, a friend called for her. She needs to know she has people on her side."

"We're on her side." Daddy's voice is louder.

"Think that's enough?"

"It should be. This is a family situation; we can get through it as a family."

"Wasn't enough for him." My mother's words are almost a whisper, but somehow they reach me. I'm about to tiptoe away, not knowing what I'll tell the voice on the other line, when she looks over at me. Daddy's gaze follows hers.

"Um—can I go out on the softball field for a minute?"

"No," Daddy says.

"What for?" Mummy asks at the same time.

"It's for . . ." My confidence falters. No matter what I say, one of them will agree and one won't. "It's for an assignment."

Mummy gets up off the sofa. "If your father says it's okay." She looks back at him. "Might be good for you to get out for a bit." She passes me in the doorway and rubs my shoulder. The smell of old sweat and unwashed sheets hangs in the air after she's gone. I turn my gaze to Daddy.

"Can I go?"

"This is really for schoolwork?"

"Yes." I hate lying, but I don't have a choice. I just know I need to go.

"Your mother thinks you should be allowed to go," Daddy says.

"So, can I?"

Daddy lifts his chin. I take that as a nod yes. I unmute the phone. "Are you still there?"

"I'm here," Alan says.

"Give me five minutes. I'm coming."

I grab the skateboard and the notebook, shove my feet in my shoes, and close the door behind me without locking it. I push off clumsily and fight to keep my balance. Push, roll, push, roll. The rhythm quiets my mind, but my body still feels like I'm running—maybe it's the exertion, maybe nervousness, maybe both. *Two things,* I hear Julian's voice say, *can be true at the same time.*

He didn't lie. I feel like the world's slowest skateboarder, but I still get to the field faster than I would have on foot. I pick up the board and hurry across the grass, scanning to see if I recognize anyone. There, by the bleachers. A guy stands up and waves. He looks short—about my height—with a pale blue shirt and jeans. He's so ordinary, it aches. To think that anyone walking around could have some memory snippet, some vague recollection, about Julian. Anyone could know something that would help me understand.

"Hey, Karmen?" the guy says when I'm closer. "Alan Jackson. Nice to meet you." He steps forward with a hand extended, his arm straight, as if his elbow doesn't bend. We shake hands as if we're here for a business interview. "So—you were Julian's younger sister, correct?"

"Yeah, I am. Were y'all in class together?"

Alan pulls his phone out of his pocket. "Sorry, I just gotta . . ."

I look away while he fiddles with it. Behind us, a group of guys kick a soccer ball around.

"Okay." Alan gives me a brisk nod. "How are you doing? It must have been so hard, with his death so sudden and everything."

Even after the girls talking with Layla on Monday, even after six weeks, even after all the *sorry for your loss*es, something about his words hits heavy.

"Thanks—I'm okay." I pull out my notebook. My mind's blank now—blank, and being pulled in two directions. I don't want to waste this chance . . . but I can't figure something about Alan out. "How'd you know Julian? Are you at CU too?"

"Uh—no." Alan tilts his head to one side. The look on his face is almost concerned. Something else, though, too. "How's your family coping?"

Is he here to help me, or to ask me questions? Ask the same question, over and over again? "How did you know Julian again?"

"Know him?" Alan screws up his face. "I didn't know him—that's why I wanted to talk to you. Someone DMed me and said you'd be willing to give me an interview. For my channel? Real Bahamas Talks?"

His words take all the breath out of my body. I just stand there, unable to gasp in or sigh out. *It's a setup!* my mind screams. *Someone did this to you.*

"They said you were willing to talk about life after your brother committed suicide."

My lungs jolt awake again. Those words. *Committed suicide.* I squeeze my shaking hands around the skateboard. My legs feel like they might give out, but they don't. "It's *died by.*"

"Pardon me?"

"People don't say *committed* anymore. Like it's a crime. He wasn't a criminal. People say *died by.*"

Alan lowers his head. He touches his phone screen and shoves it in his pocket, fast. Not fast enough, though. I saw the numbers counting up fast, milliseconds. Black bars moving across the white screen, time counting up, ticking off what he's captured from me. Sick lurches from my belly up toward my throat. I swallow down.

"You're recording?" Heat washes over me.

"It's just audio—but if you don't mind a quick video clip—"

I turn away from him so he doesn't see the tears already blurring my vision.

"Can I just get a quick picture, then?" he calls after me. "Is that your brother's skateboard or yours?" I hear the snap of his phone, but all he'll get is my back. I start to run. I have to get out of here. My stomach jolts with every step; my head pounds. Who did this? Why would they? Footsteps behind me, as I reach the parking lot's asphalt. I drop the skateboard, but my legs are jelly. For all I know, that guy is still on my tail, trying to snatch a picture of me, or video. I don't want to stay, and I don't want to fall off on wobbly legs. I grab the board and start walking.

"Hey, Karmen. That's you?" a voice calls. I don't stop. "Over here!" Girl's voice. "Wait! It's Danika."

Her words from the first day of school replay in my head: *Died in the worst way.* I pick up my pace, but her jogging footsteps are faster.

"Hey—you okay?" She leans in too close, small eyes darting across my face like I'm covered in blood.

I step back. "I'm fine."

"Who was that guy? You look so upset. He do something to you?" She sounds concerned, and I don't trust her—this second, I don't trust anyone. I shouldn't have lied; I shouldn't have come here; I shouldn't have even taken that phone call.

"It's nothing!"

"'Cause I saw him talking to Robbie. I know y'all two are kinda—can't stand each other or whatever."

"He was talking to Robbie?"

"Right over there." She points toward the tree near the bleachers. "I don't know what they were talking about but—wasn't that the Real Bahamas Talks guy?"

I don't need to hear more. I walk off through the parking lot and start trudging home. My face is wet before I've finished passing by the playing field. The shouts and cheers from some game or other seem to belong to a different universe. One where everything is right, where people breathe and run and throw balls to each other and celebrate when they're caught or hit or kicked. A universe where skateboards clack down the road. Where Julian lives. Not this twisted place where even his death is something to gawk at. Something someone wants to cash in on. Something someone wants to use to hurt me.

When I get home, Daddy's car is gone from the driveway and the front door is locked. I didn't bring keys. I knock and wait, then go around to the back door. I can see Mummy in the kitchen, moving around. From out here she looks normal, but the sheen on the glass door hides her face. I wait a moment before tapping for her to let me in.

"Did you get what you needed?" Mummy asks as I step in.

I force myself to nod. "Thanks for letting me go."

Mummy's gaze drops down to the skateboard, then back up to my face. "You learning how to ride that thing?"

I nod. The tears I wiped off on the way home threaten to spill again. She's changed since I left home—she has on a shapeless blue dress, but it's clean and it's not a bathrobe. She looks hopeful and sad. "I better get started on my school-work."

"How was counseling today?" she asks as I cross the kitchen.

Counseling feels like it happened a lifetime ago, in another galaxy. "It was fine."

"Fine how?"

"It was okay, Mummy."

"You don't have to talk to me, but I wish you would. It might help."

What would I tell her, though? That the same person I got suspended for just set me up with a tabloid to talk about Julian's death? That I can't even talk to my best friend anymore? That all I want is to understand why Julian died and why he didn't say something, *anything*, to me? That no one in the world can give me the answers I need?

"I'm fine," I say, and carry on upstairs.

CHAPTER SEVEN

I wake out of a dream, soaked. It's as if my whole body has sweated, as if my skin's trying to flush something out of me. Everything around me is deep black. I use the bathroom and catch sight of the time on the clock in the hallway. Ten to five. So, it's tomorrow now. Forty minutes before Daddy's up.

My eyes burn for sleep, but I walk downstairs anyway. The office door is closed, the steady blue light of the lock gleaming bright. I turn toward the living room. One of the lamps is still on. I step in to turn it off.

Daddy lies on the sofa, his back turned to me. A blanket is tugged up around his body.

"Daddy? You goin to bed?"

His breathing is steady and deep. His glasses sit on the side table, deliberately removed. He's asleep here. Asleep like he meant to be. There's a second where I think, *I gotta tell Julian.* Then I have to push the thought away, but instead of forgetting, a memory takes over, takes its place.

My bedroom door pushes open. Feet pad across the floor.

"Kay."

"Mm."

"You awake?"

I move over to make room, and Julian climbs in beside

me. Down the hall Mummy shouts, "Don't you dare! Don't you dare accuse me of that!"

Julian jumps up, shoves the door shut, then scrambles in beside me again. His feet are icy; I shift my leg away.

"What happen this time?"

"I dunno." Julian's voice hides something—something he heard and didn't want to, something he won't repeat. "Let's play Inspector and Ben."

A twinge of excitement—now that Julian's ten, I thought he would be too old for this game. "I ga be Inspector," I say.

"You's always be the Inspector. Anyway, all right, I's Ben. Inspector, I need to report a crime.'"

"Yes, young man—"

"I just turn twenty-six," he breaks in.

"Yes, sir. What's the crime today?"

"That's the same thing I always tellin you!" Daddy's voice this time.

"Someone take my piano." Julian carries on like we've both heard nothing.

"All right. Describe—"

"Too stubborn, just like your ma!" Mummy's voice cuts my sentence, our game, in half.

"Watch, when I pack up and go by her. And take the kids, too."

"Go ahead then, big man! Go cry to Mummy."

Tears prick my eyes. I don't want Daddy to leave; I don't want this shouting; I don't want to have to go live with Grammy; I don't want to be here without him. Who will read to me at bedtime and sneak me ice cream sandwiches? If they break up, will he get Julian and will Mummy get me? Or will I be with Daddy instead? Will he know how to part my hair straight and do it in fine braids when summer comes?

Elbow in my ribs. "Inspector. You supposed to say you could find the piano for me in three hours or less."

I blink back the tears. "I could find it in—" A door bangs into the spring stop. Feet thunder down the stairs, and the front door slams so hard, the whole house shakes. The tears break me open at my mouth and crumple my face till it aches. I cry quiet, which hurts more, but I can't bear more sound, and I can't stop shaking. Julian's hand squeezes mine.

"Daddy ain goin nowhere, you know that, right? They ain goin no place. By time's we go to sleep, he ga be back, and in the room. They always make up before they lock up the house. Lights still on. See under the door? Okay?"

When I don't answer, Julian digs his nails into my palm—firm, but not mean.

"Okay?"

"O-kay."

"Inspector, we only got two more hours. You sure you could do it?"

"Yes."

"You gotta say the whole thing."

"I could do it, but—you have to help me, Ben."

Julian pulls his hand away. My palm is slick with sweat. I wipe it on my pajama pants. My hand still stings from where he dug in his nails.

"Where last did you see the piano?" I ask.

"Well, I was at a big feast downtown for the prime min-

ister," Julian begins, and before I know it, I'm waking up. Julian's arm is flung over my neck. I step out into the dark hall and into my parents' room. Mummy snores, and on the side closest to the door, Daddy is stretched out, face down, right where he belongs. Right where Julian said he would be.

I climb up onto the bed between them and curl up, my back pressed against Daddy, my face inches from Mummy's. Everything feels calm again. Feels right. Just as I'm drifting off, I think of my brother, alone in my room. Guilt is a heavy ball in my belly, and I want to get up, to pat him awake, tell him he was right, everything is okay. Sleep is cooling taffy around my limbs, though. It wraps me up, pulls me under, keeps me still, as I slip into sleep.

I go back to my room, but I can't bring myself to stay. I grab my backpack and walk down the hall. My heart speeds up as I near my brother's room, as if the dream I'm still trying to push aside is about to play out again. Just like it did, that night.

I flick the light on. The room is in order, just as it was last time I came in. Lamp on the nightstand upright, bed smoothed out, neatly made. I sit on the bed, open the nightstand. His camera from when we were small. His passport. I open it, flip through the pages. There are a few stamps, going to Miami, up to Atlanta to visit our aunt, coming back home through Freeport. The stamps stop abruptly, three pages in. This passport is only three years old. What will we do with it? Keep it? Cut the picture out? I thumb to the signature page. He signed by just writing his name. No fancy flourish, no curls or scratches. Just *Julian Wallace*.

I put the passport back, take out the stack of schoolwork. Whole essays, pages stapled together. An English paper, a biology test. At the bottom of the pile, there's one from last year. History. I flip to the last page. B-plus.

I go through the bottom drawer. I've been here before. A broken MP3 player, a frayed charger, a Bahamas pin with the back broken off, a glass cylinder of ocean-colored cologne. These strange pieces of Julian's life, left over.

What tethers me? What weighs me down?

What didn't anchor him?

Julian is floating out there, unattached to his body. Julian exists, wherever a person goes, however they exist, when they die.

Julian is nowhere.

Julian is everywhere.

Julian is not here. I slam the drawer shut and stumble away from the nightstand. My heart pounds. I hope I didn't wake Mummy up. I listen for a few moments; no one stirs. I turn to Julian's bureau and ease a drawer open . I stare down at the neatly folded T-shirts. Julian did that himself. How do you walk away from a drawer of neatly folded shirts, knowing you're not coming back? Wouldn't you drag them all out, toss them over the floor just because? Wouldn't you just stuff them in, warm and jumbled, from the dryer? Would you even do laundry, that last week? Did he even know it was his last week? When did he decide? Did he write his plans down? Who did he tell?

I kneel on the carpet and reach into the drawer. Gray V-neck, black polo shirts, a long-sleeved red shirt. Finally my fingers touch pilled cotton. I pull out his old BahamaRama T-shirt from the festival when I was eleven. I drape it over my shoulder and slip back to my room. I strip off my soggy sheets and put on a fresh set. I lay out underwear, then reach into the closet. I push aside my school uniform and fumble around till my hand lands on a gray T-shirt dress. I lay it on the bed beside Julian's shirt. The shirt's probably a small— the tag's frayed, worn parchment-paper thin, but Julian was skinny at thirteen. Under the loose dress, though, no one will be the wiser. But I'll know. And maybe, for the first time, I'll feel like a little of Julian is with me.

I pack my bag for the day—a few assignments, a couple books to pacify Daddy in case he wants proof of productivity. My eyes go to the bag Layla dropped off. I don't even want it in my room. I think about pushing it into Julian's bedroom, but that feels wrong. I push it to the side and reach for my notebook. As my fingers close around the metal spirals, yesterday comes flooding back: Alan in my face, the phone in his hands. *He told me Julian had committed suicide.* I shove the book into the bag—I need it, but I don't even want to touch it right now. Julian was a kind of journalist. Would he ever have been like that guy? I try not to think of Alan's face, but it's etched into my memory. Not cruel, even. Just driven, just hard. Wanting a quote, a clip, from me. Wanting information he could use.

Julian, what kind of person would you have become?

Come on, don't play like you don't know me. His voice in my mind more than my ears. I can picture him on his

141

skateboard, bag over his shoulders, gliding down the road. His back lamppost-straight, so balanced, so sure.

Blue and red strobe lights slicing open the dark. Heavy knock—

I shake the memory away. I can't go there. I pack a couple more things—the history magazine, the probation letter, a granola bar I didn't open yesterday—then zip my bag closed. As I pull on the straps, I can't help the thought that comes: Julian balanced, Julian upright, Julian sure.

Was everything a lie?

As I step into the hallway, I almost collide with Daddy. He's in yesterday's clothes. He's rumpled, a pillow under one arm.

"Oh—morning," I glance at the clock. Half past six. Aren't we leaving soon?

"Morning. I'll be down in a few," Daddy mumbles as he heads into the master bedroom. He closes the door behind him. I hover for a few seconds, not sure what I'm listening for, but there's nothing, and nothing, and then the squeak of the shower turning on. I head down and grab a banana and a piece of bread. I'm halfway through eating them standing up by the glass door when I glimpse movement in the backyard. Too big for a dog or cat.

"Jul—" His name is cut off in my throat by another thought. *Robbie.* I grab the broom and stand with my back to the wall, just beside the back door. The security bars are pushed aside—we should have locked them last night; I should have closed them after I came in. I steal a look through the glass. I can't see movement, but I know someone's out there, someone who shouldn't be. *It's Robbie,* my mind screams.

Or what if it's Alan, lurking, taking pictures of the house where that guy who *committed suicide* lived? What do I do? Do I hide in here and not give him anything to see? Do I run out with the broom in hand and hope for whoever's sake I miss when I swing the handle their way? My body takes over from my mind—fingers on the lock, then the knob, and the door is open.

"Get out! Leave us alone!" My throat aches with the scream. The bushes are still; no new shadows fall. No sound, and then Ms. Wilkinson next door opens her door. Her blue sleep cap glows bright. She has on a pink nightdress and no bra. She peers out and then raises a hand.

"Y'all all right over there?"

I step back inside and close our door fast. The lump in my raw throat is too big for me to even answer her. I press my back to the wall and pound my fist against the concrete. My heart pounds fast, faster, fasterfasterfaster; everything is dark and I just want out, out out out—

"Karmen! Karmen!"

I hear my name but it's as though it belongs to some other girl in some other place. A hand on my wrist makes my eyes fly open. Daddy.

"What happened?"

"Someone—out there," I gasp. "Somebody—"

"Go in the hallway." He waits while I walk out. From the hall, I hear Daddy open the door, then his footsteps on the deck. Slowly, the high whine I didn't even know had started in my ears begins to fade. When I open my eyes and peer around the doorway, our kitchen is different in some unnameable way, as though I've been away a long time and can't remember how it was before, only that it isn't what I once knew. I hear Daddy say something, then Ms. Wilkinson answer. I can't make out their words.

The broom handle hits the floor with a thin clunk. Was I still holding that?

"Karmen." Daddy's back inside again. "I asked Ms. Wilkinson, but she didn't see anybody."

"I just thought I heard something," I say. Then I feel Daddy's hand on my shoulder. "I have to finish getting ready." I step away. My heart is starting to slow, finally.

"We can leave later." His voice is soft for the first time in days. I don't want it, this pity-kindness. I pick up my banana and almost drop it. The side of my hand aches where I hit the wall.

"I thought we had to keep routine," I say as I head to the living room. I try to hold my head straight as I pass the stairs, but I can't help looking up. I might as well not have bothered. Mummy's nowhere in sight. I imagine her door half-open, like usual, her hiding somewhere in that inner dark.

The drive is silent, but when we should turn left toward CU, Daddy continues straight. We go past our family doctor's office, and by the turnoff toward the mall. A little farther, and curiosity gets the better of me.

"Don't you have to get to work?"

"Yes, but we can make a stop first. I didn't get breakfast, and neither did you."

"I got a banana," I say.

"It'll keep." Daddy turns into a parking lot. There's a two-story building—a small convenience store and a nail salon, with a pokey-looking restaurant with heavy tints on the window and door. I want to say I'll stay in the car, but my belly growls and gives me away. I follow my father to the door. He presses the buzzer and it hisses back until he pushes the door open with a click. Inside is small but neat, bare tables wiped clean, chairs lined up neatly. A couple girls in school uniform sit near the back with a mother or aunt, each poking at their phones. There's a guy in a water-company uniform with a half-full plate. The air smells like breakfast meats and melted butter.

Daddy orders sweet-potato hash and steamed greens, then turns to look at me. I shrug. "Guava French toast with coconut whip and mango slices," he says without missing a beat. "Karmen, why don't you get us a seat?"

I pick a table not too close to the door and lean my head against the wall. It feels like I've been awake for hours, like I've been in a fight and lost. The side of my hand is bruised, and my knee throbs like it's suddenly remembered hitting the ground at school and won't be left out of the fun.

Daddy sits opposite me and sets a plate in front of me. Two huge slabs of johnnycake cut thick from a loaf. Slivers of pink guava shimmer up like sweet gems. The coconut whip is heaped into a small bowl in fluffy white peaks. The mango glows like slices of sunlight. Daddy has a small smile on his face but says nothing. We eat in silence for a few minutes. The johnnycake is perfect—thick, not quite bready, not quite cakey, not too sweet. I scoop whip onto each forkful, and slowly I start to feel like a person again.

"Your brother and I used to come here," Daddy says when we're about halfway through. I look up at him. He doesn't look angry—or sad, either. Just like he's recalling something without feelings getting in the way.

"What did he used to get?"

"Same as what you're having." He smiles now. "We got it his first day of university. I'm surprised he stayed awake all through his first class."

"Is this supposed to put me to sleep?" I ask, half joking, half waiting for him to say I could stand to be sedated. The scolding's coming any second now. I set my fork down.

"What happened, Karmen?"

The quiet, the worry, in my father's voice isn't what I expected.

"I don't know what you mean."

"This morning. I could hear you screaming from upstairs. What happened?"

"I told you that I thought I heard someone in the yard."

"An intruder?"

"I think . . ." I pause. I could keep up pretenses, but I don't want to right now. Secrecy feels like too much work, and anyway, what's the worst that can happen? I'm grounded already. "Yesterday when I went out by the playing field, it wasn't for an assignment. It was to meet someone who I thought knew Julian. I thought he knew him and could tell me how he was at school."

Daddy listens quietly, his face calm, so I go on.

"When I got there, he didn't know Julian at all. He's some guy who posts videos and stuff online with gossip about things he thinks are interesting. He just wanted to get me to say something about what it was like having Julian die. I was worried he'd found out where we live."

"Karmen. I can't believe someone would do that to you." Daddy pushes his plate away. For the first time, he looks like he might cry instead of break something. "Did you see him in the yard for sure?"

"I saw movement. I'm sure it was him. Or . . ." I stop myself from saying Robbie's name. How would Daddy react? I'm already suspended and grounded. If he finds out Robbie did this, is he gonna pull me from school to try to shield me? I don't even want to think about having to change schools. A whole new set of students whispering, making problems.

"Or who?"

"I don't know. I just feel like it was that same guy."

"What's his name?"

"He said he posts as Real Bahamas Talks."

"Never heard of him." Daddy leans in. "Listen. Karm. I know this is hard on you. But you can't go looking up random people thinking they can tell you something about Julian that's going to fix everything."

"I'm not trying to fix everything. I'm trying to understand."

"Understand what?"

How can Daddy not get it? "What he was going through? What things were like at school for him? If there was something going on that I didn't know about. Just like I didn't know he was on probation. I guess I was the only one who missed that memo."

Daddy looks toward the window. The tints turn outside purple. "We knew the second semester was hard on him even before he stopped going to classes. You mightn't have known that part, but you were in the house; you saw something was up with him. He stopped catching rides with me, said he didn't have classes till later. Didn't you notice?"

I think back over last spring, like I must have done hundreds of times over the last few weeks. His schedule was always different once he finished grade twelve. "I didn't know."

"And you didn't have to. It's not your fault, Karmen. It's no one's fault. Not your mother's, not mine, not yours. And not his." He turns back to look at me. "What do you think you'll get from this? All these questions you're asking?"

How can I explain how important answers are? Not knowing what pushed Julian to the end of his life feels like I never knew him at all. Feels like the Julian I remember wasn't real. That he not only doesn't exist—he never existed. And that's something I can't bear.

"I know you wonder, Karmen. But trust me—leave it alone. Going down all these different roads can't bring him back."

He gets up abruptly and takes both our plates to a cart near the back of the room. I lean back in my chair. I'm not getting a straight answer, then. I try to think back to spring again, to really picture how Julian was, before. In the early summer, too. All I can picture is his room door closed. I can't even picture his face.

I can't picture his face. *Julian?* I wait for his voice. Nothing. No smart answer, no wisecrack, no big-brother insight. Pinpricks of sweat dampen my hands. What if I'm forgetting him already? I reach into the bag, rummage past textbooks and snacks—there it is, the slim orange spine, black words written across: *Annals, Fall Edition XI.* I pull it out and flip straight to the back. I almost sigh with relief as I hold the book to my chest. I do remember now. His hair cut low, eyes staring straight into the camera, not scowling, not smiling. Thin-framed glasses, the mole on his right upper cheek.

I slip the magazine away and scrawl three sentences before Daddy comes back.

I'm not giving up.

I'm going to understand.

I'm going to talk to your professors today.

Mr. Demeritte's office is at the end of the history department's hallway. The door is ajar when I get there. I tap lightly.

"Come in."

I recognize the tone—Daddy uses it when he's trying to be available, but really he's immersed in marking papers, or is reading and doesn't want to be bothered. I step in. I was right. The professor beckons me into the room without looking up.

"Just a second, have a seat." He's bent over a book. I sit and take out my notebook. "Yes, all right. I'm here." He closes the book and looks at me. "Ah, you came back." He nods and folds his hands.

"Sorry about yesterday," I say. He waves my apology away. "I want to know about how Julian was here, when he was a student." I pull out the magazine. "I saw you knew him from working on this."

Mr. Demeritte smiles small at the pictures on the back. "Julian was super keen to get his first academic publication under his belt. First semester, he came racing straight out of the gate. I think he was outside my office the first day of class. I had to tell him to come back in two weeks when things had settled down."

"How was it with the magazine? Is it like a newspaper? Do you all meet in one room all the time?"

"Not really. We have a small editorial team: myself and Dr. Gibson, and one or two TAs. We accept submissions, and the entries that meet certain requirements and standards, we publish them."

"So he wasn't close with the other students here?" I touch the book and Mr. Demeritte glances down at the faces on the cover.

"I can't really say, but he wouldn't have had much overlap with them from what he wrote here. They may have had classes together."

"Did you teach him?"

"He was signed up for a class with me in his second semester," Mr. Demeritte says carefully.

"He didn't come to class?"

"Ah . . ."

"I already know he was on probation," I add quickly.

Mr. Demeritte links his fingers into each other like he's closing down a fort. "This is tricky, Karmen. I know you spoke with Dr. Fox, so you understand there's some information I just can't give out."

"I'm not asking for his grades—I'm just asking if he came to class. I just want to understand." My voice comes out louder than I mean to, but I can't help it. Why isn't he getting it? Why isn't anyone? I just want answers, and I'm tired of adults dancing around me. Why won't anyone just be honest? What good is hiding doing anyone now?

"I don't want to frustrate you." Mr. Demeritte is quiet. He leans in. "I can tell you that Julian was absolutely welcomed and respected here. He was an outstanding young man: bold, driven, curious, hardworking, talented. We're so sorry to have lost him. I know it's only a fraction of what you must feel—"

"I know Julian was all those things. I already know that—he was my brother for seventeen years. I just wanted to know what happened before he . . ."

And then I can't say the word. I don't even know which word I need to say. *Died? Ended? Suicide? Lost? Stopped?* I stand up and grab the magazine and my notebook. I have to get out of here. I trip on the chair as I rush out the door. The hallway has too many people, and there's just the one way out. I bump and jostle between them, trying to get out as fast as I can. I should be calm, I should wait here, scan for faces I recognize, but I need out, I need air, I need space. The skateboard bumps against my hip as I swing the glass door open and charge out.

"Whoa!" a voice calls just before we collide. A solid bump, but I don't fall and neither does she.

"Look out," I snap.

"Hey!" the girl calls as I start down the stairs. I can't wait. *Sorry, I didn't see you*—whatever she needs to hear, my mouth can't give it right now. I'm starting to feel that rush in me again, a huge red kite unfurling fast, catching gales, about to lift me away. "Hold on!" she calls again, but I carry on. I'm at the bottom of the steps. "Wait!"

I drop the skateboard and step on mid-roll. Pumping heart keeps me on and I push myself faster with my left foot. My heart's thudding floods my ears, I keep on, forward, forward.

"Julian!"

His name makes me need to stop in my tracks, even as my body keeps rolling forward, my legs keep me upright on the board, as I twist my head back to look, to answer. The board loses momentum without my urging it on. I let myself roll to a stop, then step off. The girl I knocked into walks toward me.

"You're wearing his stuff," she says. I look down at the board, then back up again. "His backpack," she adds.

"It's mine." I'm out of breath, but I don't have any other words anyway.

"But it used to be his." She looks at me evenly. She doesn't wince, doesn't blink. Her clothes are ordinary—blue shirt, jeans, sneakers—but she doesn't look away. She doesn't back down. She reminds me of Pru that way.

"Sorry I bumped into you. I didn't see—"

"You're trying to talk to people about him."

"How'd you know?"

"It's not a big department. Cardo was asking round. Then some people saw that guy's video with you in it—"

"Video?" My stomach churns.

"I think it was your back. There was audio, too. And he

looks like an ass for it. A bunch of us already reported it for harassment; bet you it's gonna be down by this afternoon. They called a meeting this morning, told us you were asking round, and warned us to be careful about what we say. We got a reminder about student-record and student-history confidentiality."

"They told students not to talk to me?"

She shakes her head. "I'm Camella Higgs."

"Dr. Higgs?" She barely looks older than me. "I—I didn't recognize you from the picture on the history magazine."

"People change," she says, as though it's as simple as a different hairstyle. Then she adds, "I have good genes. Keeps me looking young. My point is, you're not going to get too far asking around. Julian wasn't one to hang around with a bunch of people, and the teachers can't tell you anything you don't know."

Her words deflate me. She's being honest, and that's something—something I'd given up on as I ran out of the history building. But it's as if there's no point trying to ask anyone else anything, when Julian had a whole other life here.

"What do you think you could learn here that you don't already know?" Dr. Higgs asks.

"Just . . ." I try to find the words. New words, ones that build on my reasons, for me. "He used to be all about classes and learning. Now I find out he got put on probation. It's like this was the first place he gave up on. Like where he started giving up on living."

Dr. Higgs doesn't answer. She waits and listens. She watches.

"Is there anything you can tell me? Did you have classes with him?"

"He was in one of my classes last spring. He came a few times and stopped."

"Were his grades low?"

"There was a two-hour exam that he arrived forty-five minutes late to. I had to turn him away. He missed it, and he got a failing grade."

"Is that why he got put on probation?"

"They put you on probation for a pattern, not a single class you struggle with. I invited him to come to my office to discuss how we could move forward, and he never came. This was at the middle of term. He'd already missed assignments. Things weren't the same anymore, it was pretty clear."

"What do you think happened?"

"Some kids burn out. Some kids have something personal going on that affects their performance. Health, family situations, relationship problems. Anxiety, depression, stress, money. What was it for Julian? I honestly don't know."

"But . . ." My words peter out. I don't even know what to ask her anymore. She's the first person to be honest with me, yet she's just said she doesn't know.

Dr. Higgs steps forward so we're standing closer now. "Karmen, you were his sister. Y'all lived in the same house. Do you think anyone can tell you more about Julian than you?"

I feel like the wind's been sucked out of me, like the kite that threatened to pull me right off my feet minutes ago has been folded up into something smaller than a quarter. She's right. If I don't know—who will?

"I don't want to discourage you," she says, and puts an arm around my shoulders. I take the side-hug but I don't give it back. My arms are too loose to squeeze onto anything right now. "You have a lot of fight in you," Dr. Higgs says when she lets me go. "Don't lose that. I have to get to a class, but if there's anything you think I can do for you, come see me." I nod. "Do I need to call someone for you?"

"I'm fine." I adjust my bag. In a minute I'll make myself move forward again, make my way to the library till it's time to meet up with Isaiah.

Dr. Higgs nods and turns away. She takes a few steps, then turns to look at me again. "You really threw me. The board, the backpack . . . for a second, I could have sworn you were Julian."

CHAPTER EIGHT

saiah listens as I spill out everything that's happened since I saw him yesterday. It feels like half a week's worth of things have taken place. He doesn't say a word till I'm done, though his hand tightens around mine when I tell him what happened at the playing field, and again when I say that Alan person put the video and recording online. By the time I've brought him up to speed with what Dr. Higgs said, we're almost at a newish white building. In front, strips of metal, two stories tall, catch sun and glint white.

"How are you doing with all this?" he asks as I crane my neck up to look at the sculptures.

"I don't know. People always ask how I'm doing. How am I managing? How am I making it through? What am I even supposed to say to that? Things come so fast, sometimes I don't have time to think anything."

We carry on in silence, and I wonder if I offended him, especially when he pulls his hand away from mine. But then he wipes it on his pants and reaches for my hand again.

"You saw the video?" When he speaks again, his voice is the same as it was when I snapped at him. Even, easy, calm.

I shake my head. "Did you?"

"No." He stops. We're under a breadfruit tree. Its shade

is welcome: sweat's gathered under my arms. I only wish my hands were perspiring instead; at least they'd be easy to dry. "You wanna see it?"

I look up at Isaiah. Everything about his face looks soft—his beard, his eyes, the smooth of his skin. "I don't wanna see it. At least one good thing with not having my phone."

Near the art building's entrance, we pass a fig tree. Its branchlike roots reach from my shoulder height down to the rocky earth below, anchoring it firm into the earth. I stop for a moment and lean my shoulder against the gnarled wood. It seems so certain. So stable. So secure. Did Julian ever walk by here? He was never artsy, but maybe he walked past, prowling for skateboarding spots. Or maybe he didn't. Maybe he never knew this steady tree grew here. Never pressed against it, let it hold him up.

Inside, paintings hang on the corridor walls—pencil sketches, dainty watercolors, mammoth canvases that stretch nearly up to the ceiling, an assault of fluorescents and reds. We pass an open door with students standing at huge easels. I look back and see a male model in the middle of the room. Sun blares through the window, and I realize the model is nude. I look away, washed in heat. It's a different world here.

The pottery studio is easy to recognize. Solid glass windows flank it. Shelves of creations line the glass; clay pots, plates, mugs, and all kinds of shapes crowd the shelves, some unpainted, some slick and shimmering as if they're wet. Conch-shell pink, a deep peacock blue, green that glows, colors that make everyday life seem dowdy. Isaiah pushes a few numbers on the door's keypad lock. It beeps obediently, and we step in.

"Let me show you my spot." Isaiah leads the way farther in, to a row of cubbies. His has a chunk of grayish clay wrapped up in a plastic bag. It's almost as big as a concrete block. He pulls that away and my breath catches.

A row of delicate sculptures is tucked on the shelf. Each is curved, slightly ruffled, like flowers. The clay has been worked almost as thin as cardboard. They have a whitish, dusty look to them, but they are so lovely, I can't imagine how they'll look when they're painted.

"You made these?"

Isaiah nods. His joy radiates out, not from a smile, but from some deeper place, some source I can't see, only feel. "Very, very slowly. I work a little at a time, when I have time, so between classes or sometimes late at night."

"How? You're not an art student."

"This is the pottery club's space. That's why there's only two wheels, and it's small. The serious students work on the other side, and there's a shared kiln room in the middle."

"So club police aren't gonna come kick me out?"

"Well, technically the space is for club members. So— just don't touch anyone's stuff, and don't break anything." Isaiah reaches down and takes out a perfectly smooth bowl. He passes it to me. I cradle it in one hand. With the other hand, I rub my thumb along the surface.

"How'd you get it so smooth?"

He holds up his hands.

"Seriously?"

"I know, hard to believe these clunky things could do it, right?"

I look down at his creation. "I wonder what other secrets you're hiding." I pass the little bowl back to him and he returns it to its spot.

"We all have them." He unwraps the clay chunk. It seems impossible something so clunky and rough could be turned into something so delicate. Then my mind is on Julian again. So much in life is hidden, is secret. Am I trying to do the impossible, trying to understand what was in his life, in his mind? Can anyone ever really know? Even sharing a house, sharing a bathroom—sharing genes and memories and blood—can't guarantee.

My hands feel lonely without the little bowl. Without Isaiah's hands, too. "Does Layla know you do this?"

"I never really showed her. She knows I'm in the club, but I haven't finished anything yet, fully. I'm waiting until I have two more pieces; then I'll glaze them. Sorta nervous about that part."

"Why?"

"Never done it before with a final piece. I tried it out on just a piece of plain rolled-out clay."

"What's the worst that could happen?"

"The whole piece gets ruined. The color doesn't come out like I imagined. It breaks on the way into the kiln, or out." Isaiah laughs. "The possibilities for catastrophe are endless."

"I should be triple honored you let me even hold one."

"There's nothing of mine I wouldn't let you hold."

I burst out laughing, first at his words, then at the horror that crosses his face.

"I did *not* mean it to sound like that. Although—anyway."

He turns away, laughing and cringing. "Let's just move on."

"Anyway," I say, still snickering.

"*Anyway.*" He reaches into the clay bag and takes out a chunk. "I want you to try it. It can be really calming."

"What do you know about needing calm? You always have it together."

I expect him to laugh in agreement with me, but the slight smile on his face fades.

"Classes full-time, work shifts three days a week and hope they keep me on full-time in the summer and hire me once I graduate. I got assignments; I got exams; I got group projects where people don't pull their weight; this one professor just don't like me, and I can't fail this class 'cause it's required for the next level, which I *really* need and they only offer it once a year; gas gone up and I don't want ask my parents for money; I'm trying to save up for a new car so when Layla graduates she can have this one and . . ." He smacks his forehead with his palm. "What am I doing—I shouldn't even be complaining about this to you. Small things." Isaiah breaks off a piece of clay and presses it into my hands.

I take it. I hold the clammy, thick wad—but what I really want is to hold *him*. Hold the spot on his forehead that stings. Hold his wide shoulders. Hold his secrets, too—the smoothing-out-thin-clay part, the fretful part, the worrying-about-his-sister part. I tear the clay into two pieces and push one back into his hand. He rolls it between his palms, and I start squeezing mine. My fingers work it like they used to work Play-Doh when I was little. It feels like playing, feels easy and right. I use my fingertips to shape most of it into a small, thick bowl. I set my wobbly miniature down on the table.

"Not bad."

"I'm not fragile," I say. I keep my eyes on my tiny creation, but I feel his gaze on me. "You don't have to pretend everything in life's perfect. I hate when people do that. It's like they think I can't handle knowing that life isn't all sunshine and rosebuds. At this point, I think it's obvious I know that."

Isaiah reaches out to touch my bowl. "I won't do that, then." He tweaks a tiny bit of clay off his piece, forms a banana that could fit on a fingertip, lays it in my bowl. "What was it like, with Julian?"

I can see my brother then. Across the kitchen table, leaned back in his chair. Head tilted to one side, eyes low. His fork to the left of his untouched plate of pasta in white sauce, which I hate, and he loved.

"Julian?"

He turns toward Mummy but barely lifts his eyes.

"You're not eating, sweetheart?"

Picks up the fork and lifts a few strands of spaghetti. They dangle like guts.

"You better eat." I shove in a mouthful and gulp it down. "Only reason we havin this mess is you."

"Don't be disrespectful," Daddy says across the table.

"You don't like it either." I stab a piece of broccoli. Daddy doesn't respond, and Mummy sighs. There's a screech of wooden chair legs on tiles as Julian pushes back his seat.

The memory ends. I can't remember what came next. Did he leave? Did Mummy coax him to stay? Did he take his plate or abandon it? It wasn't that long ago—sometime in the spring when Mummy was on her vegetable-pasta kick. But my mind has pushed the other details away, or never bothered to hold on to them. All I can remember is Julian, something wrong. And me being pissed at having to eat food that resembled insides.

"He used to be down sometimes. Not always. Just"—I reach over and tweak off a pinch of clay—"sometimes."

"Like when?"

I roll a ball, then flatten it into a tangerine. "Random times. You couldn't put a finger on it. He'd just get in these moods and I couldn't figure out what the problem was."

"Would he talk to you?"

"Not about that. I mean, what do you say when you're down? It speaks for itself. When we were younger, I used to just hang out with him. Just sit and watch TV or sit outside. He wasn't home as much after he finished high school. He always had a different schedule, and then sometimes he'd be home for a couple days like he didn't have class."

"Was it worse . . . near the end?"

Summer. Waking up mornings, late, sheets sticky with midmorning sweat. Stumbling to the bathroom to pee and shower. Was his door closed more then?

"Classes were out—it was hard to say. I guess he didn't seem to be going out as much." My heart starts to speed up. I don't want to think about this, but I don't want to shut Isaiah down, either. He's the only person who's talked, really talked, about Julian this way with me. "It sounds so bad to say I don't remember. I think maybe it was worse. But then, I figured he was just taking it easy because it was summer. And I thought he'd been like that sometimes, before." The panicky feeling rises. Then Isaiah's fingers fold over my knuckles. His skin slightly sticky from the clay. Heat radiates from his palm, like he carries sunshine in the heart of his hand.

"It's hard to know what someone else is going through if they don't tell you."

"You shouldn't have to tell people everything. People who are supposed to love you, who are supposed to know you—they should just be able to tell."

"That's not always possible, though. We can't read minds. We have our own stuff going on."

"That's not good enough. It can't be. Not with family. Not when it's someone's life."

Isaiah squeezes my hand, then lets go. The rustling beside me tells me he's taking out more clay.

"You might need another ten pounds of that." My joke comes out flat.

"I don't mind if it takes ten tons." He sets a fresh wad on the table between us. I start on a bunch of disproportionately large grapes. "It's not your fault, Karmen," Isaiah says after a while.

"I know."

"Do you?"

"I just want to know why, that's all."

"Are you getting any closer?"

"I don't know yet."

Isaiah sets down something that might be a plum. "Think you'll try that pottery therapy?"

"I will if you will."

He reaches over, links his fingers between mine this time. "I'll sign us up. It's a date."

Four o'clock comes fast. I meet Daddy at the car. As we drive home, I take out the paper Ms. Rhonda gave me, trace my finger over the words Isaiah underlined. *Art therapy at CU. Thursdays, six to seven, pottery studio.* Once we're in the house, I wait till we're near the foot of the stairs before I pass the flyer to Daddy.

"And where's this?" He passes it back to me so fast, he can't have actually read it.

"It's at CU, in the pottery studio. It's another type of ther-apy . . . I thought it might help." I try not to make my voice too obviously loud. Either way, Mummy emerges from the bedroom. She's sort of dressed—an old pair of shorts and a faded pink T-shirt from church's Mother's Day breakfast the year I was eleven—and a towel is wrapped around her head. She must have washed her hair. I can't remember the last time she did that.

"Hey, Mummy. I was just asking Daddy about the art one." I bound up the steps to pass the paper to her. She blinks a couple times before she takes it. I watch her as she looks over the paper. Her face looks almost like her old self.

"Does this interest you?" She looks up at me.

"I thought I could try it. It starts tonight at six."

She wipes a drop of water off her forehead with the back of her wrist. "I guess it can't hurt."

Daddy throws his hands up. "How's she supposed to get

there? I just got home, it starts at six, and I have work to do before dinner."

"I can catch the bus," I say quickly. "Or a ride."

Daddy's eyes narrow. "Ride with who?"

"Maybe a friend from school? Or . . ."

"Or who? Go ahead, tell us." He glances up the steps toward Mummy. "Let's hear who this is you're so excited to have drop you to this *art therapy*." He says the last two words like they're code for sliding down a pole in a thong.

"Maybe Layla?" Same household counts for something, maybe?

"Layla drives?" Mummy asks.

"Nope, but . . . Oh, *Isaiah* drives, ay?" Daddy all but has an illuminated light bulb over his head. "What, now you tryin to sneak out to meet him?"

"Daddy, it ain like that, I . . . he thought it might be a good idea and I didn't want to go alone."

"You want company? I'll go with you." Daddy starts up the stairs. "Let me shower; we could all get therapied up. Fix all the problems in the world."

"Stan, you can't do that to the girl. Let her go on her own."

"For her to link up with man?"

"Isaiah's like two years older than me!" I cut in.

"That ain even the point." Daddy doesn't look my way. "She suppose to be grounded, Barb. Breaking up windows? Getting in a fight? And we supposed to punish her with dates?"

"You the one pushing for *get back to normal, get back to*

normal." Mummy's face twists as she mocks Daddy. She looks even more like she used to now. "Let her go out like the other seventeen-year-olds, then. And Isaiah, come on. That boy's one step up from a chaperone. He ain ga let her get hurt."

"Looks like you ain grounded." Daddy spins around to look at me. "Thank your mother." His footsteps thunder up the stairs.

"Thanks, Mummy," I say. She nods.

"Go. Have a good time. You need some lightness. In here always feel so heavy."

She sounds so much like herself, I decide to take a chance—to ask her what I've been wanting to ask.

"How come you didn't tell me Julian was on probation?"

"Oh." Mummy speaks like a basketball's hit her in the gut—winded, wounded, stunned.

"I found his letter."

She nods, stupor-slow. "Of course."

I made a mistake, I must have—she's only just started dressing kinda properly, it's too soon, she can't handle this. "Never mind, I—"

"No, you're in your rights to ask. I didn't think his life was in danger, that's why. Sometimes we need to step away from . . . well, what your dad's always talking about. The routine. The habitual. The expected path. Like you're doing right now. Like I've been doing. I thought Julian just needed a bit of time to catch himself before he was ready to go back."

"I feel so stupid for not seeing something was wrong. I didn't even realize he wasn't in classes anymore."

"I know how you feel," Mummy says softly. Below us, the

landline rings. The tinny trill stops our words. We stand there, waiting—for it to end, for something to change, maybe. The recording plays loud from the office's open door.

"You've reached At Peace Counseling." Aunt Glenda's voice isn't what I expect. It's always been Mummy, saying, *Thank you for calling At Peace Counseling. If this is a crisis, please call a second time. If you or someone else is in immediate danger, or having thoughts of hurting yourself or others, hang up and dial 911 or call the Suicide Prevention Hotline. . . .* Aunt Glenda carries on, on the recording. "We are closed until further notice as we deal with a family matter. Existing clients have been referred to the team at Brighter Days Healing Center." The old machine beeps.

"Hi, uh—this is Isaiah."

I bolt for the office. Daddy is on my heels, then in front of me.

"I was actually calling with a message for Karmen. I— yeah, so sorry to bother you, could you just let her know I have to take my mum somewhere so I can't pick her up, but I'll meet her there for six. I hope that's okay."

Daddy makes it to the office before I do, and stands guard between the phone and me. He grabs it without answering, holds it up high. I try to swipe, but I can't reach. Isaiah hangs up, and the machine beeps, then starts to flash.

"I must drop you for a date when you got yourself suspended from school." Daddy's voice is low. "Y'all have it too soft in here."

His words go through me like cold wind, chill me to my core. I can't look away from him. His mouth is set in a stone grimace, eyes narrowed so much, I know he can't see me. Can't even see what he just said.

"There's no *y'all*." Speaking unthaws my body. "It's only me." I turn and walk up the stairs. I look down from the top. Daddy stands outside the office, statue-still. His hands are empty, arms loll at his sides. I want to think, *serves you right*, but I can't. Instead I just feel tired. Tired, and hollow-sad. I sit on my bed and open the backpack, start taking things out. Then I stop. What am I looking for again? I push the mess aside. What happened to our family? It's like we lost ourselves right along with Julian. Even when there's a spark of good, someone else trips and falls face-breaking flat.

I move toward Julian's bedroom. I have to. I need him to be there, need to feel like my brother's here again.

Green bedspread, flattened-down pillows, nightstand clear, closet half-open. Room empty, as I knew it would be. I reach behind the door and lift his navy-blue baseball cap off the hook on the back. Pull it over my hair. I search through his drawers quickly for the Obama shirt, and still can't find it. I settle on a light blue one with Mr. Nobody printed on the front. I exchange it for the dress and the BahamaRama shirt I put on this morning, then pull on a pair of jeans. I sit down on the edge of Julian's bed. I lose track of how much time passes, just sitting there, in his stuff, in his space. I only hear when Daddy calls, "Time to go!"

On my way downstairs, I push my own room door open and grab the skateboard. I catch sight of the backpack, its contents spilled out all over my bed. I can't deal with that right now. I close the door and head downstairs.

My feet slide into my sneakers like they want out of here as much as I do.

Daddy slips on his shoes and we head out—together, but not.

Halfway there, Daddy turns down his jazz station. "You got on Mr. Nobody."

I glance down at the shirt, then back out the window. Traffic heading out of town is nearly at a standstill, but it flows smoothly for us.

"Julian lived in that shirt a while ago. When he first started university. Remember?"

This is the first time Daddy's really talked about Julian. I want him to keep going more than I want to be mad. "Yeah," I say, even though I don't.

"Wore it his first day. We had big row over it too. I told him it was a new phase, new start. I remember him sitting on the side there, just like you, elbow up by the window, just like you, looking like he rather be anyplace than in the car with me. Just like you." Daddy chuckles. "Apparently he didn't appreciate my fashion advice."

I can't imagine Julian being anything other than elated to go to college. "What was wrong with the shirt?"

"Mr. Nobody?"

"He's from the kids' books."

"I know the books. I just think . . . I thought it was morose. And in a new environment—present yourself like you're there for success. None of my kids are nobodies."

"Sometimes a shirt's just a shirt." The irony doesn't escape me, though. Is that really how my brother felt? Like nobody? I wish now I could hear him, hear his voice clarifying for me. But—nothing. I can't remember the last time I heard Julian. What if he's fading? What if I won't hear him always? What if I never hear him in my memories again? The thought makes my eyes threaten to start watering, so I push it away.

"Is this one of those times?" Daddy keeps his eyes ahead.

"It's just a shirt," I say. Daddy nods, and then turns the music up again.

At the university, Daddy turns through the side entrance instead of heading to the parking lot.

I reach down for my bag, then remember I left it back in my bedroom. I wish I'd brought it now. It's the first time I've been without that backpack since the first day of school. And the history magazine and the notebook, the letter—everything's just out there for anyone who goes into my room to see. Mummy's the only one home, but who's to say she's not finished drying her hair and turned her attention to other things? My fingers close around one of the skateboard's wheels. I pull the board into my lap. Nothing I can do about it now. I just hope Mummy doesn't pick tonight to be her reentry into the world of parenting.

"I can walk," I say.

"I'll come in and get you settled." Daddy's voice is calm, but his words are like ants on my skin. They make me feel twitchy. Can't he just back off?

"I don't need to be settled."

"It'll be evening. I'm not having you walk around campus in the dark by yourself."

"It's not even dark till seven!"

"Campus empties out in the evening."

"Can't you just pick me up when it's done?"

Daddy turns the music up higher and I slump back into my seat. We park behind the art building and he strides in like he knows where he's going. I trail behind, feeling about five. The pottery-studio door is propped open. Daddy strides in ahead.

"My daughter's here for the group session," I hear him say, and I drop the skateboard and push off down the hall. The floor is even and smooth. Julian would have loved this. I carry on to the end of the hall, then turn around and head back. No point going too far: Daddy will just hunt me down and humiliate me even more. He waves me over and I let myself roll to a stop, then pick up the board and walk the rest of the way.

The instructor smiles widely at me like we're here for ice cream and free cake.

"Welcome," she says. "So good to have you." She nods at my father, and as he leaves, I regret not staying closer to hear what he said about me. "I'm Olivia. Come on in—we have three other people here already."

I pray one of them is Isaiah, but inside, there are two girls who look like they might be students here, and a guy who's closer to Daddy's age. Olivia introduces herself first, and as one of the girls starts talking, I realize I'm going to have to come up with something to say. My hands start to sweat. What am I supposed to say? Do I have to tell this bunch of strangers about Julian dying? About getting kicked out of school? It's all wrong. Isaiah was supposed to be here—I never wanted to come by myself. I want to bolt out the door, but Daddy already checked me in like a three-year-old being handed off at day care. There's so much I have to do, so much I could be doing and need to find out, and instead I'm here.

You don't wanna be here, don't be here. Julian's voice stops my racing mind in its tracks.

And right then, something I haven't thought about since it happened plays over in my mind. We are around eight and ten. Daddy's boss is coming over for dinner when he promised he'd take us to Junior Junkanoo.

"But Daddy, you said—"

"I know, Julian, but sometimes plans have to change."

"I wanted to see the costumes!"

"Karmen, we'll go to the Boxing Day parade instead. All right? It'll be better, you can stay up way past bedtime, more people there—Barb, you wanna help me out?"

"Don't get me in that, I'm elbow-deep in raw meat. For five people. After listening to people's problems all day. Look, y'all two, go change out of your school uniforms and come down, set the table."

We drag our feet up the stairs, fueling each other's rage at the injustice. We were promised burgers and fries and milkshakes. Mummy's chicken is dry. Why we gotta be priss up like it's Sunday on a Wednesday evening? We supposed to be watching the parade and having fun. Then Julian turns around with the wicked grin that always means a good plan. He whispers his idea even though our parents are far out of earshot. I burst out laughing and clap my hand over my mouth.

We lay cutlery out on the table like obedient angels, then scamper back upstairs. We cut out paper hats and masks, staple strips of colored construction paper to our clothes, then wait. The doorbell's chime is our cue to stand by. We crouch outside his bedroom door and wait. An unfamiliar man's voice, and a woman's—adult chatter, Mummy's voice getting high like it does when she's trying to be cheerful but really is annoyed. Then Daddy calls up the stairs.

"Julian, Karmen, come down, please."

We wait until the voices trail into the living room, then tiptoe down the stairs. Julian carries the bathroom garbage can upside down under one arm, bag left on the floor upstairs. I put the freshly emptied toilet-paper roll up to my mouth. We charge, him banging on the plastic garbage-can drum, me honking through my makeshift horn.

"Oooh! Ooh! Junkanoo!" we shriek through the living room. I tread on someone's foot and Julian almost loses the garbage can, grabs it back, and knocks a drink onto the rug.

"Excuse me—y'all get back here!" Mummy shouts as we run out of the room. We know we can't run far or long, but as long as we keep moving, our laughter does too. I don't look back, just run after Julian, as hard as I can.

The room is quiet around me. All eyes are on me now.

You don't wanna be here . . . Julian's words ring in my ears again. I don't give it another thought.

"I'm Julian," I say.

CHAPTER NINE

As soon as I say the words *I'm Julian*, they feel right.

"Oh." The instructor glances down at a sheet of paper. "Julian? I don't have a Julian. I had you down as—"

"I like to go by my middle name," I break in, before she can say *Karmen*.

"I'm Isaiah." His voice behind me makes me spin around. Isaiah stands in the studio's doorway. I can only meet his wide eyes for a moment before I have to look away.

"Perfect. Isaiah and . . . is that *J-u-l-i-a-n*?"

"Yes." My throat's so dry, I can barely choke out my answer. The instructor makes a note on her paper, then looks up with a sunny smile. "Let's carry on with introductions. Isaiah, come in, get comfortable. . . ."

Please sit by me, please sit by me, I will. Whatever's going through Isaiah's head, I need him beside me. I need him to get why I have to do this. My mouth feels dry. I close my eyes for a second. Feel the hat tight around my head, too snug around my hair. I push the tightness away. Let myself imagine it fits me like it fit him.

I feel the bench beside me shudder slightly. I open my

eyes and glance over. There's a big gap between us, but Isaiah's here. I'm thankful for that.

"Julian?" The instructor's voice snaps my attention back to the center of the room. My mind is as blank as the notebook's unused pages—it's taking all my energy to hear my brother's name and not spin around to search the room. I did this, I brought his name here, and yet I still can't stop hoping the real Julian will miraculously show up. "What brings you here tonight?"

"Uh . . . him!" I point at Isaiah as heat drenches my face. Isaiah clears his throat.

"I can go. I'm Isaiah, I'm in my second year here at CU, business. I do a little bit of pottery in my spare time, which I don't have much of, and heard about the group. Thought it would be a good chance to come out and clear my head. That's it."

"Thanks, Isaiah. Anyone else want to add anything?"

"What are you doing?" Isaiah's voice is low, not exactly scolding, but close to it. "Why you using his name?"

I keep my head down. Over to our left, someone else, someone with a simpler life, is talking about trying pottery to relax before exams. I wish I could backtrack. How'd I think this would go? What's wrong with me anyway? I knew Isaiah would be here, but as I left the house, I knew I had to do this, too, step as deep as possible into my brother's head. I have to *get* Julian. He's not here in this room, with his own board at his feet. He's not in that empty house, he's . . . nowhere. Not knowing what caused all this is almost like saying it happened for no reason. Not doing everything I can is like saying Julian's death didn't matter. Saying he didn't matter.

I reach down for the skateboard and close my fingers around the worn wood's edge. I squeeze hard. *Julian, what would you say?*

"Anyone else, before we continue?" The instructor's voice drifts into my head like a whisper from another world.

"I'm in my second year," I blurt out. I wait for someone to correct me, to call me a liar, to say they just saw me in school uniform a couple days ago. "It's been hard. Something just isn't clicking like it used to, I guess. I can't keep up my grades and . . ." My words start to falter. "I guess I'm just not me," I say.

Olivia nods. "Thank you for sharing that, Julian. Thanks to all of you. I'm hearing some really common, really typical experiences that lead us, as people, to creative therapies. And there are many to choose from: painting, drawing, writing, dance, music, and, of course, working with clay. It's been found that pottery can lower blood pressure and reduce anxiety—and as someone with an anxiety disorder myself, I find it a wonderful way to get out of my mind and step back from those difficult thoughts. So, we're going to start simple tonight. On the table here, come up and get a piece of clay, a container of water, and an apron."

Isaiah stands up. I stand too.

"I'm glad you came." I make myself look up at him as we head over to get supplies. The smile he returns is small.

"Course I came. You all right?"

I nod as I pick up two clay chunks, one each for us. Isaiah grabs our aprons and water. I brace myself for his questions: *Why? How could you? What are you thinking?* Julian was right. Those *W* questions fit so many situations.

"Cool shirt" is all Isaiah adds, and I have to take an extra breath to make room in my chest for how much I like him.

"I want you to start by taking your piece of clay into your hand," Olivia says from her spot in the room. "Feel it under your palms. Now—try closing your eyes."

One girl laughs nervously somewhere across the room. I glance over at Isaiah, who looks back at me.

"Let's try it." He closes his eyes, and his face looks so peaceful. It's okay. This is okay. I lower my eyelids too.

"See where your fingers go with the clay. You can squeeze it; you can squish or shape it. Be as tough or as careful as you choose."

The clay is cold, heavy, wet. It feels—I don't want to think it, and I can't *not*—it feels dead. My fingers feel slack, and the clay thuds onto the table.

"What do you notice about the clay, with your eyes closed? Are there sounds you pick up? Do your hands want to form it into a particular shape?" The instructor's voice is closer—she's walking around the room. I try to focus on that, and on Isaiah beside me, but he's not close enough for me to feel him, and Olivia's not talking enough for me to follow her voice. All I can think of is that lifeless wad of mud. This was a mistake; I wish I'd never signed up. Wish I hadn't begged to get to come, wish—no. No. I'm not her. I'm not that sad girl from the sad family. I don't have a dead brother. I don't have a brother at all. I'm not Karmen. I'm Julian. And Julian can't sit here and cry over himself. Julian cracks jokes and pulls stunts. Julian rushes through Daddy's dinner party drumming on an upside-down garbage can.

"Are you all right?" Olivia's whisper makes me open my eyes. I nod. "If you need a minute, it's totally fine to step back from the exercise."

I nod, but I know in my mind Olivia is wrong. It's not fine to step back. I came here for a reason. I came here for Julian, and I can't step back or stop. I reach for the clay again and squeeze my eyes shut. *I am Julian.* I press my fingers into the clay. *I am Julian.* It starts to give as I squeeze down harder. Clay oozes between my fingers. *I am Julian. I am.*

After therapy, I feel exhausted. I drop my overworked chunk of clay into a plastic bag and tuck it on the shelf beside the others. Isaiah hangs back beside me at the sink as I scrub my hands.

"How was it?"

I want to ask if he means how I'm dressed—what I'm doing, trying to get into Julian's head—but that feels too raw, too far. "Intense, I guess. What did you think?"

He dries his hands. "I'd try it again. If you will. I like what she said about using creative stuff to give your mind a break."

"Julian never did that. He wasn't creative. Unless you count skateboarding, I guess. I wonder what he'd think of this."

"I was surprised when I saw you in his hat and stuff when I came in. And when you said your name was—"

"Does it bother you?"

"Oh." His focus shifts to something behind me. I follow his gaze. Daddy's come in, keys in one hand. "You in trouble?"

I dry my hands too. "I'll tell you tomorrow. You have classes?"

"Work in the morning, classes all afternoon. I'll call on your house phone."

I want to hug Isaiah good night. Behind us, my father clears his throat.

"You better go." Isaiah reaches forward and hugs me, then lets go quick. "Evening, Mr. Wallace," he says on his way out. I have to hide my smile as I gather up my stuff and head for the door too.

Daddy pulls up outside the house but leaves the car running. He passes me my jeans jacket. "Cover up that shirt. Take the cap off too. Last thing your mother needs to see." Daddy folds his arms and braces for a fight, but I do as he's asked without a protest. I've been up since five, and all I want to do is lie down. I tuck the cap under my arm and take the skateboard with me as I get out.

As soon as I open the front door, it smells like home. Not just like home—like good home.

"Hey, we're back," Daddy calls behind me. I run upstairs and shove the board and cap in my room, then head down to the kitchen. Mummy sits at the table with her purple notebook open beside her. A patient file lies beside it. Under the table, her feet are up on my chair. Her hair is parted and plaited in three.

"How was it?" Her smile is a shadow, but it's there.

"Interesting. Messy." I lift the cover off the big pot at the back. Rice tinged brown, pigeon peas with their slitted eyes winking up. Squares of diced onion, cooked translucent, and dots of white coconut milk risen to the top. "Oooh!" I grab a spoon and dig in. The first bite singes my mouth, and it's worth it.

"Get a bowl," Mummy says. There's no nip or scold.

"You want one?"

"Might as well take out three. Unless your daddy already ate."

"I didn't." Daddy's voice is surprised, from the doorway. "Smells good."

Mummy retreats into her office and comes back without the notebook. The three of us sit and eat in silence. I think of cricket-creaking at my parents, but the quiet is better than shouting, so I keep my mouth shut. Mummy finishes her food first and disappears.

Upstairs, I almost go right into my room, but turn left instead, into the master bedroom. Mummy's on the bed, but not in it. The notebook is open again, her head bent over it.

"Are you going back to work?"

She startles, then closes the book quickly like I caught her at something.

"Sorry. I thought you heard me come in."

Mummy smiles with her lips and pushes the book into her nightstand drawer. "You got enough to eat?"

"Yeah. It was good."

"Come sit on the bed."

I perch on the edge. Weeks of not being in here have made it unfamiliar.

"Think you'll try the pottery again?"

"Probably." I want to repeat my own question, but would it be too far? Mummy's only just starting to seem a bit more like herself. "What are you doing?" I try instead.

"Reading through some old notes, that's all. Thought I'd see if I could get my head back into . . . things, I suppose."

"I guess I have to do that with my schoolwork."

"It takes time." She smiles again. The sparkle goes up to her eyes this time, even though it fades fast. "What's happening with you and Isaiah?"

"That's out of the blue."

"Are you dating?"

"We're just hanging out sometimes."

Mummy nods. "Oh, Layla called. She wanted to come by, but I told her you were out."

"Thanks." My voice comes out more relieved than I mean it to.

"She hasn't been over here much lately."

"I thought I was grounded."

"Just thought I noticed something. Maybe not. I miss things sometimes."

"Miss things how?" I hold my breath. Are we finally going to talk about Julian? "Mummy?"

She looks off to the side. I follow her gaze, but all I see is the wall.

"Mummy?" I say again.

She shakes her head, smiles that shadowy smile. "I should go shower."

"What did you mean, miss things?"

"Don't stay up too late, okay?"

I want to scream. We were so close—to really talking, to getting somewhere. I was close to feeling like someone feels the same way I do. Daddy and I talk, but he just sees things so differently. Why's she acting like she can't hear my questions? "Mummy?" I try one more time. She doesn't answer—she doesn't even seem to hear me.

I give up—I'm so tired, and today's gone on forever. I get up. "Okay. Good night."

Mummy nods. Her gaze doesn't change. I'm almost out of the room before she says, "Hey, Karmen."

I turn back. My heart races—she's gonna answer. She's gonna say something.

"You tell me, all right? If anything changes."

"With Layla?"

"With . . ." She half lifts a hand, reaching for a name. "Isaiah."

I bite my lip. We've already had the talk—all the talks, actually. The no-sex talk, the safe-sex talk, the delayed-sex talk, and the *your body might say yes but your mind won't be ready until your brain fully matures in your twenties* talk. I grit my teeth and nod.

"Y'all kids shouldn't keep secrets." She says it like Julian's just down the hall. "It's my job to listen, you know." Her voice sounds constricted, like she's lying down now. Far away, like her back's turned to me. I turn around and walk away without another word.

My feet take me down the stairs, past my father in the living room, headphones over his ears, gazing at his computer screen. I step into the kitchen, empty, but with the memory of our dinner still in the air. I look at the door, and this morning's panic starts to surge over me. No—I can't. I won't. Me, Karmen, I would turn around, march upstairs, climb into bed. But my job isn't to be myself right now. Julian would open that door. He'd step outside, he'd sit down, just because he wanted to. I take off Daddy's jacket. It makes a soft sound as it hits the floor. I unlock the door and step out barefoot.

The darkness is thick beyond the square of yellow our security light casts from our door, across the yard. I lean against the house and look out over the yard, beyond the fence, toward the street. I wonder if three weeks will really be enough time away from school. If I ever have to go back again. I haven't even touched the stack of schoolwork. It feels like it belongs not only to a different time, but to a different person. The night's warm, but my arms bristle as if cold, even with the jacket still on. I take a few steps onto the driveway and sit on the cracked concrete. The shrubs planted along the side have roots that reach all the way under what people carefully poured. Quietly, over time, they have moved what no human could have budged bare-handed. Expanded gradually, determinedly. In another thirty years, there might be no driveway at all, just shattered concrete and the roots that pushed it apart.

I wonder where I'll be in thirty years. Our parents will be in their seventies. And then, some people don't live that long. If I don't have my own kids, I could be the only one. Our family will be like our driveway then. Cracked, crumbled. Mostly fallen away.

I rest my arms on my knees and put my head down. In

thirty years, will our family's breaking up, our falling apart, still matter? Will I care whether I got the answers I ache for tonight?

A car turns down our street and slows. I will it to be Isaiah—I want to talk to someone, someone who'll listen, someone who gets me—but it carries on past our home. I stay out long enough for my eyes to get used to the dark, to pick up the soft flutter of oversized moths in the air.

Another sound—a swish-whir of something rolling on the road. I turn my head. Shadowed figures—two of them—skateboard into view. Arms swinging, moving fast. One a guy, I guess. Long hair flies behind the other. They roll toward me, glide, slow.

"Pru?"

She steps off the board, says something to the other. He nods and keeps going. She walks up the driveway toward me.

"What you doing here?"

"Me and Cardo like to board at night."

"It's dangerous. And dumb."

"So's sitting outside by yourself." She plops down beside me.

"I was out all day. And in the evening."

"You ain gotta report to me. How come you got Julian's clothes on?"

"I don't know what you're talking about."

"Mr. Nobody?"

I try to make my voice convincing and calm. "It's mine."

Pru crosses her legs. "Not your style."

"You don't know me. You don't know anything about me."

"You feel better? Having his stuff on?"

Gotta find out why. Julian's voice in my ear. *That's the core of it. What, the whole what, and then why. If you understand the reasons, you can get into someone's head. See things like they do. You can understand.*

"What's with you? Why you keep showing up? My own best friend ain trailing me like this."

"Maybe that's on her, not on me."

"Why, though?" My mind goes back to yesterday, to Alan at the park. "You didn't have anything to do with that guy who wanted to interview me, did you?"

"What guy?"

"Alan? Real Bahamas Talks? Someone tricked me into meeting up with him and he just wanted to interview me about Julian dying? Ring any bells?"

"Wait—what happened?" Pru's shock sounds real.

"Yesterday, after I got home. Someone gave him my number."

"It wasn't me. He wanted to interview you?"

"I guess he thought a story with a suicide would get him a bunch of likes. I dunno."

"That's . . . I would never do that." Pru's voice almost cracks. That gets me—she's not made of rusty nails and old steel. There's something in there that bends a little.

"How come you're here, then? Why you showing up everywhere?"

"We go to school together."

"For two days."

"How'd it feel? Wearing Julian's stuff? Seriously."

Maybe I tell her because I'm tired. Maybe it's the tiredness in her own voice. Maybe I'm just curious—and the only way to find answers is to dig, to step out of comfort. Maybe sitting out here talking to someone who doesn't quite make sense feels like something Julian would do. Maybe it's because she knew something about him, about my brother. It's not just that I *know*, that she's told me—it's that I can feel it too, in the swish of her board over the road, the way she's blunt and raw and always there. "It feels . . . right. And wrong. And hard, I guess. Everything's hard."

Instead of answering, Pru lifts the hem of her dress. Her legs are muscled and lean; a wilted rose is tattooed on her left thigh. Then—sky-blue ruffles? The edge of something way too long to be panties, too satiny to be exercise shorts. She pulls her skirt back down. "Bloomers," she says, like that explains everything.

"Why . . . ?"

"My cousin—she was like my sister, she used to live with us and all—she was a dancer at her church. Her favorite dress to dance in was this ridiculous long blue thing. Long like she just come out the nunnery, and these trumpet-looking sleeves. She was mad this one night. I was supposed to hand-wash her dress for her rehearsal the day before and I didn't, so she had to go in a long T-shirt and leggings. I told her she was carrying on over this dress like somebody dead. Then she didn't come home."

"Until when?"

Pru reaches into her pocket, pulls out a big pin-on button. A photo is printed on it: a soft-faced girl about our age, hair pulled back in a ponytail. Even in the small picture, even under the plastic coating, her eyes glint like she's holding in a joke she shouldn't tell. Underneath the girl's face it says RANAE DAVIS. Then two dates—the year she was born, and two years ago. She never came home.

Pru pulls her hand back abruptly. The pin disappears back into her pocket.

"I'm sorry."

Pru gives me a look like I've just insulted her. "You took her? What you apologizing for?"

"I mean it sucks. I wish it hadn't happened—whatever happened."

"Better."

"Do you know? What happened?"

Pru shifts to lean her back against the wall. "My mummy told the police that same night, when she didn't get dropped off after practice. She was supposed to get a ride from the worship leader but she didn't. Someone saw her get in a car they didn't recognize. The police put out a flyer and stuff, but you know." She shrugs. "Girl goes missing, everyone says the same thing. Either 'Praying for her safe return home!' or 'These girls too like mess with big man.'"

"Y'all never found out anything?"

"Nope. Did they find anything with Julian?"

"Well, he wasn't missing. The police just found him, after. Wasn't any question; they were sure it was suicide. I never talked about this with anyone before. Not even—"

"Layla?"

I was going to say Isaiah. "Yeah."

Pru laughs softly. "You're a really bad liar. Just like Ranae."

"So those were hers—what you have on?"

"Worship bloomers?" Pru laughs again. "Not a thing."

"I didn't think any bloomers were a thing, but apparently . . ." It feels weird to be joking. Weird but good. Like it's okay for there to be a little extra air in the world.

"I made these." Pru's voice goes serious again.

The why that keeps nagging me is back. I try to answer it for myself. "To remember her?"

"It's my penance."

"Penance?"

"Punishment. Consequence. Absolution."

"She's gone. Isn't that enough?"

Pru shakes her head. "Everybody has something they do for penance. Your mum, your dad, you. My mum. Everybody punishes themselves somehow."

"That's—" I start to argue, but the front door opens abruptly. Daddy looks out.

"What you doin out here?" His eyes land on Pru. "Who's this?"

"This is Pru. She was just in the area."

"Good night, Pru. Karmen, come inside. We have to get up early tomorrow, like normal. One minute to say good night to your friend." He pushes the door half-closed.

Pru glances over at me. "Like normal, ay?"

I feel suddenly protective of Daddy. Close as we just felt, I don't want her picking at his words. "He wants us to stick to our regular routine, like if I was in school."

"Your brother died. Nothing's regular routine."

"That's just how he is."

Pru's mouth twists to the side like she's about to say more, but she must rethink it. "Well, it actually is a school night for me," she says. "If that makes me *normal*."

I get up. I'm tired again—or maybe still. Too tired to take her bait. "Cardo coming back this way to meet you?"

Pru stands too. "I'll catch up with him."

"You really was just in the area, or you came this way just to talk to me?"

She drops the skateboard, holds it steady on the driveway's slope with one foot. "See you, Karm." She eases toward the street. Where gravel and asphalt meet, she pauses and looks back at me. "Trying to be normal can be penance too."

Then she's gone, swooshing down the road until distance swallows her sounds. Inside, Daddy looks at me without a word. I clean up in the kitchen, then peer into the living room. The lamp is off, and Daddy is curled on the sofa again. His body is a Z of contortion, knees bent awkwardly, elbow crinked under his head. Pru's words pop into my head. Is there something wrong with trying to do things the way we did before Julian died? Is it better to get up early and go out like our whole world didn't implode? Or is it better to lie in bed all day?

I head upstairs and turn off my own light. I lie down, feeling the interruptions of the backpack and all it holds, pushed on the other side of the bed, weighing the cover down. I close my eyes, but it's a long time before I get to sleep. A new question circles in my mind now.

If everyone has a penance, what's mine?

I reach beside the bed and feel for Julian's skateboard. The sandpapery deck is worn, but still rough against my fingertips. I let go and turn over in bed. My foot brushes against something soft and bowl-like on top of the covers. Julian's cap. I sit up, slip it over my hair in the dark.

You know what yours is. Julian's voice is matter-of-fact, and low. *You doin it right now.*

For the first time, I push his thoughts away. *This isn't penance,* I tell myself. *It's understanding. There's a difference.*

CHAPTER TEN

When I wake before six, Pru's words pop into my mind, as if they swirled around the bed, waiting to leap into me at dawn. *Trying to be normal can be penance too. Your brother died; nothing's regular routine.* I sit up in the bed and reach a hand up to scratch my head. My fingers brush the cap. I take it off, hold it in my hands. I look down at Mr. Nobody sprawled over my chest. I think of Pru, the flash of sky-blue satin, the memorial pin with her cousin's face on it. Penance. Punishment.

I jump out of bed. Forget her. She doesn't know me. It sucks that she lost her cousin, but I'm not her. Me trying to get into Julian's head? That's different. That's solving a mystery. That's figuring out something I should have seen while he was still here. That's the birthday gift I'm giving him. It's not punishing myself. It's a good thing.

I make up my bed, smooth the sheets, shake out my pillows, then tidy up the stuff I left on the top. When I get to the history magazine, I flip through the pages to Julian's article. I stare at his shadowy picture.

What's stopping you? Julian whispers.

I don't wanna read this, I think back at him.

What you scared of?

Everything. Seems like this was the last thing you did that was you. Before I don't know what messed you up.

You wanna know me? See me here, he whispers through the page.

I already know you, I think, but something deeper, something I feel in my bones more than in my mind, murmurs, *If you did, you'd have noticed. You'd have known.*

I squeeze my eyes shut. I have to do this. I flip to his pages and begin.

Free Towns: Echoes in the Present
By Julian Wallace

Freedom was nothing but scrub brush and forgotten coastline when a hundred and thirty-one liberated Africans who overthrew an illegal slave ship were granted the land to settle as their own. The tiny community in a remote corner of New Providence became one of a few of its kind.

I keep going, through Julian's words, through his eyes. He writes about how Freedom remains unique as an isolated village, more like a settlement on a rural Bahamian island than a far-flung corner of the capital.

The isolation has allowed well-preserved artifacts from the early emancipated African settlers to be unearthed. Residents with roots stretching back those nearly two hundred years proudly believe they still live steeped in the traditions their ancestors brought. For them, history is woven through rituals and routines that remain intact today. But is it possible for the past to be retained in the present? Where does identity blend with true historical preservation within a living culture?

This is the Julian I know—thinking, questioning, excited. His passion leaps off the page. There's something else here, though. Something surer than I remember in him. Like I'm seeing a little of Julian as he would have been, as a man.

I thumb through the photos. His name is in the credit under each image. One is of a building made of crumbling stone, roof long gone. The structure is simple and square. A girl, a couple years older than me, looks out through one of the windows. The sun is behind her and I can't see her face. The next picture is of a well built of rocks. The roof is wood and has green shingles on the top. *Historians say this well provided fresh water for many of the early residents.* The third picture is of a motherly-looking woman standing next to a girl—the same one as in the first picture, I think. They're in front of a newish building, a restaurant, that the article said serves dishes from recipes brought by the freed people.

Did Julian talk about this place? It seems like he would have been excited, but I can't remember him mentioning it even once. I try to think back to last September. I had soccer; he had late classes. Mummy took on more evening clients, and Daddy was in full swing with office hours and teaching and working on his doctorate. Sometimes it seemed like we didn't all see each other for days.

I close the magazine and get out of bed. I want to be up now. But I can't go back to the university, not a third day in a row. After reading Julian's words, I know what my next big step is. I shower and get ready. This time I don't flinch as I take a plain red shirt from Julian's drawer. I hold it to my heart for a second, then tuck it, and the cap, in my bag.

At the bottom of the stairs, the aroma hits me. Boiled fish. Again. I brace myself for a huge pot and a steaming bowl at my place. I tell myself I'll be kind. I'll smile through every fishy bite.

Mummy sits at the table alone. There's one bowl—hers—and it's half-empty. No pot on the stove, nothing in the sink. Her feet are propped up on Julian's chair again. She has that notebook in front of her. She's so immersed, she doesn't even see me.

"Morning."

She looks up. "Hey, morning. I didn't hear you come down." She's dressed—all the way dressed. A yellow skirt with soft pleats, a pale green blouse with white flowers. Her hair is in a French braid. No earrings, no lipstick, but I can smell her peach lotion.

"You made boiled fish?"

"I heated up some I had in the freezer." She rests her spoon in the bowl. "You want the rest? I know y'all don't like it."

"It's okay. I just thought . . . it's okay." This Mummy—the one who eats whatever she pleases and leaves me and Daddy to fend for ourselves—feels new. Feels different. Like she won't crumble if I bring up September fifteenth. I take out the bread and push two slices in the toaster. "You look nice."

"I'm going to see my counselor today."

I turn around to look at her. "Really?"

Mummy nods. "Feels like time. Well, anyway, I have to start sometime."

"Are you gonna start seeing clients again?"

She follows my gaze to the notebook, and rests it on Daddy's empty chair. "Not yet, Karmen."

"I saw you had that book a couple times, is all."

"You're getting more like your brother. Inquisitive."

I turn back to the toaster. The squiggly wires inside are already glowing red. "Speaking of Julian. I asked Daddy if we could have something to remember his birthday. He said you might not want to." The kitchen is silent. Maybe Daddy was right—maybe it's too soon, even with Mummy up and about. But I feel like we need to do this, like *I* need to. "Ms. Rhonda suggested it," I add.

The toaster's sharp beep rescues me from the quiet. I drag a buttery knife across the slightly burnt bread, then bite in.

"What'd that toast do to you?" Daddy walks past me to the fridge. "Barb, you made fish?"

"Just for me." Mummy gets up. "I'll wash the bowl out; I know y'all don't like the smell." Her voice is even, like I've not said anything.

The bowl clatters lightly as it lands in the sink. I should have skipped that question. I should have picked another— should have asked if she read the article Julian wrote about Freedom.

"I'd have suggested that to a client, when I was practicing." Mummy's voice is soft, but it still takes me by surprise.

"What's that?" Daddy leans over and takes the second piece of toast.

195

"Having something on the fifteenth." Mummy squeezes dish soap onto the sponge and starts washing. "Karmen asked. I think it's a good idea."

"We spoke about it." Daddy's glower burns into the side of my head. I keep my eyes on my plate.

"We have to find new rituals. This could be one."

"I think it's soon." Daddy opens the cupboard and takes out peanut butter.

"It'll always feel soon. Karmen, you put your ideas together; I'll think about it today too. We can all of us sit and talk about it this evening."

"She's still under suspension," Daddy cuts in.

"Life itself is punishment enough." Mummy flips the tap on. I can feel the argument brewing. This isn't what I wanted—for them to disagree. For them to take up this polite, angry tiptoeing around each other.

"Can I go out to Freedom today?" I blurt out.

All eyes are on me. I wish I'd put the cap on so I could half hide under its brim.

"Go to Freedom for what?" Daddy's voice is sharp, even with his mouth full.

"Julian wrote something about it for school last year. I want to go see it for myself."

Mummy sets her clean, wet bowl on the side of the counter.

"Y'all know he printed something on Freedom in his department's magazine?" I ask.

"He brought it home and showed us. Remember, Stan?"

"I remember."

Why didn't Julian show me? Were we really all that busy? Were we fighting about something? We didn't fight like that, though. I push through my questions—I can't afford to get bogged down. "Did we all ever go out there together?"

Mummy shakes her head. "He learned about it in one of his classes." She turns off the tap and dries her hands on her skirt, then frowns as if she's just remembered she's not wearing a kitchen towel.

"We got five minutes." Daddy drops his plate into the sink and heads to the living room.

"Can I go?" I call after him.

"You got schoolwork," he calls back.

"Your dad's right," Mummy says, but she sounds tired out, like she's been awake since long before sunrise. "Take a couple minutes to think about what we should do for Julian's birthday."

"Can you tell him I can go out to Freedom?" Now I'm pushing too far—I know I am, but I can't stop myself. If I don't push, who will? And if I do, I might get what I need. It's worth the risk.

Gotta at least try. Julian urges me on.

Mummy smooths out her rumpled skirt and picks up her notebook. She holds it to her chest, protecting something— or using it to protect herself. She takes a few steps toward the doorway and stops in the middle of the floor like she's forgotten something, like she's waiting.

"Mummy?"

She shakes her head, disagreeing with some phrase I can't hear. Then she's gone, with her notebook and whatever is in it. She might be upright and dressed nicely, but she's not back to her usual quizzical self. *Maybe she never will be,* I think, as I pull on Julian's red shirt with the cutoff sleeves, as I gather up the backpack, the magazine, the skateboard—everything that made him him. Everything that'll help me.

I skip the library charade altogether. Campus is still quiet, and I can roll for several feet without having to adjust left or right. There's moments of lightness, when I find an even patch of road, or where the sidewalk isn't too interrupted by divots and cracks. On campus, no one gives me a second glance, not like at school. How can a year or two make such a difference? At school, everyone cares so much if you do something even slightly different, slightly strange. Not that skateboarding is strange to me—it wasn't strange even when it was him, jogging a few steps before dropping it, all four wheels down, then hopping up as if the hard, rolling slab were a detachable part of his body, magnetically drawn to reunite with the rest of him.

I'm not there by a long shot. When it's time to cross the road, I step off and carry the board under my arm. Then I get back on and glide, push, glide, push my way toward the base of the hill that leads to Isaiah's work. On the way, I near two guys walking. I brace for them to hiss or call out to me.

"Yeah, king," one says as I pass. I lift my chin to greet, hope they can't see my plaits sticking out under the hat.

Outside the white office tower, I bend down and grab the skateboard's edge. Pick it up, examine its worn red wheels and scuffed top. How much banging around, how much beating, can a thing stand up to before it breaks? Who broke Julian?

I walk past my room and the bathroom. Before I reach his door, the smell hits me. Unwashed body, farts, stale sheets, windows closed up, old sweat. I grimace.

"He's depressed," Mummy said earlier.

"Hey." From the doorway I can see him, or his outline wrapped in a sheet, facing the wall, back to me. "I brought food."

"Not hungry." He doesn't sit up.

I step in and rest the food on the bureau, then push the curtains open. "You ain gettin up?"

Julian groans, covering his eyes. "I tryin to rest."

"For three days straight?" I crank the window as wide as I can.

"That's too much draft."

"It's almost July, and in here smell like horse backside." I run down the hall, grab room spray from the bathroom, and charge in, nozzle blazing. Now he's upright.

"Don't spray that in here! I don't like that stuff." He coughs. At least he's sitting up now.

"Yeah, methane's toxic too." I pass him the plate. He fans the air as he slumps past me out the door. He sits right outside the room, cross-legged. I sit opposite him. The spray does kind of stink.

"Old roses, Grammy's soap, and—"

I sniff, then splutter, pulling the door shut. "And a hint of Baygon."

"Memories. And the roaches should be dead in there, too." Julian half smiles, pushes a curl of pasta onto his fork,

199

then another. He eats quietly, head back against the wall, eyes closed while he chews. For a minute I feel like I fixed him. Then I see his face. How tired his shoulders are as he leans back. How he looks thinner, like it's been months instead of days.

"Bey. What happened?"

Julian bumps his head back into the wall, one, two, three. He closes his eyes. "You ever feel like you wanna just . . . stop?"

"Stop what?"

"Everything."

An ache opens in my belly. What does he mean, stop everything? Julian opens his eyes and frowns at me.

"You should see your expression." Julian scoops pasta into his mouth. Downstairs, the dryer whirs on. Should I tell Mummy what he said? "Mummy sent you up here?"

"Of course."

"Yeah, she was in here fifteen times yesterday."

"You counted?"

"Ain nothin else to do. I was just dozing, not like I was passed out. I was tired, man. End-of-school exams wipe you out, ya know."

"Yeah." I want to believe him, this upright brother.

He finishes off the last of the food, then sets the plate down. "I might as well shower."

"Please, for the love of breathing humans everywhere."

He looks like he always does, as he walks back into the room, as he comes out with clothes under his arm. The bathroom door closes; the toilet flushes; water runs. He's fine, I tell myself. Just tired. Makes sense. Nothing to worry about. Nothing to tell Mummy. Nothing she doesn't know.

How could I not see through my brother's act? Anyone with a brain and a knack for acting can fool a parent, but not a sister. You can't help but be close—maybe not tell-each-other-everything close, but still. You share a bathroom; you bring stuff to each other. You have a whole lifetime of grimaces and bouncing knees, nervous twitches, the words *ever feel like you wanna just stop everything* to warn you.

I take a breath and step inside. I ask the person at the front desk for Isaiah. She scrutinizes me under half-lowered eyelids as she presses a few buttons on her phone.

"Isaiah? Someone's down here to see you."

I wait by the door. When the elevator door opens and Isaiah comes out, he looks at me, then around. The receptionist points my way.

"Hey—Karmen?"

The receptionist humphs.

"Let's talk outside," Isaiah says pointedly.

"Gladly."

Outside, he hugs me awkwardly. "I didn't even recognize you for a second."

"The skateboard wasn't a tip?"

"When I think about you, I don't always think skateboard."

"Maybe you should."

"Are you allowed to be off campus? I thought your dad . . ."

"I want to go out to Freedom. That's what Julian was writing about, last year this time. I read the article he wrote. I just thought maybe I could see it through his eyes."

Isaiah nods. "How you getting out there?"

"Well, my mother was busy, and Daddy didn't even answer when I asked."

"I'll take you."

I look over at the university. It feels distant already. "Don't you have to work?"

"I'll leave early. Just this once."

"You don't have class?"

He smiles. "Not till later. But for you, I never have class."

We burst out laughing together.

"This is your fault, Karmen. I don't say this type of corny stuff when I'm not trying to impress you."

"Don't blame me," I say as he unlocks the car. "You really don't have any place to be?"

He holds my door open like we're out on a date. Like I'm in a fancy dress and heels instead of jeans and an old shirt. "Promised I'd do anything I could to help you. Let's go."

CHAPTER ELEVEN

Two ways into Freedom," Isaiah says. "Which one you want?"

"You got a map?"

He chuckles like I've suggested we lick our fingers and hold them up to the breeze to find north. "Coral Harbour Road, or Cowpen Road and Bonefish Way."

"That means nothing to me."

Isaiah tosses me his phone. "One-seven-eight-three."

I put in the code and check maps, stifling my smile. He trusts me with his phone. And his PIN. I zoom into the southwest part of New Providence. "So, cut through a bunch of bush by Coral Harbour or . . . what?"

"Go by the cliffs."

I gasp. He might as well have said *go by where Julian died*. I imagine those cliffs—the steep drop, waves lifting and crashing, churning water sapphire-deep. Slabs of rock unforgiving below. I close my eyes. Isaiah lays his hand on mine and squeezes hard.

"Oh, Karmen. I wasn't even thinking. I'm an idiot. We'll go Coral Harbour."

"It's okay."

"It's not okay. I shouldn't have forgotten. *You* can't forget."

We drive in silence, taking quiet roads I don't recognize until we slow near the end of a rough side street. We pull up outside the place in Julian's photograph—a small, tidy wooden building painted in exuberant vertical stripes: blue, yellow, orange, green, pink, red. The hand-painted sign above the door reads RONNIE'S RESTAURANT. Inside is white, and almost plain compared to the zealous exterior, but the tables are clean. A few have a clear vase with two or three hibiscus floating in water.

"Sit anywhere," a voice calls from the kitchen. "The patio's open."

We step in.

"You know who you want to talk to?"

I look in the magazine at the photograph. "One of these ladies."

An older woman appears. "Morning. Early lunch or late breakfast?"

"I came to see if you remember my brother." I hold up the article. "He came out here last year to do an interview."

The woman takes the book. "Aha, yes, I remember this young man. Krissy," she calls through the window. "Come here a minute." She passes the book back to me with a strange glint in her eye. "Better you talk to my daughter."

"What was that about?" Isaiah whispers as she starts setting flowers out on the rest of the tables.

I look around us. The yard is neatly maintained, the grass cut low, the bush cleared back to what must be the edge of the property. I peer through the surrounding greenery for a glimpse of old ruins or artifacts, but it looks like it's just trees and overgrown vines around here.

"First time here?"

I turn to see a younger woman—more of a girl, really—with a grocery bag in one hand. The girl from the photo, hair trained into thick dreadlocks that she wears tied back from her face, and she has on a long, loose orange dress and flat sandals. Her face is small, chin pointed. A glittering stud shimmers from one side of her nose. As soon as I see her, all I can think is that Julian must have thought she was beautiful. "Uh—yeah, first time."

"You early for lunch. If you come back around eleven, we can take an order then."

"Are you Krissy?"

She nods as she carries her bag behind the counter. "I am."

"My brother talked to you a while ago. Julian." I rest the history magazine on the bar's countertop. Its orange cover almost glows against the beige, a small rectangular sun. When I open it, it falls right to the pages, the path worn well by my fingers now.

Krissy takes out a large pack of napkins and looks over. She smiles, and the closedness in her face opens like a flower just feeling morning light. "I remember him." She bends down to get something under the counter, but I already know. She liked Julian. Whatever happened, if anything happened, she saw something in him, something that, months later, could unlock that smile. She straightens up and sets two napkin holders on the counter, then pulls the magazine over. "I was waiting to see the story when it came out; he said he was coming back with two copies, but he never brought them." Krissy looks up at me. Her eyes are warmer now, a warmth I know isn't for me. "How's he doing?"

I don't know how long I stand there, looking back at her face. It could be thirty seconds, or five minutes. All I see is the open door to her hope, knowing I've brought nothing but news that will slam it shut. "He couldn't come," I say finally. My voice sounds like it comes from someone else's body, distant and strange.

Her smile fades, eyebrows knit together. "Is he all right? Did he get sick or something?"

I feel Isaiah before I see him, hear him before I feel his warmth beside me. "Julian died, unfortunately. I'm so sorry. End of July."

Krissy's fingers tighten around the counter's edge. She holds on as though that will stop the floating feeling, the sense that everything is falling away. I do the opposite. I can only stand there unrooted, ungrounded. Krissy shakes her head, denying the news. I turn away, toward the open door, but my eyes are welling up too, not only for Julian, but for this warm, sweet girl. A girl Julian might have liked, might have one day brought home. A girl who obviously liked him. Everything becomes background as I walk outside—Isaiah talking low, Krissy's mother, and sobs that can't be suppressed. I only get as far as a table and chair set in the grass. I stand there, but the greenery, the salt air and warm breeze dissolve around me.

Blue and red strobe lights flash outside the window. I sit on my bed and strain to listen.

". . . it's him?" Daddy's voice, choked.

". . . need you to come down . . ."

No.

"Barb?" A tight bark, constrained throat.

". . . have to identify the . . . body."

Daddy's sobs are loud like coughs. They won't stop.

No, no, no.

I cover my head with the pillow. I squeeze my eyes tight. No, not immovable. No, not breathless. Not still, not nothing, not dead. I do not see red and blue lights ease away. I do not hear footsteps rising like smoke, hear a tap at the door. I do not feel a hand on my arm, warm droplet, someone's tear. On the other side of the bathroom, my brother lies, laughing into his pillow. What a scare. What a joke. Through the concrete, he breathes. He is there, snuck in through a window, cut the burglar bars and pried off the screen. He's been there all the time, behind the dresser. Under the bed. He's alive. He has to be.

Warm arms pulling me close. Warm chest, warm chin over my shoulder. I'm back but I can't stop shaking. I can't unsee, unhear, unforget.

"Sit."

I can only sink down to the grass, rest my head in my hands. When do I stop remembering? When does all this stop feeling raw and new?

After a while, the woman comes out with two glasses. Isaiah takes them and he sips. I hold the glass, feel its ice turn my hands numb.

I feel Isaiah's eyes on me. "This was a bad idea. I shouldn't have brought you here."

"I asked you to."

"This can't be good for you, Karm. You were shaking. Let's go."

Doesn't he know the shaking is in me, whether he sees it or not? It's like tears. They don't just get invented the moment your eyes get wet. They wait, locked somewhere low in your heart. The right key, the right twist, and they're set free.

A shadow falls over us both. From the way Isaiah looks up with a sad smile, I know it's Krissy.

"I didn't know. I'm sorry. I never thought he'd passed," she says. "Your friend told me what happened."

"We didn't mean to come out here and spring that on you."

I flinch at Isaiah's words. Why's he apologizing? What is it about death that makes everyone act so weird, as though there's no way to be sad without faking responsibility?

"We just came because we had questions," Isaiah continues. "We only found out about the magazine this week, and Karmen—she just wondered—"

"Did Julian come out here often?" I interrupt.

Krissy sits beside me and stretches out her legs. The long dress drapes over the grass. "He started coming last year. I saw him whiz by from inside like he had wheels on the ends of his legs instead of feet. Then he came in for something to drink. Brought out this big huge textbook and slapped it on the table like he was planning to read the whole thing while he had one coconut water and a side of plantain chips. I think around September or so we got to talking more."

Isaiah gets up quietly, touches my shoulder to let me

know *giving y'all space*. I watch him head out toward the road before I continue. "Were y'all dating?"

Krissy picks at a blade of grass. "I mean, not really. I thought he was cute. I think he liked me. Neither one of us really said anything about it, but he'd come in sometimes two, three times a week. Sometimes it was busy, but if I had time, we might talk."

I look out toward the bush at the edge of the yard. How many realities did he shatter with what he did? The girl he could have gone out with, could have fallen in love with, married? The babies he could have helped make, the stories he could have told? What about our parents, when they're like the man in the picture on the wall, very gray, very old? What if they can't stand that upright and strong? What about when they're gone? What about me?

I push my anger down. "I wish you could have known him more."

"I wish I could have known him more," Krissy echoes. "What was he like at home?"

There should be whole libraries worth of things I can tell her, things that would warm up her sad eyes, things she'd fill her mind with, things that would make my brother more real, more . . . here. But right now, sitting in the grass, sitting where he should be, my mind is as emptied out as his room—things in it, but the essence, the life, gone. *I don't know* is what I want to say.

Instead I close my eyes. "He was smart," I start off. "He was always way smarter than me—got As all through high school. And funny. You know those heavy, awkward moments?

He just knew how to make it light and silly again. This one time we were supposed to do laundry, but we wanted to go swim with our uncle . . ."

As I tell her the story, my anger melts away. I'm back at home, Julian beside me. I'm twelve; he's fourteen. We're standing in front of the washer, a mound of sheets on the floor. Julian's already in swim trunks, towel over his shoulder.

"Mummy say we had to wash all this, plus mop the floor."

"Yeah, and Uncle Ellis ga be here in ten. You want stay here and watch the machine agitate, or you want go to the beach?"

"So what we supposed to do?"

Julian pops open the dryer and starts stuffing sheets in.

"That's nasty, bey!"

"Toya ga be there so, you want stay home and be clean, go ahead. I ain missin seeing Toya in a two-piece."

"Gross." I grab a dryer sheet anyway, toss it on top.

"Ah, now you're thinkin." He sets it on high and presses start.

"What about the floor?"

He tosses me the broom and I sweep. He comes right behind me, a wad of paper towel under each foot, the spray cleaner in his hand. Four minutes later, we're speed-folding. I change fast while Julian stuffs the sheets back in the linen closet. When Uncle's rattly truck pulls into the driveway and the horn toots twice, we thunder down the stairs, already laughing, wind already on our skin. We might as well already be by the water for how light we feel.

As I remember, as I talk, I start to feel lighter. Part of it

210

is easing Krissy's sadness, seeing her smile. It feels good to remember him too. Not just remember, but remember good. To let him be alive for a while.

By the time Isaiah strolls back into the restaurant's yard, Krissy and I have been talking for what feels like ages. Another car pulls into the parking lot and she stands up.

"I guess I better get in for the lunch rush. Are you guys gonna stay?"

"I don't think we will today," I say. "I'm not that hungry."

"You should look around, at least. You ever been out this way before?"

"I picked up a brochure." Isaiah holds it up. Krissy takes it and circles a few spots on the map.

"Check out the ruins, and the cliffs."

I swallow. Isaiah didn't tell her that part, then. His eyes meet mine, fast, and I shake my head so only he sees. I don't want her to know he died so close to her.

"This is a shortcut to the caves," she carries on. "They're gorgeous. You can walk there from here." Krissy passes the map to me. "I still can't believe it. I'm so sorry—I should be comforting *you*."

I take the map and tuck it in my pocket, then give her a hug. "At least I know someone else misses him."

Krissy nods and goes back inside.

Isaiah offers a hand. I take it as we head back to the car. He squeezes my fingers gently. "Should we go?"

It's almost eleven. A tiny part of me thinks about my appointment with Ms. Rhonda later. But I don't feel like the answers are in that stuffy little room, any more than they're in my school classroom or the university library. I want to be out here, like Julian would be. We wander around and find the ruins we passed on the way in. We avoid the path leading to the cliffs, and instead loop around through the trees and back to the car. I'm antsy, though, and not ready to go. We head back to the restaurant and order food: okra and rice, accra fritters. By the time we are done, I feel more like myself.

"This seems sort of weird." Isaiah finishes off his ginger lemonade.

"How so?"

"Everything. Off campus in the middle of a school day, skipping work. Hanging out with you."

"Oh, spending time with me is weird?"

His laugh is as quenching as my mango-mint-infused water. "It's your fault. You have me saying stupid stuff all day. Hanging out with you is weird in the best possible way." He takes a swig of lemonade; a trickle escapes down his chin, through his beard, and trails along his neck. Before I can stop myself, I reach over and brush the droplet aside. The light curls tickle my fingertips, and I pull them away. I keep my eyes on my water glass; suddenly I'm hot again, hotter as I feel him looking at me. He reaches a hand across the table, just barely grazes my fingers with his.

We pay, then leave. On the way out, I try to catch Krissy's eye, but she's sideways to us, in the middle of taking an order. I wonder if her shoulders are always rounded a little that way, or if the news about Julian did that. At the car, Isaiah hovers by the door.

"I feel like walking this food off a bit. What you think?"

"We could try to find the water." I reach for the door handle. "Let me get something first."

With the skateboard in my hand, I feel whole. We head the opposite way from how we came, down a slight incline. Isaiah points left. "I think that way."

We turn, and after a minute I put the skateboard down and step on. I roll slow, keeping my pace level with Isaiah's steps, only shifting slightly to avoid pits and cracks. The swoosh of wheels on road fills the space where words might be, their scrape-clack on old asphalt as unobtrusive as background music. The board's gentle clatter keeps my mind steady too. Keeps it from wandering where I don't want it to go.

"Can I ask you something?" Isaiah keeps his eyes straight. Ahead of us: casuarinas shift their branches in the breeze. "What if you can't find what you're looking for?"

I lose focus a moment and almost end up in a small pot-hole. I swerve and put my foot down in a jolting stop. My body keeps going forward. I fight to keep myself upright.

"You all right?" Isaiah reaches out for me. I pull away from his outstretched fingers, then wish I hadn't. *What's wrong with me?* I think, except I know.

"Yup." I get back on the board. We both start moving again. "The water," I say finally. "I think it's through the trees."

"Think I see a little blue, too. That's not what I meant, though."

We go a little farther, and the trees thin out. It's not beach access, but rocks that end in deepish water too rough to invite swimming. The salt air feels fresh, though, and we stop. He leans against a tree. I stand with my arms around the skate-board. "I dunno." I pick up a stick and toss it into the water. The waves swallow it without stopping. The stick is there a moment; then it's gone. Beside me, Isaiah studies the ground. A plain little bird, stubby wings only good for short flaps, pecks near our feet, flutters back, pecks a little more.

"I don't want you to get hurt is all."

"Too late for that."

"I mean hurt more. What more do you think you'll find? What have you found that you didn't know?"

"You think I'm invading his privacy."

"That's not what I'm saying." Isaiah's words feel like tiny ants scuttling under my skin. But his voice is cotton-ball soft. That's the only reason I can keep listening. "All I mean is, whatever you find, don't let it change what you think about him. He's your brother; you loved him."

"Love."

"I know."

"No, present tense. It doesn't go away."

Isaiah gets up. He sits on the tiny bit of stump beside me. He doesn't say anything, just leans a little closer. I tilt my head over until it's resting on his shoulder. When he eases away and stands up, I pull him back. Isaiah rests a hand on mine, but he doesn't lean in.

"Maybe we—"

"Of course." I let go. I feel like I shrink three inches. I was reading him wrong, then. And I just made an idiot of myself. "We should go; you got stuff to do."

"It's not that, I just . . ." Isaiah looks away. "You know I like you. I been tripping over my words around you for days. And I don't skip work or class for anything or anyone."

"What's the problem, then?"

"I don't know if this is a good idea!" His words burst out of his mouth like he's been holding them there for too long. "Don't get me wrong, I want something with you—something real, not just hanging out—but I don't know if it's . . . a good idea?"

I should be happy-dancing, even just on the inside, at *I want something with you*, but it feels like we're in danger of having nothing at all. "Why wouldn't it be a good idea?"

"I mean, you're dealing with everything with Julian. I don't want to take advantage of you being fragile right now."

"If I was gonna break, don't you think I'd have done it by now?"

"Karmen, you're wearing his clothes. You said you were *him* last night at that pottery class."

"I'm trying to get into his head so I can understand!"

"I know, I know you wanna understand—I just worry that it's just not the right time. I don't want to rush things and then you regret it."

"I'm not gonna stop trying, you know."

"I'm not saying you should. I'm just saying . . . I want you to be okay before anything were to happen for us."

It's already happening, I want to say. I get up. "We should go." I should start back toward the road, hide how much I want him to say *never mind,* to say *I was wrong.* Instead I look out at the sea. The water's rhythm holds me in place, the forever lift and tumble of waves, the way they exist and then don't, but somehow still do. The blue, churning and deep, keeping secrets in its constant motion. I lift another stick and throw it out to the water. Wind interrupts its path and it doesn't go far, falling to the waves nearer to the edge.

"Maybe," Isaiah starts, and hope flutters up through me. I take my eyes off the coast. I look at him, and it's better than the ocean's hypnotic dance.

"Yeah?"

"We could just pass by those caves. For a minute."

Something unsnaps in me, something that wants to move—fast. Something that wants to make my own breeze through motion. When I look at him, I feel that spark I know so well flare up. A spark Julian always had. Now it ignites in me.

"Race you," I say. Isaiah breaks into a sprint like he's been waiting for the chance. I skip over pine needles and onto the road, drop the board and step on, push off so fast, I almost overbalance right away. But I find my steady legs. Then I pick up speed.

Isaiah's a block ahead; he looks back and laughs—once, sharp—and increases his pace. I pass houses, new, half-built, old with crumbling walls and missing roofs. Wind whips by me, or because of me. Half a block between us—Isaiah makes a sound, something between *oh* and a laugh, and breaks into a full run. I push faster, faster, air whizzing by me. Then— wham!

I hit a pothole and the board goes one way and I go another. I sail through the air as if gravity has loosened its grip on me. Thrill and terror rush me—*I'm flying, I'm gonna die*. Then the ground surges up and I land on my hip and side with a thump.

"Whoa, you okay?" Isaiah jogs back. My breath is heaving, my chest pounding; my pulse is fifty steps ahead of the rest of me. Isaiah pulls me up, hands on my waist. His face is earnest, concerned. "You hurt?"

Right now, nothing hurts. I catch my breath a little as he lets go of me.

He bends down and picks up the board. "This thing ain safe." He hands it back to me. "You might get hurt."

"I'll show you hurt!" I take off as hard as I can, on foot.

"What!" I hear him shout, and I push harder. Feet pound, body jolts, the board slows me, and then we are racing neck and neck, scalding sun, asphalt burn through our shoes. Our bodies know the way: toward the sun, curve left, follow fizzled-out road—gray pavement faded to pitted white. We run on the skeleton of the street, old stone structures standing firm in the bush. My chest burns, sweat stings my eyes, my thighs ache and I'm sore where I fell, and I am so, so alive and I never, ever want to stop.

But it does—the running and the road. We peter out as the path turns sandy. We stop, and Isaiah makes another of his sounds—*Whooh!*—and tugs at the collar of his sweat-soaked dress shirt. No breath in me to laugh, but it comes anyway.

He eases off his glasses, wipes his face on his sleeve. "You—whooey—ain tell me—oh boy. You never say you got back on the track team."

I grin. "I didn't."

"And I guess you don't skateboard."

"I don't."

"Except now you do."

"I'm a living mystery."

Isaiah studies me with those steady eyes, that small smile. "I wonder what else you don't do."

I look away, heat all through me, and then I look back.

"Come." He reaches out a hand, and my calming heart jumps again as our palms touch, as his fingers lace through mine. Together we weave through the scrubby pine trees. Out here, there are no noises—the pine forest swallows up even the sound of our feet—and now that my heart has calmed to its regular pace, I feel hyperaware that we are alone. Not only alone, but *deep* alone. A bird zips overhead, quick on its way, as if the air around us is too thick to fly through.

The cave entrance is low. We step in, and instantly it's cool. Quiet, too, as though no one has spoken here in years. We move slow, stop to gaze up through holes in the roof. Tree roots snake through the space and down, anchored strong in the damp. As our eyes adjust, I realize how much light seeps in through these spaces, the cave ceiling's crannies and holes letting sun in.

"How far do we go?" My voice is too loud; the blackness splinters around us and the pieces fly over our heads, squawking like weird birds. Bats rise through one of the cracks and vanish to the hidden sky. The cave narrows, the roof lowers, we duck, and then we are in an opening. Beams of sunlight seem to hold up the cave's high ceiling. There is a pool, clear water glistening, still. We slip off our shoes and tiptoe to the edge, then sit. Near the edges it is shallow and light, by the look of the blue, but at its center it is ocean's-heart deep.

Isaiah's voice is reverent and chapel-low. "It's a blue hole."

I look over at him, and for a moment his eyes are hidden as his glasses reflect blue. He nods and smiles. The space left between us could melt away so easy.

"What?" Isaiah says. "You sighed."

"Oh?" The light shifts above in a blink; something passes a hole in the cave, a shadow soon gone. I take my gaze back to his face, to his eyes. "I'm just—happy."

"Good." A pause. "I mean, I wouldn't want to upset you. Bad girl and all."

"Bad girl!"

"Suspended from school . . . beating people in street races . . . fall down and don't even flinch . . . I don't usually hang with such a tough crowd." He bumps me with his shoulder, and I lean into him. "Just kidding," he says. "You're nothing but good."

"What do you mean?"

"Name one bad thing that wasn't completely understandable."

I slip one foot into the water. The dark keeps it cool, even though it's shallow. "I broke that window at school."

"Understandable."

"I haven't even looked at a single piece of homework."

Isaiah slides a foot into the water too. His toes nudge against mine. "Understandable."

"I skipped counseling today."

He laughs. "You don't really think that makes you even remotely bad. Do you?"

"Not really." Something else hovers in my chest, threatens to weigh me down. Waits for me to speak, to say it, to let it out or keep swallowing it down. I don't want to be heavy anymore. I want to find that crack in the ceiling. I want the way out. "I don't know how I can ever go back to regular life. This non-suspension suspension, trying to talk to people on campus, even the pottery group—it's not real life. It's not getting up and going to school. Some people are all about me getting back to normal, even when I'm off and supposed to be clearing my head. But the truth is, I don't think I can."

Isaiah looks over at me. This time I can see his eyes. I watch for pity, for sad. I can't see either. "That's what I was trying to say earlier. This is so important to you, and I understand it—I mean, as much as I can. But you might not find what you're looking for, and if you don't . . . I mean, with you being so caught up in this, I just worry if it's really . . . healthy."

"Nothing about this is healthy. Mummy washed her hair yesterday for probably the first time since Julian died. Daddy just wants to power on through and leave early every morning like he can't wait to get to someplace that isn't our house. Me borrowing Julian's shirt is pretty okay compared to all that."

I set the skateboard on the cool ground, then put my other foot into the water. "If I tell you something, you promise not to say I'm crazy?"

His other hand folds over the back of mine. "I would never even think that."

"I'm pushing so hard because I kind of . . . owe it to him. I couldn't help him in time, but maybe this is a gift I can give him now."

"A gift?"

"He was supposed to turn twenty next week." I look over at Isaiah. "You probably think I'm being ridiculous."

"I think I've never known someone to love as hard and as wide as you do."

I feel my eyes start to water. I don't want tears—not now, not here. I look down into the still, cool water. I reach down and scoop up a handful. As I lift it, I feel that again. That spark. That urge to push. To play. To live loud.

"Really think I'm bad?"

"What—hey, you wouldn't dare—"

I send the water flying. It spatters his face; droplets speckle his shirt.

"You wait!" He's on his feet as I bend down to scoop more. "Watch—it might get deep!" He grabs me, and we both go down. The water is still shallow where we land. We scramble to our feet, soaked from the waist down. My back's wet too, and his glasses are drenched. We stumble back to dry ground, and our laughter rings through the dark, echoing as though giants inhabit the space. "You all right?" he splutters.

"I'm drenched."

"Me too. Can't go to class now." Isaiah pulls at the front of his wet shirt. He lifts it to wring it out. That strip of exposed stomach again. He looks up and catches my eye. I look away, but he reaches for me.

We meld like there's nowhere to go but into each other. His shoulders are strong, and his hands on my waist anchor me like I could stay here in this cave forever. When his mouth brushes mine, I want to melt. So I do.

• • •

We are late back to the car. The sun is lower than midday-high. The restaurant's parking lot has emptied again. I catch a glimpse of myself in the window before he opens my door.

"Look how you got me all rumpled up."

"You?" He gestures down at his shirt, sweat-stained and beyond crumpled. "I can't even go to class like this." He climbs in on his side. "I don't even know what class I'm supposed to be in right now. I never do this." He starts up the car, then reaches for his phone. As he unlocks it, it starts to buzz. He frowns, then swipes. The dash clock says half past two. "Time to pay the piper."

"They looking for us?"

"It's like twenty texts here. 'Isaiah, have you been in contact with Karmen today? Her dad called me looking for her, she missed her counseling session today.' My mum. 'Couldn't reach you at work. Where are you?'"

My heart sinks. All the lightness is gone. This is bad.

"'Giving her dad your number.'" He checks his voice mail as we back out. Daddy's voice pipes out of the speaker: "Isaiah, this is Mr. Wallace. Please contact me immediately, I'm trying to locate Karmen." "Mr. Wallace again. It's after noon; Karmen's mother is very worried. Return my call, please."

We pull onto the side road, turn the opposite way from where we came. He knows I don't want to go by the cliffs; it's a shortcut. It must be.

Isaiah's father's voice blares out of the phone. "Mr. Wallace been by your class; you didn't show up. I been by your work; they say you left in the morning with a girl in a red shirt. Where are you?"

Panic flares like fire. Isaiah speeds up—he feels it too, whole body leaning toward the steering wheel. I wish I could slow us down instead. I don't know what waits for me in my house. But I know it's going to be bad.

My father's voice again. "Karmen, this message is for you. Your mother and I are waiting at home for you. We let the police know you're missing, and apparently there's not much they can do since it's only been a few hours. I'm trusting that you will come through that door. Come home now."

I press my back into the car's seat, but that can't stop Daddy's words from squeezing my chest. I know that feeling—of waiting, of watching. I know what it means for him to talk to the police.

This was important, though, a voice in me says. On the drive out, as I flew down the road, and back there in the caves, I agreed. Now, though, I'm not sure anymore.

We cut back toward the coast, and along. The water is shallow, and then obscured by shrubbery. "Where are we going?"

"You gotta call them." Isaiah takes the curve fast. On our left, the water is deeper now. The road slopes up: my fear bursts into a full blaze.

"We're going the cliff way."

"Shoot. I wasn't thinking." Isaiah picks up the phone with one hand. "If I turn back now, we'll be even later. Sorry, Karmen, this is such a mess. I shouldn't have brought you out here." He pokes at his phone. "At least call my mother." It rings twice.

"Isaiah!" Relief in her voice. "We been trying to reach you all day. Is Karmen with you?"

"She's with me in the car. We're about twenty minutes away from her house. Can you call her daddy?"

We turn a corner. Sun blares right in our faces. There's no beach, just steep drop-off. A few high pines teeter on the edge, one storm away from falling to the deep.

"You need to talk to him yourself. Where were you?"

"We just went for a drive, Mummy."

"For three hours? What kinda drive—Isaiah, if you slept with that girl, I swear—"

"Mummy! You on speakerphone!"

How can you care, I want to scream, *how can you even care about that when we're passing where—where Julian—* My palms are sweating; I wipe them on my pants, then keep them plastered there. I want out of the car. I can't seem to breathe in, only out. I squeeze my eyes shut. It'll be over soon.

"I don't care if I'm on megaphone. Y'all out having good times and her parents just about having a heart attack? You can't mess with that girl." His mother's voice is loud, distant though. "That family been through enough."

"I'll call you later." He hangs up. There's a thump behind me, on the back seat. Must have thrown the phone back there. Isaiah's hand touches mine. The sun paints the back of my lids sparkling orange-red, glitter dots against black. "We passed it."

Before I can reach for his hand, he pulls it away. Maybe he wants two hands on the wheel while we speed toward my house. Maybe he realizes getting tied up with me is too much trouble. I keep my eyes closed for the rest of the drive home.

"Here we go." Isaiah sounds like we've reached the edge of a gangplank we're about to have to walk. I open my eyes as we pull up to my house. Daddy is out front. He kneels beside the driveway, cutlass in one hand. He raises it high, then swings down, whacking into the long grass. "Uh . . . your daddy . . ."

Daddy stands up. The cutlass is still in his hand. His face glistens with sweat and fury. He glowers through the car window at us.

"You don't have to come out." I pull my backpack onto my shoulder.

"No, I'll come, I'll come." Isaiah shuts the car off. I reach for the skateboard. My fingers close around air.

"No. No, no, no." I turn around to search the back seat. Isaiah's abandoned phone, and a box of tissues—nothing else. "Julian's skateboard!"

"You don't have it?"

"I must have left it—" Before the words *in the cave* can leave my lips, my car door is wrenched open.

"Come out of the car." Daddy's voice is low.

"Good afternoon, Mr. Wallace," I hear Isaiah say. I pull Isaiah's seat forward, push mine all the way back. No good— it's not there. I know I left it in the cave. It was in my hands— and then, stupid me, it was not. I was too distracted to look down, but I can see it there, on the ground in the cave, near the slab of rock. I want to scream and cry all at the same time.

"Karmen. *Now.*"

It's no use. I get out. Daddy tosses the cutlass toward the hedge and points to the front door.

"I'll go back after my last class, see if I can find the board—" Isaiah begins.

"Goodbye, Isaiah." Daddy's words are a growl.

"Uh, Karmen, I guess I'll talk to you . . ." Isaiah's voice fizzles. "Uh—I'll—later—sorry, Mr. Wallace."

I step in the door first. Julian's shoes are the first thing I see. The gaping holes waiting for his feet, heels worn down from feet shoved in too fast, sides and toes scuffed.

"Unbelievable." The door slams behind me. Daddy turns the lock, like there was a chance in hell anyone could go anywhere today or in a decade. "Barbra, she's home," he shouts into the hallway, then turns back to me. "You care to explain?"

I feel bare without the board. Will Isaiah really go back? He has his own family to answer to, or class to get to, or work. Now Daddy looks ready to explode. How could those moments in the cave have brought me here?

"Karmen?" Mummy's voice behind me is almost welcome—until I turn to see her, shoulders hunched, arms across her chest. Her eyes are red; her cheeks are wet with tears. I brace for her to come toward me, to hug me. Instead she cowers in the doorway. "How . . . ?" She shakes her head.

"Answer me." Daddy's bark makes me turn back to him.

"I—we just went for a drive."

"Out to Freedom, where we *both* told you not to go?"

"It's not like it's dangerous, I just—I had to clear my head."

"So you ran off with that boy for hours? No counseling, no text, no asking, nothing."

"You took my phone! And I asked you to take me out to Freedom!" My voice pitches—I know he's mad, but I can't handle it, not right now. "You didn't even answer!"

"I thought you were gone." Mummy's voice shakes. "Hours went by, we had no idea where you were. Only to find you were out doing who knows what, why you couldn't be reached."

"We wasn't doing nothing!"

"Don't shout at your mother!" Daddy barks back.

"You don't even—" I can hardly speak. "You don't even wanna know why I wanted to go to Freedom?"

"Well, I saw you get out that boy's car. What else I need to know? Y'all sleeping together? How dumb can you be, Karmen? And inconsiderate!"

"We weren't—I wanted to—"

"It doesn't matter. You shouldn't have run off. You shouldn't have left campus. You shouldn't have skipped out on your counseling session. You shouldn't have been doing *whatever* why the boy couldn't even answer his phone. You're so far out of control, I don't know what to do with you." Daddy isn't even looking at me anymore.

"Mummy, I . . ." I turn to her, I don't know what I'm asking, what I'm hoping for from her. Mummy shakes her head.

"I know you're hurting, Karmen, but you have no right, *no right* to make us worry like that."

"Go upstairs to your room. I can't even look you in the face right now." Daddy brushes past me and back outside. The door slams so hard, it shakes the whole house.

"Mummy, I didn't—it wasn't to hurt anyone. I just wanted to find out about where Julian used to go."

"It's too far." She wipes her face. "Wherever Julian used to go, it didn't do him any good. Maybe your father's right. You're out of control. You need more rules, not less."

I feel like a half-blown-up balloon someone's dropped—deflated, slobbery, worthless. How can they so completely not understand me? How can they not even care? I'm right in the same house—I was right in front of them both—and they won't even let me speak. All that matters is what I did, not why I did it. They don't know me at all. And what's worse? They don't *want* to know me. I look at Mummy, but there's no way anything I say can make a difference right now.

Her office phone rings.

"Who is that now?" she snaps. The call goes to voice mail, and my aunt's voice rings out, with its matter-of-fact reminder that Mummy isn't taking clients currently.

"Shut that thing off, Barbra!" Daddy bellows through the window. "If I have to hear it one more time—"

Mummy dashes for her office and slams the door behind her.

"And we ain having a thing next week. No party, absolutely not. You out of control as it is; we can't handle that right now." Daddy's voice is ready for a fight, but I'm done. I don't even have it in me to argue back. I listen to him open the car door, start it up, pull out of the driveway. Let him go.

All I need to do now is go upstairs, shower, and lie down. I turn away from my father's words and take two steps toward the stairs before I see a rectangle of purple on the floor. It's Mummy's notebook. As I pick it up, a manila folder slips loose and spills a page onto the floor. It's covered in Mummy's handwriting. As I pick the paper up, phrases jump out at me: *Feelings of hopelessness mounting. Unsure of reason; no changes in relationship, school, family.* Guilt warms my face. I slide the page back into the folder. I shouldn't be reading this person's file. Then my eye catches the name on the tag, a name that stops me like a kick in the gut. It can't be. But there it is, in my mother's steady print.

Julian Wallace.

CHAPTER TWELVE

Julian Wallace

Feb 1: Engaging in regular activities but something seems different. Relationship breakup? Not aware if he's seeing anyone. Possible rejection?

March 7: another three days in his room. Didn't come out except to use the bathroom, not interested in eating. Skipping classes. Friend came by the house, would not go and meet him. Obviously depressed, refuses medication. Won't see own counselor.

I flip through my mother's notes. They go back through the spring, then before that to last year . . . I turn to the first page. Five years ago. Five. There's nothing in any of them I don't know—Julian sleeping in, Julian missing class, Julian's quiet spells, Julian's moods. What's new is that our mother was recording them. Can she even do that? Counselors aren't allowed to see their own kids as clients. But if she was, why didn't she *do* something? Why didn't she help him?

The office door opens suddenly. I look up and into Mummy's face. The weariness slides into shock.

"What are you doing with that?" She reaches for the file.

I step back. "You lied." My fingers tighten around the paper. She grabs the edge of the file. I hold on tighter.

"You said you were just trying to get your head back into things."

"Don't—you'll tear it!" Mummy grits her teeth, then lets go. "Pass it here, please."

"You lied! You knew something was wrong, and you didn't help him."

I can't get my words out fast enough to make room for the fresh ones forming. "You said you couldn't treat family."

"I wasn't treating him, Karmen; I was just trying to figure out—"

"You said—"

"Give it to me!" Mummy's face twists—her mouth wrenched open, contorted into a monster's snarl. She yanks the file out of my hand so hard, she tumbles back into the wall. My fingers burn from the force of the paper slipping away.

"You didn't help him—you knew stuff and you didn't say anything—all this time I'm trying to find answers everywhere and the whole time . . ." My skin, my arms, my throat, everything feels like I'm about to burst into flames.

"I did everything I could!" Mummy screams back so loud, it feels like a full-body slap.

"You supposed to help people!"

"Not everyone can be helped! No one knows that better than me."

"And I don't? He's my brother!"

"He was my *son*!"

"You should have done something. I didn't even know anything was wrong, but you did." I know I should stop talking, but I can't help myself. The words leap out like flames to gasoline. "Might as well have pushed him yourself."

Mummy freezes like I've speared her through her heart, from behind. Her eyes are wide and wet, her mouth slack. The anger is gone—and the sound, and the air, all sucked out through the vacuum I've opened wide. The sob that rises out of her is like everything in her is being wrung out. Mummy runs up the stairs, but her wailing trails after her. It fills the house—that and my knowledge that *I* did this. I caused that sound. I said those awful words I can't take back.

Part of me knows I should follow her. I should say I'm sorry. The other part of me can't move, not in that direction.

I catch sight of Daddy's work bag. He never leaves it when he goes out. But we live in never, now. *Go,* my mind tells me, as I rummage through the bag until I find my phone. I shove it in my pocket. *Get out. Get out of here.*

I scrawl a note on a stickie. *Went to Layla's.* Leave it on the calendar, in the middle of our broken July. I hoist the backpack onto my shoulder and shove my feet into Julian's sneakers. When I close the door behind me, I wonder: Is this how Julian felt living here? Did our family stifle the life out of him? Did he always want to run, the way I do now?

After a few minutes, I slow to a walk. I dial Layla's number, then hang up before she answers. I need a friend I can see. When I finally reach Layla's house, I'm soaked in sweat. Isaiah's car isn't in the driveway, but their parents' truck is.

I knock on the door. The old me would be praying neither of her parents answers, not after they were calling all around looking for me too. This new me doesn't care.

The door swings open. Layla stares back at me. She almost looks like she doesn't know who I am.

"Hey. Can I come in?"

Layla steps outside. She pulls the door closed behind her.

"So I guess you heard." I try to make my voice sound light.

Layla cuts her eye at me. "I can't even believe you. You had us all scared silly."

"I didn't mean to scare anybody. I just asked Isaiah to go out to Freedom with me."

"Right. 'Freedom.'" She air-quotes, but her tone's full of a different finger sign.

"That's really where we went! Come on, what you think we were doing?"

Layla looks over at me, then away, like she can't stand what she's seen. She shakes her head. "I heard him tell Mummy y'all made out in the caves."

"Well—I mean, yeah, but that's not why we went there. We—"

"You don't have to tell me anything. Good thing *he's* your best friend now."

"What was I supposed to do, ask you to cut class and steal a car? I needed to get out there to—"

"Yeah, I know, to ask questions about Julian. Know how I know that? I heard it. From my brother. Seems like I might as well not even be your friend anymore, since you rather talk to literally *anyone* besides me."

"I talk to you."

"Really." Her voice is flat.

How can I even explain it to her? That it calms me, the way he asks. Without pity twisting his voice. Without helpful hints from experts and books. Without quotes and tips between us like a dusty sheer curtain that keeps billowing up in my face. To him, I'm not irreversibly broken. I can handle a conversation. I'm like everyone else.

"Why are you even here, Karmen?"

"I forgot my skateboard in the cave, and I wanted to get out there."

"Isaiah's supposed to be in class till eight, and I wouldn't even ask Mummy. You're not exactly her favorite person right now."

I turn away from Layla and walk back down to the main road. I perch on a bus bench and take the phone out again. I go to my chat with Isaiah. *You there?* I type, then delete it. I already messed up his day enough.

But I need my skateboard back. My fingers hesitate, then I scroll to another number. The phone rings twice before it's answered.

"Hello?"

"Hey. Pru? It's Karmen."

"I know. What's up?" She sounds a little warmer now.

"I left my skateboard way out by Freedom."

"All the way in the back of the bush? How you get out there?"

"I'll tell you later. Can you maybe come out there with me?"

"Where are you?"

"I'm by the drugstore on Marsh Road."

"Isn't that by where your friend lives?"

"Yeah, it's not too far from Layla."

"I meant the other friend, but okay. I'll see you there."

A gray car pulls up in the drugstore's parking lot. The front window goes down and Pru waves me over from the passenger seat. I get in the back. Cardo sits in the driver's seat. He nods hello.

"Thought you was grounded," Pru says.

I lean back in my seat. "Long day. And ain finish yet."

"What'd your mummy say when you left?"

I lean back into the seat. "I wrote a note. Layla'll probably call and tell her. Apparently she hates me now."

"Musta been pretty distracted to forget a whole skateboard." She turns back to give me a knowing look.

"Ah . . ." I glance up at Cardo.

"Oh, don't be shy around Cardo. He knows the ways of the world. Hold on." There's a click from the front seat. Then Pru's climbing over the center console into the back.

"Pru!"

Cardo glances in the rearview mirror. His expression is unchanged: apparently, this happens every day.

"It's just easier." She settles in beside me. "So, what? You just blowing everything off today? Hitting bridges with matches left and right?"

"I just couldn't be home."

"Why?"

"Everything. Where you want me start?"

Pru waits, silent.

"I said something to my mother before I left."

"What?"

"Told her she might as well have pushed Julian herself."

"Oh wow." Even Pru looks surprised.

"And my parents said no to me doing a birthday celebration for Julian, so I guess now I have nothing to lose."

"How you feelin?" she asks.

"Awesome," I say, and we burst out laughing, together.

Cardo takes the Coral Harbour route without my even asking and parks by the caves. Pru doesn't even ask, just hops out of her side and strides in alongside me. We find the board easily, and relief floods through me, but the caves don't feel like the place I sat in just hours ago. Pru pulls a dress out of her bag.

"I didn't even change out of my prison clothes," she says, unbuttoning her blouse. I look away while she changes. "What are you doing the rest of the day?"

"I don't know—go home and get yelled at some more, I guess?"

"How about this?" Pru straightens out the dress—it's just below mid-thigh and red, with a golf-shirt-style collar. A hint of the pale blue bloomers flashes out as she moves. "You can hang with us instead."

I think of Julian, always doing everything so properly. I think of all the good he's not here to do. What's the point, living perfectly, trying so hard all the time? When you're gone, that's it. No more fun. Not for you, not for anyone around you. Except today. Except me.

I straighten my shoulders and hold the board tighter under my arm. "Let's cheat death," I say.

A whole new sun opens up in Pru's face. "Let's."

Cardo parks by a grocery store. Together, we skateboard through the empty half of the parking lot, then over to a drive-through. The three of us laugh our way through ordering food, and laugh harder at the look on the woman's face at the window as she passes us our bags of burgers and fries. We eat under an almond tree, skateboards wedged around the gnarled, woody roots.

"Ever been by the Cellar?" Pru balls her bag up when she's done.

I look from her to Cardo. "What's the Cellar?"

"It's a club, bar-type place. I ain know 'bout that, Pru. It's after six thirty. I'm tired. Plus I don't like taking my car out there." Cardo jangles the keys in his pocket.

Pru pokes his board with her foot. "We ain gotta drive. It's not far. Fifteen minutes max." Pru stands up. "Time for street riding. Ain that much traffic out this way. Plus, it's not so bad with three of us. And there's smooth sidewalk along that whole stretch by the Ministry of Culture."

Cardo gets on his feet too. "I guess we don't have to stay long. Only if both of y'all want go, though."

I don't want to. But would Julian hop on a bus and head home? Or would he go for the adventure? I reach down for his skateboard, hope I'll feel an answer somehow as my fingers touch the scuffed wood.

"There's some nice ramps by the ministry building,

though," Pru says with a wicked grin. "I don't know any boarder that'd pass up a good ramp."

I get up too. I feel like I have to. "Let's go."

To get out of the parking lot, we have to cross a four-lane street. I step off my board, half expecting Pru to launch into traffic, but she does the same. Once we've walked to the other side, though, we take a long, mostly straight road with few cars. Pru and Cardo alternate going first, the other always behind me. I could let them make me feel inept, but I like the sense of being surrounded, of having someone show the way and another watch out for me. By the time we reach the long white-and-blue wall that marks the start of the Ministry of Culture grounds, it's starting to get dark. The gates at the front are locked, but the wall is low. Pru looks back at Cardo. He shrugs.

"What?" I look between the two.

"When God closes a door . . ." Pru sets her board on top of the wall, then hoists herself up. There's a flash of shimmery sky-blue satin as she scrambles over. "Who's next?"

Cardo points at me. "Ladies first."

Pru guffaws from behind the wall. "You see any of them, Kay?"

The nickname is a key notching into a lock. I set my board on the wall and pull myself up. There's a moment, at the top, where I feel both tall and little, feel like Julian must be right behind me whispering plans. I jump down and look back. Only Cardo, but it's somehow okay. I feel Julian, still. I know he'd approve.

There's a row of a dozen or so parked cars with government license plates, then the empty buildings beyond.

"Where are these ramps?" I ask. Pru deposits her bag on the ground near the wall and points toward the entrance. I shrug my backpack off too. Cardo drops his board and sort of run-steps onto it. Boy and board are metal and magnet: one calls the other and, snap, they are together and then up a curving ramp. He curls around toward the five stairs, then does something with his feet, so fast I can't see. The board flips—then his feet reconnect at the bottom and he rushes toward us, then stops, board angled like a jacked-up car.

"Look at you, stuntin." Pru's grin is all approval.

"It's like you were flying—how do you get it to swivel in midair like that, and then how do you get your feet to connect with it again?" I'm babbling and I don't care.

"Practice. Lots of falling." Cardo's off again.

"I wonder if Julian was that good too."

Pru starts moving again. She doesn't answer. I follow her, slow at first, letting her stay in front. Then my confidence picks up and we ease through the lot side by side, no talking, just fresh warm breeze, wheels whooshing, and freedom— nothing to carry, nothing to say, only thoughts and moving bodies cutting through air. This is Julian, I'm sure of it. If he stunted like Cardo does, he would have shown me. *Would he have?* my doubt whispers. I shove it down. *Yes.*

"Hi! Y'all can't do that in here." A woman's voice behind us. Pru keeps going, of course, but I stumble off my board too fast. "That's the same reason right there. Y'all don't come out here and kill y'all-self on government property."

I spin around—head on fire, heart about to jump out of my

chest. "We look like we came to kill ourselves?" I shout back. Darkness interspersed with streetlight. I can't see this idiot.

"Kay. Let's go." Pru's hand on my shoulder.

"Y'all want me call the police?" The woman won't even show her face.

"We're not suicidal!" The words tear up out of my throat. "It ain no joke!"

"Calling 911 right now." The voice is singsongy, smug. I could swing at her if I knew where she was. Tears are starting to blur my eyes—Cardo's beside us too, grabbing our bags and tugging at the gate.

"Ma'am," he calls, "you want open the gates up?"

"Yes, we have intruders at the Ministry of Culture building. Main entrance."

"Let's go." Cardo scrambles over the wall and Pru tosses our bags to him. Somehow I get over—half climbing, half pulled, with a little shoving to make it over. Pru is last. Cardo hurtles down the street on his skateboard. Pru reaches for my board.

"We could run it. You could run, right?"

I make my feet go forward, go fast till we've passed the wall, then farther. Cardo waits by a side street, and we cut through there, then slow at a shadowy house.

"So, sometimes you get chased," Cardo says finally. "Y'all all right?"

Pru nods. "Don't worry about me." When I don't answer, she leans her shoulder into me. "Come on, let's go." She doesn't wait for my response. She lays my board down, back toward the main street.

I look at Cardo. "We're not gonna get arrested if the police see us?"

"It's not a crime to skate on the side of the road."

I carry on with them then.

The Cellar is small and crowded, though it's still early. The place reeks of alcohol and sweat in a hot, confined space. Cardo disappears into a group of guys, and Pru leads the way to the bar. She mouths, *What you want?* I shake my head, but when she waves the bartender over, he still comes back with two drinks and a knowing smile. She pushes one my way. I take a sip. It's iced tea, spiked with something strong. The night gets loud fast. Cardo pulls Pru onto the dance floor. I sit with our bags for a while, but then two girls in spiky high heels work their way over and one claims Pru's chair. I shove my board into my backpack. It's too long for the bag: it sticks up like a skyscraper in a suburb. Whatever. I just need out. I close the zips against the board as best I can, then hug the bag to my chest as I work my way toward the bathroom. The line of girls waiting snakes into the narrow hallway. I turn back to the bar, and of course my seat is taken. Pru's board, and Cardo's, are still there. My head's starting to whirl, and I wish Isaiah were here with me. Except he's probably on his way home after class, where he should be. Where he belongs. *Where do I belong?* I wonder. Not here. Not in this din, not alone. It's the alone part that gets me.

Someone steps on my toes, hard, and I yelp. The sound is swallowed up by the music's blare. I worm my way through gyrating bodies toward Pru, but every time I get close, someone gets in the way.

"Watch it! You got shelves in your bag, ay?" someone complains behind me. I push toward the exit and into the night. I yank my phone out. I call Isaiah, but no answer. I text *hi* instead, and wait.

The dark is persistent. My mind starts toward home—Mummy and Daddy will be so far past mad by now. Layla probably called them after I left. When I get home, it's going to be bad.

Pru and Cardo stumble outside, all wrapped around each other.

"Girl, where you been? I was looking all over for you!" Pru staggers toward me. "You have our stuff?"

Is she serious? "It's inside. I couldn't carry it all." I watch Cardo head back into the building. "How do we get back to the car from here?"

"Car? It's right over there." Pru points toward a red car beside me. It feels like my whole body shrinks a size as I realize—she's drunk.

"We parked by the grocery store. Remember?"

"Grocery store? Right, right. You so smart. We could ride back." She looks around. "Where my board gone?"

"You can't skateboard drunk." It's a fight to cling to my patience. "Especially at night."

"Course you can. Well, *I* can." She trips over nothing. "What the hell? You see that?"

I roll my eyes as Cardo reappears. He can walk straight, at least. There's another guy with him.

"How y'all getting back to your car?"

"Sorta far to go. We could catch a ride with my boy Marco."

Marco nods my way.

"You okay to drive?" I ask.

"Better than walking." Marco unlocks a green car and climbs in.

"Marco only had a couple beer or so." Cardo climbs in the front. "Pru! Come on, get in."

Pru makes her way over. She looks sort of stable for a moment, then pitches forward beside the car and moans.

"Hey, y'all, don't puke in here." Marco is not amused. Someone a car over shouts. It's just a hello, but it sounds like they're inside my head. I take Pru's arm and help her in, then get in beside her. Inside the car, all I can smell is beer, bittersweet. Marco starts out even, but then we get to Go Slow Bend and he veers across the line. A car honks, passes close on the blind corner, and Marco straightens up, then overcompensates, and for a second we're almost on the seawall. A wave splashes up, taunting—calling. We're nowhere near the spot where Julian died, but suddenly I can't breathe. This is dumb. I can't be here—I can't be in this car with this idiot. I have questions to ask, questions no one else cares to get answered.

"Look out!" My voice comes out like a squeak, my throat too tight for words. Marco slams the brakes at a stop sign. "Wait," I say, fumbling with the door.

"What you doin?" Cardo cranes his neck around.

"I didn't leave my house for this boy to kill us on the

road." I open the door and step out into the night. "Pru. You coming?"

Pru looks up at me. She opens her mouth to say something, then pitches forward. The wet slop of vomit hits the car floor. "Oh . . . sorry . . ."

"I can't believe I ever thought you were anything like him." The words tumble out of my mouth.

"What you talkin about? Look, if you goin, go. Pru, you with us or not?" Marco cranes his neck, then gags. "Cardo, deal with your girl, please."

Cardo reaches back and slams the door shut from inside, and they pull away.

I move forward through the dark, but my heart doesn't stop pounding the whole way. Anything could have happened— we could have gone into the wall; we could have gone over, hit the rocks, kept tumbling. Could have plowed into a car coming toward us, spun out and hit a lamp. Anything could happen now—a car hitting me from behind, someone jumping out of the bush and grabbing me. I could trip and fall in the road, and no one might see me. All for . . . what? A stupid adventure? Following behind Pru? I can't believe I thought she was a friend. Can't believe I ever saw any similarity between her and my brother. He'd never have taken a chance like that.

If *I'm* gonna take a chance, it has to be *for* something. For Julian. That's what it's been about all along. If Julian were here—pounding heart, aching legs, rushing wind, empty streets in the dark—he'd be doing it for something. Wouldn't he?

I was *out here. What you think happened that night?*

The thought terrifies me, nearly sends sick climbing up my throat. But I can't look away any longer. I get onto the main road heading out toward the cliffs. As I do, Julian's voice grows stronger in my mind.

I was out here. I know. For more than adventure. I was out here for the thing I couldn't find.

I push the thought away, like I push away the agitation, the pulse of fear. I push on, through aching legs, through thirst that makes me cough, makes me glad to swallow spit. I push on.

Julian, I think, *I didn't know. I didn't know anything was wrong.*

Julian's voice comes back, clear and calm. *Didn't you?*

The memory that takes over me is old. I am small, maybe four or five.

Cold floor under bare feet, tiptoeing across tiles, something stuck—cat, mouse, puppy stray, singing moth, something with feathers and fur. Call his name, erase the sound. Now tracking silence, sense a feeling, a shift of shoulder, cotton against wood. A warmth of air from nostrils. Try playing "Peekaboo!" and the word falls like a book dropped, perfectly flat. He's not under the table or in the closet or any of the cupboards, his usual spots empty. Walk faster, heart hurrying ahead, body cannot keep up. Look back over my shoulder; nothing's following me. The office door is closed. In the living room, the TV whispers stories to the empty air.

What makes hand reach for the kitchen door's knob, push it closed? He is there, except it is not the brother who crosses

245

his arms at the wrist, hands holding my hands, and spins us around, his feet and mine dancing in a circle, the direction silently agreed. This is not the boy who stands on the Y of the guinep tree's branches and launches himself off, shouting, I can fly! This boy is not a boy. These curved shoulders, buried face, limbs folded in on each other. He cries like someone has taken Mr. Fluff and sliced his teddy ears off, pulled the soft stuffing out onto the floor. But Mr. Fluff is on his bed; I saw him there before I came down just now. What happened to him? I take a step toward him, and as I do, I start crying too. I curl up beside the body I know as well as my own, try to curve my shoulders too, bury my face and sob. Except my cries are loud—they will pull our mother out of her session, and her skirt will be wet with two sets of tears.

I will never remember just why I was crying, except that he was. But the greater question is always—why was he? His sorrow is the core of my own, and to have no answer feels like standing on the Y of the guinep tree, looking back at nothing, certain something without hands waits to push me.

My heart is racing again, always racing, always running. Like there's something in me besides me, something too eager to leap to a sprint. I can't remember the last time I felt even, felt calm, felt like me.

Yes you can, he whispers. *You can remember. You better remember. You have to.*

I'm back in summer then, and I don't want to be, but I'm there anyway: Layla's room, its luxurious mess—the thick carpet, air cool from her AC, the scratch of wool against my fingers.

"This is just ridiculous." Blue stitches pushed on her finger like bright rings.

"It's fine. Wait, don't undo it!"

"Not like you could help me!" she protests, as I try to anyway, her blue yarn tangling with my deep orange. "Hold on, before we make some mega-double-twisted new color. Have to use our legs."

"Thigh workout?"

She bops the door open with her hip. "Zaiah! Come here."

My phone buzzes, beeps.

"Who's messaging you? Secret lovah?" Layla shimmies her shoulders.

"You tryin to make it worse? This tight on my wrist, girl."

"Where my big-head brother? You call him—you know he's the only man for you. Maybe your distressed maiden cries could bring him running. 'I-zaiah! Oh, help me, Zai-ahh! I'm a-trussed and a-tied and a—'"

"What y'all guffawing about!" Isaiah appears. I elbow Layla hard.

"Shut up, girl," I hiss, but she's laughing too hard to hear. I can't quite look at Isaiah, and can't quite look away. Singlet, and pants on, but no belt yet, so they're low on his hips. Smile can't be bitten back quite all the way. "Trying to knit without needles."

"Karmen, how you let my silly sister get you in this. That's what I always say: don't get tangle up in art." He's over, smelling like fresh soap and sunshine.

"Actually, this was my idea."

"Boy, you couldn't put on clothes?" Layla interjects.

He kisses his teeth. "You want me help you or what?" Oh, to be his teeth right now. He reaches around me to lift the orange wool; it's almost like he's holding me.

"Hurry up before this one melt," Layla says.

"What's crazy talkin about?" Isaiah's in front of me now, looks me right in my eyes. My tongue might as well be wool too, thick and twisted all up on itself. I shrug, and a garble comes out.

"What's that, Karmen?"

"I said I don't know." I cut my eye at Layla as she pulls free.

"I gotta go pee." She tosses her yarn on the bed. As she passes, she whispers—not quietly enough—"You're welcome."

"Almost there." Isaiah's face is inches from mine. He reaches around, lifting the orange around from behind me. "Uh-oh. Think I made it worse."

"It's okay." I can feel the shower's warmth radiating off his body. Should I step closer? Away? Now he's slipping the stitches off my fingers. His hands are warm too. "Oh, someone trying to reach you." He looks over at the bed—my phone lit up again. Don't get it, I plead. Don't get it, don't walk away. I'm free then, stitches removed. I can't step back from him, and he doesn't move either. Am I here? I feel like the room's melting away, like it's me and him and we could be literally anywhere. He holds the pile of wool out to me—it's so huge, it's touching my belly. And his. I push my hands into the soft.

"Hey, Layla, y'all want pizza?"

We spring apart at Mrs. Parker's voice, my heart pounding so loud, it drowns out nearly everything. My face is hot with guilt.

"Isaiah?" Mrs. Parker's voice is knowing. "Thought you were getting ready to go with your dad to Men's Study."

"Um . . . yeah. I was just helping with a little tangle . . ."

"I see that." His mother's eyebrows go up. He slips out past her. I stuff my yarn into my bag, hoping Mrs. Parker will just melt away too.

"Where's Layla?"

"Ah—she just went to the bathroom."

"Mm-hmm." That knowing-mother voice is obliterating the bliss I want to hold on to so badly. "When she comes back, y'all come tell me what pizza you want."

"Okay."

She turns to go. I suppress a sigh of relief as I reach for my phone.

"Karmen?"

I drop it onto the bed, heart pounding. "Yes, ma'am?"

Mrs. Parker eyes me, head tilted like a dog picking up a voice three blocks away. "I'm always around. In case y'all need anything." She raises her eyebrows. "Always got my ears and eyes open."

"Yes, ma'am." I watch her retreat, then plop onto the bed. I just want to sit with all these new memories in my head, on my chest. My phone buzzes again.

"Who this is?" I mutter, and pick it up. Messages—Julian. I open them up. Three, all deleted. I should call.

Layla comes in. "Y'all wrapped up your lil love fest?"

"Shh."

"What?"

"Your mummy."

"What? She catch y'all?"

"We wasn't doing anything." I touch Julian's name. *A gap in sound—silence? Pause?*

"The person you are trying to reach is not available." Mechanical voice. *"Please try your call again later."*

"What's wrong?"

"Julian texted me a bunch of times. Now his phone's off."

"Maybe his battery died."

"I guess." My head's starting to ache. I dial Mummy's number. It rings, then goes to voice mail. Right—she has sessions. Daddy's at school. I try Julian twice more, then give up. Layla's right: his phone probably just needs to charge. Everything's fine. I push the thought out of my mind, or try to. Everything's fine, I tell myself again. Why wouldn't it be?

High beams flash in the dark; blaring car-horn blast. "Get out the road!"

Legs ache. Push, glide. Push, glide. Almost there.

"Hey! Go on the side, miss." Car swerve. "You got a death wish, ay?"

Sweating. Cold. Ocean air, breeze off deep sea.

Stop.

I've made it. This is the cliff. The place. His place. Chose it, thought of it, skateboarded to it, got to it, and—

This is where—

The scream tears out of me without words; I can't even think anymore.

Water below roars; dark blurs rock into ocean into air. The scream lifts free and billows and still I can't stop. I scream until I'm hoarse, until I can't anymore. Worn out, I step forward, rocks shredding my sneakers. I walk. To the edge.

"Why?" I open my arms. "Why?" I lift my face. All that's left to do is step out. Is fall. I can't feel. Not anymore. Not again. I don't want to be here. I don't want to hurt. I want it all gone: the pit in my belly, the hollow in my chest, the way my head swirls, the dreams. The memories, all nightmares.

Then it hits me: I'll never know for sure why Julian ended his life that night in July.

But standing here . . . in a flash, I think I understand how he might have felt. How he was willing to do anything to make the pain go away. Anything for peace. Anything.

I step out of the shoes and hold them by the laces. I stand like he did. Feet bare, chalky stone cutting into my skin, making me feel once more. Taking one shoe in each hand, I draw my arms back. Lift them over my head. Then I let them fly.

My brother's shoes sail through the air. As they arc overhead, fear rushes me. They are airborne and helpless and I want them back. It's too late—I reach out as they hit the water. They don't even make a splash, swallowed whole.

I step back. There's a steady, low clicking. No—chattering. My teeth call to each other as if somehow that makes warmth. My whole body shakes. The skateboard shifts slightly in the buffeting wind. I reach down for it. I hold it to my chest. I cling to it for dear life. I dare not let it be blown away. Dare not let me be blown away.

My legs keep taking me back, back, back from the edge. My arms feel weak, like they belong on someone else's body.

What just happened? What almost happened just now?

I reach for Julian's voice. And . . . nothing.

"Julian?" Out loud—maybe that way he'll answer.

Nothing.

"Julian?" Shouting now. I scream his name over, over, until there's no breath left. I hug his skateboard to my chest. I think of those shoes—his shoes—and then I can't think of them anymore. I need to get out of here. I need help. I need to be me.

My fingers almost shake too much to dial. They swipe past, somehow, all the missed calls that've come in. I don't wait for an answer, just gasp into the open line. "I'm by the cliffs. You gotta come for me."

CHAPTER THIRTEEN

saiah doesn't hang up, doesn't come off the phone, until the crunch of wheels over the line matches the crunch of wheels beside me. Even then, his breath reverberates through his phone to mine as he runs to the bench, as he wraps his arms around me. The skateboard's wheels dig into my flesh as we hold on to each other. When he pulls away to lead me back to the car, my legs give out, and I have to brace myself on him to take the few steps to the open door. Inside, he locks the doors, then hangs up from our call. Dials another. My mother's voice is miles away.

"I found her, Mrs. Wallace. I'm bringing her home."

I hear my mother thank him, and then I lean my head back against the rest. Then I let myself feel nothing but the jostle of road patches and the odd pothole, the squeeze of Isaiah's hand on mine.

Close to home, the shaking starts again.

"It's okay," Isaiah says again and again. "It's okay." Trying to convince me. Trying to convince myself. He pulls into the driveway. My parents are waiting outside for me.

"Twice in one day." I mean it as a joke, but it doesn't come out funny, and it doesn't stop the trembling that takes over my whole body. The car isn't even shut off before Mummy pulls my door open.

"You're okay," she sobs, and falls on me. I hug her back and hold on. I let her absorb my shaking. I lose time, holding her. Daddy's hand squeezes my shoulder, reaching around Mummy, holding her, too.

When we finally get out, we go inside. I hear Daddy thanking Isaiah for bringing me home. He sets the skateboard down, closes the door, then leans against it, sealing the world out.

"You don't have on shoes." Mummy's voice is stretched thin. My eyes go to the empty spot where Julian's shoes stood.

Daddy steps forward. "We need to sit and talk."

"You need to shower first, Karmen? Wash your feet?"

The choice feels like too much, right now. "We can talk," I say. It feels easier. Part of me's afraid to be alone with my thoughts. With what happened out at the cliffs—what could have happened too. Mummy leads the way to our kitchen table. I sit, and she sits beside me. Daddy pulls out a chair opposite us both. At least we all know where to sit. One thing that doesn't require a big choice.

"Why?" Daddy's voice is more worn than angry. "What's happening, Karmen?"

I look over at Mummy.

"I want to know the same thing. Why would you do this?" Her voice cracks. "Isaiah said he found you out at that . . . that place?"

"I just couldn't be here."

"Seems to be a trend with our children." Daddy keeps his eyes on the table.

"What do you mean you couldn't be here?" Mummy presses.

"It's—it's too much sometimes, around here." I look at Daddy. "You can bury yourself in work, and Mummy"—I turn to face her—"you just lay in bed all day. But you expect me to go on like nothing even happened."

"No one expected that." Daddy's voice is small.

"You keep going on about normal. Get back into normal routines, get back to doing regular stuff, wake up the normal time. I know I messed up this past week, but . . . nothing's how it was. And it's never gonna be."

"Can you blame me?" Daddy's eyes search mine out. His are such a deep tired. It seems new lines have deepened between his eyebrows, just since morning. "First Julian, and now I see you slipping into someone I don't know? The acting up at school, and since you've been home it's almost worse, even before you ran off today. You think I don't see you trying to be Julian around here?"

"I'm not trying to be him, I'm—"

"Wearing his clothes?" Mummy cuts in. "Your sudden interest in skateboarding, which you never cared one bit about before?"

Her words leave me feeling naked. "I didn't think you saw."

"I'm grieving, Karmen. But I still see. And I don't know what to do anymore. I'm afraid of what's happening. I can only imagine how you feel. Missing Julian so much you're literally trying to *be* him."

I look up at the ceiling and take a breath. I let it out, and will myself calm, or as close as I can be. "I was trying to *get* him. There's a difference."

Daddy reaches over and folds his hand over mine. "You're not going to, Karmen. You're his sister, and you're left behind, like your mother, like me, trying to pick up the pieces, and trying to live even though you feel guilty for even drawing breath when he's not here to—" Daddy's voice snags like cloth on a rusted nail. "When he's not here. We all feel it, Karmen. We have our different ways. But we feel it. We can't fix it, and we can't get it. We just go on."

"Going on without him is like leaving him behind." My throat feels so full, I can barely get the words out. The thought of tomorrow, and the next day, and the next week, and October, and next year, without Julian, and without knowing *why* he can't be here, feels like more than I can bear.

"All I know is, we have to try to function." Daddy's voice is tired. "What you call getting buried in work, that's functioning to me. I make that choice because I don't want Julian's legacy to be that after he died, I fell apart. Or that our family's going to fall apart."

"*Going to?* You and Mummy don't even sleep in the same room anymore! Y'all can't agree on anything; someone in here always mad." The words spill out of me so fast, I can't stop them. "You got so mad at me for breaking that window when that kid said what he said about Julian to me, but you went and threw Julian's skateboard out the door! And Mummy, you broke up the bowls from the boiled fish, remember? Why would I even want to live in this house anymore?"

Everyone's quiet then. Hear-the-clock quiet. Its ticks feel

more like clacks, banging out from the hallway, trying to fill the space. I should feel lighter. But maybe I just made things much worse.

"What'd he say?" Daddy breaks the silence. "That kid at school. What'd he say about Julian?"

"You can tell us." Mummy's shoulders curl forward like a plant weak for water.

"His ball caused me to trip, and this girl Pru told him to say sorry. He said, 'Why? Nobody dead.' He knew about Julian—everyone knew, the teacher emailed the whole class before school started—and he still said that. Like Julian was nobody."

Daddy shoves his chair back and storms out of the kitchen.

"I knew there was more to it." Mummy's voice is so soft, so stripped down of the anger, the sadness that should be there. It's like Daddy's taken everything in, and her feelings have all fallen away, like the inner parts of a leaf. Like all that's left behind is the feathered skeleton of what was living and green.

"You were already so upset, I didn't want to make it worse."

"I'm your mother. Whatever you can take, I can take."

"It hasn't felt like it." I can't even look over at her—what if looking is the thing that makes her break?

"It'll get better. I'll get better. I have to do that, for you. And for me. But Karmen—you know Julian was more than just *somebody*. He was ours. Whatever anyone else says, you know that. And you know you're ours. We can't lose you."

"You won't."

"I'm scared." She touches my arm, and I have to look over. I expect to see the sad, the hunched, the frail. Instead I see her eyes clear—for the first time in forever. Clear, and really seeing me. "You were in trouble at the cliffs. Real trouble. Right?"

"I . . ." The answer, the real answer, feels like too much to say. I stop, try to find the words I need. Instead, the shaking starts up again.

Mummy lays her hand on mine. Her fingers are cool, her touch light as dry leaves, until she squeezes my hand hard and doesn't let go. "What were you doing out there?" she presses again.

I pull my hand away, cover my face. I can't hold it in any longer. "I wanted to see how he saw things—to get into his mind, so it would make sense. I was just standing on the edge. Like he did. And then . . . I threw his shoes in the water. And for a second I just . . ."

A sound in the doorway makes me turn. Daddy leans, listening. Beside me, Mummy's voice is a whisper I can't ignore. "Were you thinking about going in too?"

I don't want this dragging, this nagging, this pull that's been on me. I don't have the energy to pretend, or to hide. Even though it was only for a second, even if it was only to understand what my brother felt, even if it was just because I thought maybe, *maybe* him not being here would hurt me less if *I* couldn't hurt anymore . . . even though, even if all those things, I nod. "Yes."

Daddy moves back into his chair. We sit for a time I can't measure, both their hands touching mine. Sit in our three seats, sit with the fourth chair empty, our new always. Mummy gets up first. I hear her on the phone to Ms. Rhonda. "Emergency appointment for tomorrow morning," she says.

"I left a voice mail for your principal." The calm in Daddy's voice surprises me. "Told him what you told us. Told him what that boy said."

"Does that mean I have to go back to school sooner?"

"You won't go back to school until we've talked to Ms. Rhonda." Mummy answers. "Until things are more settled. Until you're ready."

Daddy gets up. "Let me pour you some water." He opens the cupboard and takes out that last purple glass. He fills it and sets it in front of me. As I lift it, the table, the oven, the walls, even Daddy—everything I look at is tinged purple too. Immediately, I'm back to one of our last good memories. One of our last times being whole. The night of our parents' last anniversary.

"Okay, okay." Daddy's standing, a beveled tumbler in his hand. "All right, y'all younglings settle down."

"Gather round, gather round, fireside chat time," Uncle teases from the side. His eyes glow from the bonfire. Sand under our feet, people paired off all over—Uncle Ellis with Aunt Glenda, cozied up with a blanket around their shoulders, other friends, faces turned to my father.

"In honor of my beautiful wife," Daddy says, "I'm gonna tell you all a great love story to inspire you all."

Julian elbows me, rolls his eyes. He cups his hands over his mouth, amplifies his shout. "Ay! You don't have no fresh story, Daddy?"

"How long you been married, small fry?"

"Daddy, we could tell this story in our sleep," I call back, but I snap my mouth closed because I know the rhythm of the tale. Told round the dinner table, on long car rides, when we're being tucked into bed, and at dinners, and around beach bonfires at night.

"Go ahead, then." Daddy sits down. "Ladies and gentlemen, give it up for my smart-mouth kids!"

A smattering of sassy family applause. I look at Julian. He looks at me. "Let's do this thing."

"It all began," I say in my best old-timey story voice, "with a single glance."

"Have you ever had the experience of seeing someone, and feeling you knew, in that instant of time, as your eyes met, that they were your destiny?" Julian's eyebrows are raised, his mouth twisted in a playful grin. "Welp, if you haven't, you're about to hear . . ."

"The greatest love story ever," we chime.

We go on, retelling how our parents met at a bonfire a lot like this one, at the beach a short drive from the university. How their eyes found each other across the flames, but she was there with her boyfriend of two years and he was just out of a relationship, and supposedly heartbroken. How they kept meeting at the refreshment table—fingers brushing as they reached for the same cup of punch, how they both went for the last corned-beef sandwich. And how, finally, they both wandered, separately, away from the crowd and down to the water. A stingray swam up close to the shore and they stood there, toes in the water, watching it move by.

Edged closer and closer until their hands touched for real.

"And there was a spark of electricity. Not just passion, friends. Not love at first sight. True destiny." All the mockery is gone from my brother's voice.

"True destiny," I echo.

Julian raises his glass. Bonfire orange glows through the translucent purple at the top, through the red punch. "Mummy, Daddy, thanks for getting together so us two could be here."

I raise my cup too. Like mirrors, I think, as I lean against my big brother. Everyone's cheering and laughing and toasting whatever they scrounged up from the mishmash of mugs and glasses and old plastic cups, drinking to our parents, with their arms looped around each other, and it feels like when Julian and I would draw stars together on a picture when we were little—so many lines, in so many directions, all crisscrossing and overlapping at their middle, at that single pivotal point. So many lines intersecting. So many lives. So much love.

"Y'all brought our good glasses out here?" Mummy appears beside us a few minutes later. A half smile dissipates the frown in her rumpled eyebrows.

"You said bring what we need from the kitchen." Julian shrugs, with that get-out-of-jail-free grin.

"I meant the big pack of plastic cups and plates. I told Karmen."

"Oh. Why you didn't tell me that?" Julian looks over at me, mischief dancing in his eyes like reflected fire.

"Don't you do it, boy. I ain tell you put all them breakables in the box."

Daddy tiptoes up behind Mummy, finger over his lips. He covers her eyes and she shrieks, then melts into laughter and play-scolding.

"Turned out nice, though." Julian looks around.

"Sure did." I lift my glass of punch. "Actually, I rather drink outta real glasses. Can't get a good clink outta plastic."

"Hear, hear." Julian raises his glass. We tap purple to purple, and sip.

"Ding!" I say, giggling. Julian obliges, and we tink our matching glasses again.

"Like an infomercial out here. 'It cleans and shines in half the time!'"

"Ding!" We're both giggling inanely now. We clink again and again, laughing harder and harder. Someone shouts something about cutting us off at the punch bowl, but it's not the punch, and anyway, we're in it now. We clink again and there's a crack—Julian's glass splits off a jagged third and the chunk lands on the sand. Shock on his face mirrors my mouth.

"Oooooh . . . Mummy ga kill us, Karm!"

"What us? You! That's your glass."

"That's how you ga do me?"

"You brought it out here. And she ain ga do you nothin. Her golden child?"

Julian bends to pick it up.

"Don't get cut!" I bend too. The breaks are angry and deep, the teeth of some monstrous animal no one saw coming. I still hold my unfractured glass, but I trust it less. They are from the same set, washed in the same sink, stood up side by side in the same cupboard for years. If one could just shatter,

how secure is its kin? "Throw it in the garbage?" I query.

Julian looks out to the water. Waves lift and ride to shore, rising up the sand in frothy breaks that glow white in the dark. Together we wade in calf-deep. I hold my hand out and he lays the broken-off piece on my palm. I draw my hand back and fling it as far as I can. It lands without any splash we can hear. The water is rougher than it looks; it takes focus to keep our footing with the sand beneath us shifting, always.

He is next. He hurls the body of the glass. The waves swallow it whole.

"What if someone goes swimming?"

Julian's face shows no fear. "Too late now. And people throw glass in the ocean all the time. It'll smooth down."

"Let's go." I turn to the shore and wade back onto land. Julian stays a minute longer, looking out into the dark water and all it hides.

I fold my hand around the glass. What stands between a safe grip and the squeeze that's too tight, that shatters smooth safety into knifelike shards? What turns familiarity into danger? What stands between smooth and snapped? How is it possible that I am here and Julian is not?

But, impossible or not, Julian is gone. Possible or not, I am here.

"Your appointment's at ten." Mummy lays her hands on my shoulders. "We all need rest now. You especially. Come on."

Mummy guides me upstairs, holds my hand like I'm four, and I let her. The whole time I'm in the shower, I can sense her just outside the door. Know she's watching. Listening. Waiting to be sure I'm okay.

Back in my room, she tucks the sheets around me. I feel her nearby, watching, waiting, as I drift into sleep.

Come morning, the sun is too bright, and my mind feels too blank. Ms. Rhonda greets us at the door. I brace myself for her to scold me for missing yesterday, or at least to give me one of those pitying smirks, but instead she smiles her always-wide smile. Today her lipstick is fiery red. She grips her parrot cane tight. "Come in, love. Mrs. Wallace, Mr. Wallace, if you don't mind, I'll talk to Karmen first, and then have a word with you both afterward."

I follow Ms. Rhonda toward her office.

She pauses by the door. "You want outside or inside today?"

"Can we sit outside?"

She leads me past the office and through a side door. Her limp seems more pronounced. She's never told me what happened, why she walks with the cane, why something's different in her left leg from her right. It's one of the weird things about counselors, I guess. They know everything about you, and you know next to nothing about them. Maybe that's why some people prefer clay. Maybe they like the even terms.

I follow her into her little side garden. The fountain is on beside a night-blooming jasmine. An enterprising hummingbird, smaller than my thumb, noses around the flowers' closed mouths. I sit on a wicker chair with a faded red cushion.

"So." She settles into the seat opposite me. "Where are you at today?"

I don't know where to start. "Okay, I guess."

"I hear you had an eventful day yesterday. Tell me about that."

"So, right into it, then."

The cane is still in her hands. "That's what we're here for." Her smile is kind. She folds one hand over the other so both grip the carved parrot head. "Go ahead."

"I went out to Freedom to see if I could talk to this girl Julian interviewed for a history article he had published. Turns out she out she didn't even know he had died. And it seems like maybe they liked each other."

"Romantically?"

"I think so."

"Would you like to talk about that, or shall we move on to talking about your second trip out to Freedom? I'm sure you know your mom spoke to me last night, but I want to hear from you."

My shoulders feel heavy. "The second time, I snuck out and left a note saying I had to go out. I met up with a couple . . . people I know, and I had to make my own way home. But I decided to go out to the cliffs instead."

"The cliffs?"

"The cliffs where Julian died."

"That's a hard thing to say. Why did you go to that place?"

"Just . . . to understand? I keep saying it, and people don't get it. They don't get why I need to understand Julian."

"Tell me."

I feel like I've said it over and over. I think, try to find a new way of explaining. A way someone can finally understand.

I think of the purple glasses. Of how once there were four. Then three. Of the two of us, clinking the pair against each other, toasting our parents. Of how now there's just one mismatched glass in the cupboard, alone. "We were like a set," I say. "If you can't understand the people you belong to, what's the point of even belonging?"

"So you deeply need to understand Julian's death in order to make sense of what he meant in your life?"

Julian's death. Julian's death. Can we stop saying that? He was more than just the end. He was a whole person. A whole person I thought I knew. Now I'm here left with this half, the other part a big, mysterious chunk. "To understand *him*," I say. "There was more to him than just that."

"By 'that' you mean his suicide?"

I look away, to the fountain. The water rises from the middle, spouts up, cascades down, cyclical, certain. "I mean Julian." My voice comes out more annoyed than I like.

Ms. Rhonda leans in. "I wonder, Karmen. About how you're coping with your grief. With those feelings, those so natural, so understandable feelings of frustration. Of rage. Of abandonment. And of the trauma and grief of Julian dying in such a sudden, tragic way."

There's something about this I always find so artificial, so weird. A near stranger asking you about the parts of yourself intentionally kept under the surface—even if they keep resurfacing. "Can we talk about something else?"

"I know it's hard, Karmen. Your mother told me you went out to the cliffs, though. And she told me you considered ending your life. Is that right?"

Her words make me feel itchy. "I'm not Julian. I'm not going to hurt myself."

"Is it right, though? Is this something you considered, however briefly?"

"I just couldn't be where people wanted me to be, yesterday."

"Go on."

"I asked my dad to take me out to Freedom; he wouldn't take me. I got a friend to drive me there instead, and we stayed out longer than we meant to and my parents were pretty upset."

Ms. Rhonda nods. "I can imagine." Her face is that therapist face I know too well from Mummy, or at least Mummy before. Calm, even, smooth. Not too happy, not too sad. Just neutral-sympathetic-listening. I shift my gaze to her hands wrapped around the top of the cane. Her fingers are a little more relaxed now. Her red-painted nails are smooth, almost perfect. Then I notice a slight chip on her thumbnail. A chip like someone would get trying to dig a string of food from between their back teeth, or scrape old food dried on the side of a glass. *She's a person,* I tell myself. *She's like me.*

"Can I ask you a question?"

Therapist face—open, pleasant, unsurprised. "Of course."

"Would you ever counsel your own child?"

Ms. Rhonda smiles. "Well, officially, it's much like a medical doctor. Treating family is a huge conflict of interest. That said, I think we're all human. It can be difficult to keep things in their separate columns. My turn. I have a question for you."

"Yeah?"

"Why do you ask? I get the sense this isn't a random inquiry."

I shake my head, but I can't stop myself from going back to yesterday. To the folder, to screaming at Mummy. To what she did for so long.

"I was just curious."

Now her smile is more knowing mother than neutral therapist. "I think there's more to it than that."

"What?"

"You're very bright, Karmen, but you're not *just curious* about anything. You have reasons. Very carefully considered, very thoughtful, very weighted reasons. As evidenced in the huge, painful—and very unsafe—lengths you've been going to in your quest to comprehend your brother's journey." She leans the cane against the side of the chair and grips one wrist with the other hand. The chipped nail is hidden now. "Tell me about your parents being upset. How did that go?"

"Not well." I can feel her *What happened?* lurking behind the end of my sentence, and push on before she has to ask. "I wasn't in the mood to get lectured. For one, I caught Mummy . . ." There we go. I have to talk about it now anyway—about the reason for my question about counseling family. *Well played, Ms. R.* Julian's voice, in my mind, is grudgingly admiring. It's half-comforting, half-agitating, though, which is new. Can I trust Julian's voice, when trying to hear it took me *there*? Then, for an instant, I'm back in that buffeting wind, the water raging below.

"You caught Mummy . . . ," Ms. Rhonda says gently.

"I found out she'd had a file on Julian for years. Like she

was counseling him." Saying it feels like a lifted weight, and like a betrayal. Like I'm forgetting Mummy's gentleness since I came home last night.

"How did that land with you?"

"Like she's a liar. Even though she was really nice to me later on, I just—I dunno. Anyway, I guess now you have to report her or something."

"It's not like that, Karmen. It's confidential."

"Unless someone's breaking the law."

"Confidential unless there is real risk of violence toward others or self."

"Well. He's already dead so I guess everyone's safe."

"I'm not sure about that, but we'll get to that. Did you see what was in your brother's file, Karmen? You don't have to tell me the content if you don't want to."

"I saw enough."

"Do you believe your mother knew Julian was considering suicide?"

"I don't know. Maybe? I didn't see the whole folder."

"Have you asked her?"

"She just said she didn't realize, and at the same time that we all realized. Like we all knew."

"Knew that . . . ?"

The chair feels uncomfortable now. I wish I'd asked to sit inside. The wicker is too hard for the flimsy cushion. There's a soft whir behind me. I turn; the hummingbird is back. When I face Ms. Rhonda again, she's leaning forward again. Waiting for me.

"Knew he wasn't okay? I don't know. I'm not the one

who had a file on him. I thought I knew him. It doesn't make sense. To me it just doesn't make any sense. I don't get why. I keep trying to get it, and I can't."

"Get why Julian ended his life?"

"Yeah. I never thought things were that bad. I can't figure it out."

"Let's talk about the lengths you've been going to, looking for answers."

I shift in my chair.

"I know it's uncomfortable."

"It's annoying," I blurt out. "Obviously Mummy already told you everything. She told you I went out to the cliffs. She probably told you I've been using his skateboard and wearing his clothes. . . ." A tiny flicker of surprise on Ms. Rhonda's face. So I guess Mummy didn't tell her about the clothes. And I guess it's possible to shock Ms. Rhonda after all.

"I hear you've been looking for those answers hard. Driving out to Freedom. Scouring his old stomping grounds. Trying to get into character—"

"It's not a game!" The way my words bark out of my mouth makes me sit back.

"What are you thinking right now? Something surprised you."

"How my words came out. I sounded like my daddy."

"And?"

"And I don't want to be him." I don't want to be anyone else, I realize. Not even Julian.

"Tell me what you're thinking."

"That I don't want to be Julian, either. That being him

won't bring him back. And if I try any harder . . . I might lose myself."

"Karmen—that's huge. That's an enormous realization. And I agree. None of us want you to lose yourself. Not your parents, not your friends . . . and I'm certain Julian wouldn't want that either."

"It's so empty. Just not having an answer to why Julian ended his life."

"Sometimes you can't get an answer—it doesn't make the loss any less meaningful or painful. If anything, it complicates it. It compounds it. These are the things we sometimes have to carry with us, Karmen. And it's heartbreaking and hard, and it's heavy. It's so heavy."

She stops talking then, and I'm glad. I can't handle more words right now, just want to sit with these ones she's unloaded on me, with the ones I've let out of myself, words I didn't know I was carrying.

"If Julian were here right now, and you could ask him, Karmen—what do you think he'd say?"

Julian? What you say, then? What's your answer? What's your reason? All you putting me through, you owe me an answer. You owe me. Julian?

Nothing.

Answer me!

The water trickles. The hummingbird returns, buzzes, departs.

"I wonder what you're thinking right now."

A smattering of ani birds land on the lawn, their dark feathers gleaming brown and blue, and pick through the grass like shoppers digging for firm onions on a hot August day. Thinking. I don't know. Right now it's like my brain is on pause and my eyes, my ears, the parts of me that beat and feel have taken over instead. Ms. Rhonda follows my gaze.

The ani seem satisfied that the lawn has no food to offer; they turn their attention to calling *Mine? Mine? Mine? Mine?* in a chorus of rising whines. We watch the birds together. I can remember my grandfather pointing to them, telling me their name.

"When my granddad died, it wasn't like this." The words fall out, surprising me.

"Like what?"

"It didn't follow me everywhere. He was gone; I missed him. We kinda knew it was coming—my parents didn't say, but he slowed down, and then one night, I guess, it just . . . happened. This is different."

"Julian was young. And it wasn't expected."

Curved-shoulder Julian crying behind the kitchen door.

On-his-bed-in-the-dark Julian.

"You ever feel like you wanna just . . . stop?"

Sweat, beginning to bead at my hairline. I wipe it dry.

Mine? Mine? Minemineminemineminemine? The birds are an arm's length away. What are they calling for, unsure it's theirs?

"Karmen? What are you thinking?"

All these questions. Time stretching out—isn't it time to go?

The fountain trickles steady, water going nowhere but around and down again.

Was it always this way with my brother? Something in him meant to fit got tilted a different way? Were we always going to end up here, him gone before twenty, all these questions left where he should be? Was it always bad, really? What did I miss? Did I miss something? Why didn't I catch it?

What did he text me, that night, when my arms were wrapped in wool? What did he delete? What were the words he took back?

"I don't know anymore. Maybe it should have been expected."

"Go on."

"I feel like maybe he knew. And I was supposed to know too. He was . . . sad, sometimes. More than just sad. Depressed, for reasons I didn't get. We didn't have such a bad life, I thought. But I guess I always thought that was just him, and that it'd be different one day. Or that it would always be the same, but that was okay."

"Do you feel responsible for his death?"

I think of all the versions of Julian I've known. Laughing till he gasped for breath, bickering over dishes, glued to election results on the TV, hunkered over his computer tapping something out, flying past the window on a skateboard I couldn't see, like his body moved forward by some even-keeled mystery power. And curled up in his room for weeks, and slumped at the kitchen table, his usual self locked away. My throat tightens, makes it hard to speak. "I feel like I missed it. It was right in front of me—he was depressed; he was struggling—and I missed it." I wipe tears away, but more come. "I should have helped him and I couldn't, because I didn't see that he needed help. And I didn't, so the least I could have done now was to understand."

"I'm going to suggest that your greatest responsibility is to accept that you can't ever know, and to love him anyway."

"That's not good enough."

Ms. Rhonda nods. "And yet sometimes that's just where we find ourselves. In the middle of 'It's not good enough.' It's a hard place to be. I wish it weren't. There'll be a time when you won't be in the middle anymore. Maybe over to the side a bit instead. But one day it won't feel quite as raw as it does now." She pauses, then says, "I want to bring your parents in for a few minutes. I want to continue seeing you for sessions, and I want you to try out a group for young people with struggles similar to yours. It's important you feel both supported and understood—especially with understanding being so close to your heart. How does that sound?"

I reach my hand into the backpack. I show Ms. Rhonda my phone. "I took it back yesterday before I ran out. I guess my parents didn't get around to bringing that up yet."

"I know they want you to take your time away from school seriously, but we can all talk together about some compromise that has you supported, not isolated. Let's go inside; I'll phone them from my office." She scrabbles for the cane, for a moment too far out of easy reach. A small, sharp exhale as she strains; then her fingers close around the wood. "And I want you to be extra gentle with yourself for the rest of the day. It's time, now, to step back from your knowledge quest."

I stand up too.

"Anything else you'd like us to discuss together with your parents?"

I tuck my skateboard under my arm and sling my bag

over my shoulder. I don't answer right away, and I don't push, but as we walk together to the office, I glimpse the calendar hanging on Ms. Rhonda's wall. My eyes go straight to September fifteenth. "I still want to do something for Julian's birthday," I say.

CHAPTER FOURTEEN

I sleep most of Sunday and Monday, as if my mind and my body have agreed to take a break. On Monday afternoon, when Daddy taps on the door and asks if I want to join him for a meeting with the principal, I shake my head. I have the first group meeting later, and I want to clear my mind. I take the skateboard out onto the empty driveway. I can feel Mummy watching through her office window. I haven't touched the board since I got home on Friday night. I wonder if it will feel right anymore, being on it. If that's something that belongs back in last week, when I felt like it was vital, or even possible, to see things as Julian did.

I push the front door open. "Mummy, can I just go down the road and back?"

Mummy hesitates. "I suppose so," she says finally, "but be back in five minutes."

"I will," I say. I mean it. This is part of what we talked about with Ms. Rhonda—rebuilding trust, and giving me a little room. I close the door and set the skateboard down on its wheels. One foot on the board then, and one on the ground. I push off, glide down the driveway and onto the quiet street. The road ahead is wide and clear. I pick up my pace, first tentative, then faster, faster, keeping on the side, keeping safe. Maybe Julian felt this once—but it was when he was first learning, when he was still shaky like me. But his skateboarding was different from mine too. Julian skated for himself—not to pick up the pieces of sadness left behind by someone else breaking. I reach my arms out, forward, back, pushing on. Wind on my face, in my ears. Arms pumping, body finding balance. Feel the ache in my still-tired legs, feel the way the air tries to beat against my hair—longer than Julian's was. What I feel might overlap with him some. But it'll never be the same. We aren't the same.

At the corner, I turn back and head home, like I promised I would. I stay on the board, up and down the driveway, keep in front of our house. I'm so immersed, I don't hear anyone approach. I just look up and see motion by our side gate, the one near the kitchen, where Mummy wouldn't see. A girl's back. Long braids trailing. Blue school uniform rolled up too high. I abandon the board and follow.

"You lost?"

Pru turns around. "Thought you didn't see me." She looks scared, not defiant. She holds a piece of paper in one hand. "I was gonna leave this for you."

"Where?"

"Just—by your kitchen door."

Something clicks into place. The sound, the rustling in the yard that day. "That was you, that morning. What's with you? Why you always hanging around me?"

"Sorry. The other night? Sorry. I was kinda messed up."

"You were kinda stupid."

She looks away, then back at me. "You got home okay?"

"I took a detour."

"Where?"

Hiding doesn't feel important anymore. And anyway, no matter how Pru messed up on Friday, I've made mistakes too. At least she's one person I know understands how that feels. And understands how it feels when someone close dies, too. "I went out to the cliffs."

"*The* cliffs? Where Julian died?"

"Yeah. There was a second where I thought I might not come back." I wait for her to gasp, to tell me I was dumb to go out there.

"I get it," she finally says.

"Do you?"

"More than you think."

"What's on that paper?"

She looks down at it like she forgot it was in her hand. "I wanted to tell you something. I was gonna just leave it, but . . . you know what, I had enough of conversations we can't have. I had enough of that with my cousin being gone."

"Me too," I say. "So. Just tell me."

A sound from inside reminds me of Mummy, waiting. Listening out. I crack the kitchen door open. "Mummy, my friend Pru came over. We're just in the backyard."

"Okay," Mummy calls back. I hear the relief in her voice as I sit on the deck. Pru sits too.

"So?"

"Remember how you asked me if I knew Julian? If I knew anything about why?"

I nod. My heart's already pounding. I wait.

"Something I didn't tell you. I wanted you to know, and I was waiting till maybe I got to know you better. I didn't just know Julian from skateboarding and stuff. I met him before, actually."

"Where?"

"We met a few times at a support group for high school kids. Some people there were depressed; some had really bad anxiety. I was there after everything happened with my cousin. I said something in the group about having thoughts about . . . you know, hurting myself. One time afterward, I was waiting for my ride and he was messing around on his skateboard. I thought it was cool, having your own little set of wheels. I was just watching, and he started talking to me. He said he'd thought about it too."

"He told you that? When?"

"About a year ago, maybe. We didn't talk about it after that, and I stopped going to that group, but I started bumping into him at skateboarding stuff. Then I stopped seeing him. I just figured he got busy or whatever. I should have told you—I don't blame you if you never wanna talk to me again. I thought maybe I could try to help, but I don't know how to help, and . . . I should have known. If I'd known you then, I'd have told you he was in trouble."

I struggle to take her words in. To accept that Julian confided in Pru that way. Someone he barely knew. Someone who wasn't me.

"Do you hate me?"

I shake my head. The answer comes without thinking. "At least you told me now, I guess."

"Me and him, we promised each other, you know? That we'd stop each other from . . ." Her words fade away.

"I don't know how you could have stopped Julian. I think . . ."

Ever feel like you wanna just . . . stop?

"I think he'd been trying to be okay for a while," I say.

"Wish it worked that way. Wish trying was what it took."

"I've got this support group tonight," I say.

"Which one? Out west?"

"Off Soldier Road. You should come."

"The last one didn't help. Didn't help me or Julian." Pru's voice is sad. I get how she feels—or maybe I don't.

"It'll be better if we both go. We could give it a try."

She looks over at me. For the first time, her face seems bare—not hiding behind a sarcastic half grin, no bloomers or props, tricks, surprises. No snickers or smirks. Just a girl. Like me, and not like me. A girl who once crossed paths with Julian. A girl who, like me, is still here. A girl who, like me, might not have been.

"I guess we could. But . . . you really don't hate me for not telling you?"

I think about what Julian would have done. I already know, really. He would have understood her why. He would have seen how she did tell me, when she could, and seen who she was—struggling, like he was, like I am. Like who knows who else might be. I think he wouldn't have had room to hate. I think about how I don't either. "I don't hate you at all."

Pru smiles small. I smile back.

• • •

Wednesday afternoon, I'm in the yard, tidying up, when Mummy calls, "Layla's here!"

Layla stands on the deck. She looks almost like a stranger—it feels like we haven't seen each other in months, not days. I try to squelch the disappointment I feel. "Hey."

I nod. "Hey. How are you?"

She shrugs.

"How's school been?"

"All right."

"Nothing to say?"

"I don't know what to say. Not since . . ."

"Since when?"

"Since you turned into a different person. I don't even know you anymore." Layla's voice isn't angry. If anything, she sounds tired out.

"Sorry if I changed too much for you because Julian died." It sounds more sarcastic out loud.

"It's not just because Julian died. It's just—you're not you. You always seem mad; you're doing weird things, hanging around *Pru*, sneaking out with Isaiah. Seems like you rather be around literally anyone but me."

"I'm grounded."

"But when I do see you—"

"When you do see me, you're acting weird too. Quoting books and grief advice."

"I was trying to be there for you."

"Yeah, but it feels like I'm being treated by an unqualified therapist."

Layla all but wilts. Her face looks like I've slapped her.

"I'm not trying to hurt you," I say.

"I wasn't trying to hurt you, either."

"I just—I don't need you to tell me what some grief book says about me. Just talk to me like before. It's not like I'm a totally different person."

"You are, though. I mean, last year this time, we were messing around with wool after school, and talking about what we wanted to do when we graduate. Everything's changed."

Her words stop me short—because she's right. "I guess *I'm* different."

"I'm still your friend." Layla's voice is small. For the first time, though, it sounds like her. At least what I remember of her—from what I remember of me.

"I should finish cleaning up."

Layla nods. "I'll see you some other time."

"I mean, if you wanna stay and help me clean up out here . . ."

She hops down off the deck. Together, quietly, we pull greenery away. While Layla clears vines from the fence, I pick up the shears and snip back the overgrowth that looms low from the trees. Each snip comes hard and fast. It feels good to reach up, to yank down the vines, to feel how they resist, then come free. To let the branches breathe. To let light in.

On the morning of Julian's twentieth birthday, I take the stairs down, two at a time. Once I'm there, though, I stand in the foyer, like I did one night that first week. I remember the first fight, after the funeral.

Daddy in the kitchen with a laundry basket full of things harvested from around the house. Anna Karenina, *now closed, swept up from the kitchen counter. A stack of history notes from the table. Laundry folded and unclaimed. The blue sneakers Julian left on the rack. Mummy screams, her arms raised, hands like claws ripping at the air. "What you think you doing? You trying to erase my son?" Mummy said.*

"What you mean?"

"Put it back. Put every single thing back!"

"We can't pretend, Barb. He's not here." Daddy is so calm. "You have to come to terms with it."

"Don't you tell me what I have to do. I'm his mother—I know! I know what he needs."

Daddy stands there, silent, as she screams about Julian in the present tense. I want to get up from my chair and slap my father myself, slap the hysteria he should feel into him. He sets the basket down on the counter. The shoes gleam up at me, the reflective strip designed to provide night visibility, to prevent the wearer from being run down. To protect him. The shoes he walked past, the last time he walked out of our home. Walked out barefoot with no plan to come back. Daddy opens his arms, walks toward my mother. She pushes him away.

"Don't you dare touch another thing. If you want me to stay, leave my baby's things alone."

Daddy grasps the hamper, fingers so tight, the plastic should break. He lets go, lets a breath out. Daddy lifts the sneakers out, cradles them to his body. He walks past me and to the shoe rack. Lays them down. He stays bent over, fingers

283

touching them. Then lifts the right one, just a bit. Settles it at an angle again.

Looking at the shoe rack now, I realize I'm not sorry Julian's sneakers aren't here anymore. There are a thousand different ways I'll remember my brother every day. Looking at the sneakers he left behind, the shoes he was too broken to wear on his last walk? That's not how I want to start or end another day. I bend down and pick up my school shoes. They seem dusty from not being used. I lift them onto the top shelf, just the same. I'll wear them again one day.

There's a throaty noise behind me—a clearing, a shifting kind of cough. Daddy steps past me and lifts his shoes from the floor. He sets them beside mine. Mummy moves last. She walks to her office. She comes back with the soft-soled slip-ons she wears for her appointments. She sets them down on the other side of Daddy's.

I grab a bucket and squeeze in dish soap. I add hot water, and a canopy of bubbles rises. The iridescent dome shudders as I tote it back to the foyer. Plunging the mop in, lifting the water over the floor, feels like a fresh start. It would make sense to lift the rack out of the way altogether, but I don't want to disturb our shoes. I work around it.

It doesn't feel like a shrine anymore, though. Tomorrow, more shoes may be added—tatty flip-flops or dressy ones. And other people's, as they come and go. Shoes, and more shoes, added and taken away. And always Daddy's, Mummy's, mine. Just us three, and our shoes. We will get used to it, even if it never feels right. We have to.

Last, I reach for the calendar. My fingers tremble as I take it down. I turn the months forward, one at a time: August, then September. At December, I stop. We're not there yet. But maybe we'll get there one day. It's something to move toward anyway.

CHAPTER FIFTEEN

Layla and Isaiah relax with me in the living room. It's a far cry from the party I wanted—we watch a movie, eat pizza. Layla's phone buzzes so many times, Isaiah threatens to loan her out to a beehive, and she retreats to the hallway. He and I are alone.

"How was the group session?"

"Not bad for the first one, I guess. I like one-on-one with Ms. Rhonda, but it's interesting being with people who get it. Not that you don't, but . . ."

"I know what you mean. When you live it, you understand more."

I lean my head against his shoulder. "You understand pretty well." He's right, though. There's something about people who've lived it. My mind goes to Pru, but we haven't spoken since that night. I feel sadness that I don't want to make room for today. "Been doing any pottery lately?"

"I went to the art therapy group yesterday. If you ever want to go back . . ."

"Maybe. Probably. But right now I have group on Mondays, and I see Ms. Rhonda on Wednesdays and Fridays. Maybe you can sneak me some clay."

Layla reappears in the doorway. "So, I have to go."

She glances at Isaiah. "You could drop me by . . ."

He nods, and gives me a quick kiss on the cheek as he gets up. "I'll be in the car."

I turn to Layla. "You got somewhere to be?"

"Kind of."

I try not to let it sting. Of course she'd have other plans. I haven't been in school for a week and a half. It still hurts, though. I watch as she gathers up her stuff around the room—a thin sweater, pink lip gloss, her sketchbook—and wonder if we'll ever be the same again. She leans forward and a shadow falls over her face and hides her expression from me.

"Hey. We still cool?"

She doesn't look surprised by the question. "Of course."

But despite her words, I know something's changed between us—changed in me. I swallow hard. I have to live with it, then. I'm working on accepting that sometimes we can't put things back the way they were. Sometimes we can't fix what's been broken. Sometimes we can't get the answer we need.

It's just coming up to six as Isaiah and Layla pull out of the driveway. I stand in the foyer long after they're gone.

There's a knock at the door. I swing the door open. "What did y'all forget?"

Robbie stands outside my door. The words all drain out of my mind. My hand tightens on the doorknob. Why? Why is he in front of me? Why is he at my home?

"What are you doing here?" My words come back at last.

He holds a small yellow book out to me. I stare at it, then back up at him.

"It's from school." He takes a step back.

"What do you mean?" I don't know whether to take it and hurl it as far away from me as possible, or just slam the door.

"Just . . . some people wanted to put together something for you." His voice isn't the angry Robbie I know. He sounds quiet, subdued. He sounds like life's mashed him up and he's trying to talk through the crumpled-up bits. "I—I came to say sorry. For everything."

I don't know what to say. An apology from Robbie is the last thing I expected. I don't even think I want it.

"I messed up a bunch of times. I shouldn't have said . . . what I said that day at school."

"Hello?" Mummy's voice floats in ahead of her. She steps into the foyer. "Robert—I'm not booking sessions quite yet—" She catches herself, looks from him to me. "I'll give you two a minute," she says quietly. It clicks, then. I look down at the book, then back at Robbie. I still want to slam the door in Robbie's face.

Instead I grit my teeth. Julian's not here—I can't ask him for answers. But Robbie?

I'd rather Julian a billion times over. But that's not a choice I have.

"Why'd you set me up with that guy? To interview me about how Julian died? How could you even do something like that?"

Robbie looks like something's just been broken in him, and like tears are about to spill out of the cracks. "I was . . . I dunno. I was messed up. Still messed up. It's better when I can see . . ." He looks up, quick, toward the foyer's doorway. Mummy's office is just beyond. "It's better when I can talk to someone. I know you probably wish I was dead—"

"Don't say anything like that. To anyone."

He nods back. Hesitates. "Which part?"

"All of it. Everything you've ever said to me."

Robbie nods again. "Sorry, Karmen. Really." Then he turns and is gone. I lock the door and press my back against it. I open the book and flip through. Different handwriting fills its pages. I pause on one page.

Julian was funny and smart as the newspaper editor. He had such a gift for making us laugh when we had to work a little longer to meet a deadline before we went to print. I recognize the name beneath: a girl in our grade. I thumb through. There are notes from teachers, even one from Principal Gardiner. I keep looking, searching for familiar names. I recognize classmates, kids from other grades. Among the names, the different colors of ink, careful script and sloppy scrawl, the same messages repeat, page after page. *I'm so sorry, I can't imagine.* I turn page after page of those lonely words. Then Layla's careful, perfectly vertical cursive jumps out at me. *I might not know the best way to be there like you need, but I love you always.* I look up, toward the window, though of course she's long gone to whatever else she has planned tonight. Her words warm something deep in my chest. I feel a small smile starting. I let it spread, then go back to turning pages. On the back page, there's a little cartoon guy with glasses and a short 'fro on a skateboard. Behind him, a cartoon girl with a messy puff bun—I guess it's meant to be me. Pru's name is scrawled underneath.

Nowhere can I find Robbie's name, or any explanation of what he has to do with all this. Behind me, Mummy comes into the foyer. She leans over my shoulder. I hold the book up for her to see. She takes it, looks through a few pages.

"Robbie dropped it off."

She nods and hands it back to me.

"What did he used to come see you for?"

"Karmen. You know I can't say. Just know this—a lot of people are hurting. We can't always know why. We can try to help, but we don't always succeed."

As I take the book upstairs to what used to be Julian's room, I do what everyone says they can't. What I've been trying to do all this time, for Julian. I imagine. Imagine a boy with his own hurts, hurts the people closest to him can't even know. Not even his counselor mother. Not even his sister, his friend—maybe even his best friend. I lay the book on top of Julian's bureau.

I could stay there in the settling dark, straining to feel some last spark of what made these walls his. Some whiff of hair oil. Tilt my ear for a whisper, try to stretch my mind to meet my brother's, try to *be*.

I could switch on the lamp and thumb through the little yellow book's pages, scouring stories and remembrances from all the people who knew Julian, who know me. Try to piece together some bit of knowledge I've missed.

Instead I backtrack.

I go into my own room. Into my own dark. Here, my feet

know the way to the window—over the stack of books, past the backpack half unzipped and gaping, by the bed's sharp corner. I reach onto the bureau until my fingers close over softness. The yarn glows orange—warmth I can feel more than see. I hold it anyway, as I move to the window that overlooks the backyard. I stare up, through the security screen's looping cage, to the freedom of the sky. My hands remember the movements: find the loose long strand—end or middle, hard to know. My fingers count the waiting stitches, even in the dark. Push it through, wrap it around, pull it over, and let it go. I could keep going, but I let myself be still, just hold it to my heart. Let there be softness. Let there be love. I wait for the first pinprick of light to appear—a white dot, distant, shifting. Nothing—nothing.

I give it time.

I keep looking up.

SUICIDE PREVENTION AND CRISIS SUPPORT RESOURCES

Some of the many organizations that work to help those in crisis and to improve the lives of people suffering from mental illness are listed below. These resources are provided for informational purposes only, and their inclusion is not intended to be an endorsement or promotion of any particular organization. It is also not intended to be a complete or exhaustive listing or a substitute for the advice of a qualified medical or mental health professional. The information below was accurate at the time the first edition of this book went to press.

GLOBALLY
Find a Helpline: findahelpline.com/i/988

UNITED STATES
988 Suicide & Crisis Lifeline (24 hours): call or text 988
Crisis Text Line (24 hours): text HOME to 741741
National Alliance on Mental Illness HelpLine (weekdays 10 a.m.–10 p.m. ET): 1-800-950-NAMI (6264) or text HELPLINE to 62640
Teen Line: 1-800-852-8336 (9 p.m.–1 a.m. ET) or text TEEN to 839863 (9 p.m.–midnight ET)

CANADA
Crisis Hotline (24 hours): call or text 988

Kids Help Phone (24 hours): 1-800-668-6868 or
text CONNECT to 686868
Talk Suicide: 1-833-456-4566 (24 hours) or text 45645
(4 p.m.–midnight ET)

BAHAMAS
Bahamas Crisis Centre (24 hours): (242) 328-0922
**National Hotline for Crisis Intervention—Grand
Bahama (24 hours):** (242) 351-7763
**National Hotline for Crisis Intervention—New
Providence (24 hours):** (242) 322-2763 or (242) 422-2763

ACKNOWLEDGMENTS

Thank you to my editor, Catherine Laudone. It's been a wonderful three-book ride together! To Rachel, my agent and dear friend: your expertise is a treasure.

My profound gratitude to Karen Letofsky: your decades-deep expertise in suicide prevention and crisis support profoundly shaped this story for the better.

Thank you to early readers and writing buddies Alison Acheson, for skateboarding checks and balances, and Terry Dove, for encouragement and thoughtful feedback.

To Jason, my husband: you give me the space and peace to write. What a gift you are.